a
proclivity
to
prurience

a proclivity to prurience

Cheryl Butler

The Book Guild Ltd

First published in Great Britain in 2017 by
The Book Guild Ltd
9 Priory Business Park
Wistow Road, Kibworth
Leicestershire, LE8 0RX
Freephone: 0800 999 2982
www.bookguild.co.uk
Email: info@bookguild.co.uk
Twitter: @bookguild

Copyright © 2017 Cheryl Butler

The right of Cheryl Butler to be identified as the author of this work has been asserted by her in accordance with the Copyright, Design and Patents Act 1988.

All rights reserved. No part of this publication may be reproduced, transmitted, or stored in a retrieval system, in any form or by any means, without permission in writing from the publisher, nor be otherwise circulated in any form of binding or cover other than that in which it is published and without a similar condition being imposed on the subsequent purchaser.

This work is entirely fictitious and bears no resemblance to any persons living or dead.

Typeset in Minion Pro

Printed and bound in the UK by TJ International, Padstow, Cornwall

ISBN 978 1911320 579

British Library Cataloguing in Publication Data.
A catalogue record for this book is available from the British Library.

*To all those who have supported me throughout
– you know who you are.*

1

"Hey, Joe, could you just zip me up? I don't know what's taking Eddie so long." Abbie's blasé attitude disguised, she hoped, her desire to feel him so close. She knew she was teasing him, but she didn't know what else to do; it had been nine years since she'd seen him walk out of the bathroom, towel around his waist, skin still damp, water-droplets accentuating his lashes. She'd hoped her involuntary gasp had gone unnoticed, but no... Eddie, thankfully, had been desperate for the loo so had missed her reaction, but not Joe; he'd turned round, smiled knowingly and sauntered in to his room. *Shit!*

She'd been struck by his beauty the first time she'd met him, but he was just a boy then. At fourteen, when many of her neighbours had benefitted from his burgeoning talent, she'd drawn a line (although he'd opened her eyes to the splendour of young men and they'd suddenly become more appealing, albeit, those of a more suitable age...) but had practically counted the days until he was eighteen. Now, five years later and, aside from an occasional suggestion, nothing! Maybe he simply wasn't interested...

Joe did as he was asked; he welcomed any chance to get close to Abbie, but they were, unfortunately, a little too infrequent. God, she smelled good! It was one of the things he'd noticed about her when they first met, waiting with Eddie outside the school gates. He'd spotted them from a way off but could see, even from that distance, that she was...well, just lovely, and when he got close, he could smell that sweet, warm scent that, no matter what perfume she wore, remained her. He resisted the urge to kiss her neck…this time. How, was a complete mystery; it had been long enough and he'd take her right now if they were alone, but he knew Eddie would be down within the next couple of minutes and that might prove a little awkward. If the wedding went well, though, he'd have her tonight – women love a good wedding! He wanted her so badly…and he wasn't used to waiting, but somehow she'd managed to elude him for so long. Sharing her with Eddie was bad enough, but at least he would never touch her like Joe wanted to, would never be inside her…like Joe wanted to. Whether Eddie was aware of how he felt was irrelevant – he wasn't about to let that stop him. With any luck, he'd be so wasted tonight he'd go straight to bed. Conscious of that familiar sensation in his crotch, he stepped away from Abbie.

"Come on, Eddie, we're going to be late!"

"OK, Mum, calm down; I'm ready. It's only a wedding and it's not like it's yours!"

"I asked Joe to be ready at one o'clock, so we could leave soon after, and he was; I asked the same of you, but you can't manage it – why?! AND, it's not just a wedding, it's Frankie's wedding, and if we're late…"

"Well, I'm sorry, Mum, but it's clear Joe didn't make an effort. I didn't want to let you down." He smiled like a choirboy, waiting for the inevitable retort.

Joe laughed in response and winked at Ed. "Some of us don't need to make an effort, my friend…" An irrefutable statement, but a fact that had benefitted them both countless times. "But, don't worry, Abbie, we won't be late; I'm driving."

"There you go, Mum, so what's all the fuss about?" Abbie smiled and gave her son a gentle tap on the back of the head. "Hey, mind the hair!"

She opted to sit in the back of the car. She knew her son

would want to sit in the front and chat to his friend and she didn't mind; it would give her a chance to watch them as she had for many years. Joe had become a permanent figure in their lives over the past twelve years and he and Eddie were like brothers, despite their obvious differences but, having been shaped by their early start in life, it gave them a bond that was clear to everyone. Eddie's father had been a user and had regularly beat his mother, though, thankfully, he'd never witnessed it, and when he was eight, the man died from as overdose and left them penniless; Abbie had brought them back from the brink of homelessness with a determination she'd never previously felt, but Eddie would never know how close they were, and he still missed his father immensely. Joe's mother had died when he was just seven, protecting him from a drunk-driver and his father had blamed him ever since; he never spoke about her, but Abbie knew they'd been close. Finding Joe had been the best thing for Eddie – Abbie had no complaints either – and the boys had become inseparable. Before long, he was living with them, though nothing was ever formalised and once he was old enough to support himself, he turned his back on his father for good, but in the years in-between Abbie had brought him up and shuddered to think what would have happened if the two boys hadn't met. She hadn't just provided a safe-haven for him, she'd been a mother to him; she'd discussed his grades at school, she'd fed and clothed him, and cried at his graduation as she did for Eddie. Countless nights she'd sobbed when, checking him before she went to bed, she'd found him clutching the only photo he had of his mother. But he'd been happy living with them and she'd given him a small chance to be a child again, though it didn't last long. As they grew up and their group of friends expanded, they would meet at her house for BBQ's and occasional parties, many of which were impromptu, and they had treated her like royalty, full of respect and good manners. Luckily, most of the group was male and there had even been the odd moment with one or two of them when Eddie wasn't around, but she was effortlessly discreet and they were too scared of her son, and quite possibly Joe, to brag.

"This is it, Mum, isn't it?"

"Yep, but don't turn in here; just drive down a bit further and the car-park's on the left."

"I do believe we're early – happy now?"

"I'll be happy when you stop your cheek!"

Hayward Manor was a stunning medieval manor house, with beautiful grounds that sprawled in all directions; there were seven separate gardens, all themed and individual, that lead to the woods and paddocks that bordered the perimeter; two huge lakes were home to at least a dozen different varieties of birds, and horses and donkeys – used mainly to aid rehabilitation and therapy for several charities nationwide – roamed freely. Still owned by the Hayward-Smythes, it had been in the family for at least six generations, and had served as a hospital during World War Two, and, now, as then, they were passionately patriotic and community-spirited. Aside from the annual festival, which was free to the locals, they held a party for every season for the wider community, again, with no charge and the current occupants, Mr and Mrs John Hayward-Smythe IV, not only funded these events but were involved in every aspect of the organisation and clean-up, often seen assisting in the dismantling of marquees and props and wandering around with black sacks, picking up rubbish, before hosting a lavish buffet for all staff who had given their own time voluntarily. They were well respected and loved by all who knew them, and they treated their staff as family. Less than a half-hour drive from her home, it meant a great deal to Abbie; many an hour had been spent playing hide-and-seek and rolling down banks with the boys, climbing trees and running races. There had been picnics and parties in the summer months, and it was where she'd met Rose, her closest friend. Rose's daughter, Francesca, had been running around, as had the boys, when she and Eddie had bumped heads. There were tears and apologies all round as both mothers blamed their own child for not paying attention and despite being three years older than Eddie, Frankie was almost half his size and had come off a lot worse, fracturing her arm as she fell. Abbie was concerned for her, and amidst protests from Rose, she'd driven them to the hospital and waited with them whilst Frankie was treated. The two mums swapped numbers and Abbie demanded she be kept abreast of Frankie's progress; Rose kept her promise and they soon became inseparable.

A few years later, when the boys were older and she had more time on her hands, Abbie had worked at the Manor – occasionally still did – organising and running events, and had finally found her niche. It was there she had 'discovered' Jesse, who had begged her to let him perform for free at the annual festival when he was just nineteen. She'd let him and what a performance he gave! Despite the big names she'd attracted, it was he who'd stood out and within a year he was a household name…and he'd never let her forget, only too pleased to show his gratitude whenever they met. He had agreed to come back to perform at Frankie's and Danny's wedding…and Abbie was rather excited!

She thought about their first…encounter: after an exhausting three performances at the festival, Jesse had stayed at the Manor with his family, courtesy of Abbie, and on the morning he left, he'd gone in search of her to thank her for her support. Finding her in her office, he'd wandered in, beaming in the aftermath of his success and she'd hugged him tight…a little too tight. "Oh my God, Jesse, you were amazing! Did you hear that crowd?!"

He laughed bashfully. "Yeah, it was amazing!"

"But they kept calling your name inbetween sets! I've had tons of emails about you, and have you seen Facebook? Have a look…" As he analysed every comment, standing just a little too close, she could feel the heat from his body and wondered if she should offer to cool him down...and God, did he smell good!

"Abbie?"

"Er...sorry, Jesse – miles away... Sorry, what did you say?" She boxed the image of him half-naked for now.

He smiled, oblivious to her reverie. "I don't know if I can ever thank you enough..." There was an innocence to him, and his words were delivered with total sincerity, but as Abbie bit her lip and dropped her eyes, it became clear it would be easier than he thought. His smile grew...*that* smile. A dangerous combination, coupled with the face of an angel, the smile that would open bedroom doors for him once he realised its power. To some, it was sweet and warm, sincere and friendly; to others, however, and, in particular, Abbie, it was full of mischief, full of dissolute promise and open to suggestion, but then he was, if nothing else, somewhat paradoxical. Looking like a boy scout, who'd lived in the wild a little too long, when he sang, his voice was sweet enough to melt your Granny's heart, but it would change without warning and he suddenly became a banshee, his voice coarse and loud, exuding passion, and his face contorted as if feeling the pain of his lyrics – unnerving for the faint-hearted... but exciting for the more reckless, and sex was just the same: he pulled you in with a soft touch and gentle manner, but once he'd succeeded, he became primal, intense, almost aggressive...and Abbie found that an irresistible mix.

Heeding her silent suggestion, Jesse kissed her gently, moving her back towards her desk, looking deep into her eyes, smiling all the time, and, pulling him close she tried, unsuccessfully, to slow her hands as they reached for his belt, unbuttoned his jeans and felt the hardness of her reward. Enjoying her touch, and her tongue, he let her guide his cock out of his jeans and then took control, pushing inside her, playing with her, sensing how badly she wanted him. He was, however, a little surprised; he hadn't anticipated her payment methods, but was happy to be indebted to her. Abbie, however, had hoped he would feel a little gratitude.

"Is this how everyone thanks you, Abbie?" His soft tone increased her longing. "If I'd known this was the arrangement, I would have approached you sooner..." He smiled, knowing she needed his mouth as much as his dick, and leaned in close to tease her, whispering gruffly. "Do I have to pay for each performance? I wouldn't want you to feel short-changed." Whilst she very much enjoyed his jesting, she was concerned they'd be heard, but her attempts to encourage taciturnity were failing. Silencing his words with her mouth, the inevitable rapid breathing and groaning would be a little more difficult to disguise. As he thrust brutally, his hands were painfully gentle on her skin and he continued to tease her with his tongue and his lips, arousing her more, but when she begged for his mouth, there was a knock at the door, and, feeling audacious, he whispered again, "Let them in."

Composing herself, she prayed she could prevent an intrusion. "I'm in the middle of something. I'll come and find you in a minute..."

Jesse couldn't resist: "I'm the one in the middle of some—" Her hand flew to his mouth as his smile spread across his face and, pushing deeper inside her, he watched her struggle to keep quiet.

Stifling her cries, she waited until it was safe. "You want another audience?" She was a little surprised but not displeased.

"I give a pretty good performance..."

Their child-like giggles soon stopped as, finished with the games, he was determined to make the most of this woman. With her breathing heavier, her contentment was evident and he enjoyed the unexpected impact he was having. This was a first for him: his skills had been practised on his peers, and they'd been pretty few, but now he wondered why when, without inhibition, Abbie had made it perfectly clear what she wanted, and when…and he liked that. The smile disappeared as he kissed her hard. God, he wanted to make her come, and as he rammed her hard, he awaited admonishment, but it seemed rough was what she wanted, and he was happy to indulge her. Feeling the pain of her nails digging deep, forcing him further inside her, he, like she, wanted more; wanted those nails piercing his skin and, pushing down on her hands, she responded well, delighting him as he watched her climax, clutching him tight. He found her mouth, needing to taste her breath as she came and, increasing momentum, he watched her squirm as her pussy throbbed, knowing he was responsible for her exhilaration and desire, and, as he marvelled at the events of the past few days and today's culmination being the highlight of what had already been an incredible experience, he welcomed his orgasm…and boy was it sweet! Relishing every second, he closed his eyes to heighten his buzzing senses and as he slowly opened them, he kissed her passionately, before the smile reappeared and his ego swelled.

As she controlled her breathing, Abbie stroked his chest, desperate for more and disappointed he would have to leave. "Your debt is partially satisfied, Jesse, but we can work something out for the rest." She laughed; she would obviously need to add interest.

"Well, I'll agree to whatever terms you have, but I'm sorry, I've got to go. My family are waiting outside…" He dressed himself as she realised what he'd said.

She gasped. "What? Why didn't you say anything?"

"You didn't give me a chance…or a choice, but don't worry, they'll understand! I'll see you soon. And thank you…for everything." He kissed her again, but she stopped him.

"Christ, you can't tell them…!"

Kissing her hand, he smiled as he left the office.

She closed her eyes and chewed her lip, unsure if he would, indeed, confess. She straightened her clothing as Grace, the mystery intruder, walked in. "Is that what you were in the middle of? Honey, you owe me. Next time, you let me in, OK?!"

***

Back from her reminiscence, Abbie was keen to find her friend and, having greeted several familiar faces, she hugged Rose tight. "How are you, my darling?"

"So glad you're here; it's bad enough being polite to my family, but for some reason Michael's are here too! Hi boys, you OK? Looking good, Eddie; Joe…" She sighed – what could she say?

"You look divine, Rosie, but I'll try to restrain myself." He knew she adored him but equally adored her husband; maybe one day…

"Come on, Rose. Just think of Francesca; she's paid a lot of money for this wedding. I'm sure you can be civilised for one day."

"Well, if she hadn't invited the whole bloody family it would have cost a hell of a lot less!"

Rose was straight-talking, honest and open, but it met with disapproval by a lot of people. Clashing frequently with her own family, she hadn't spoken to most of her husband, Michael's, for years and making small-talk was not her forte at the best of times, but to keep the peace, it was an intolerable ask, and seeing her in action was a source of constant amusement for Abbie. She could never quite understand people's perception of her friend. She had a heart of gold but spoke her mind – where's the problem? Rose, however, was indifferent to the various opinions of her: "If you don't like what I have to say then don't ask my opinion". Good point.

"I'll get you a drink, darling, but just the one for now; we'll have a few more later, I promise, but you need to take it easy for now; I'll be watching you…"

"What happened to you, Abbie? You used to be fun... Hi darling – mwah." As another tedious relative engaged Rose in another tedious conversation, Abbie laughed and headed to the bar.

Back with a small glass of something mildly alcoholic, she interrupted politely, ignored the disapproval from her friend and left her with her inadequate drink and, along with the boys, went to find Danny in the orangery.

They embraced him, shook his hand and engaged in pleasantries. He was his usual calm and charming self, but it was clear he was extremely happy: Frankie was his world and he wasn't afraid to show it. He'd had a promising political career when they met but had given it up to help her, with no regrets, choosing instead to support her as her online catering business became hugely successful, making her very rich, very young. She had, however, handled her wealth well and once the business was thriving, she'd set up workshops locally to teach people to cook, but only those with a real need – single parents, low-earners and troubled teenagers – and they were free, funded by her ever-expanding business and various fund-raising events, including an annual cake-baking competition that was taken very seriously by the locals. Danny co-ordinated these workshops and was just starting to move them further afield; he and Frankie promoted them, unashamedly, at every chance, including today at their wedding, with a post-box for donations instead of gifts.

Having set the budget for her wedding, Frankie had booked the Manor, asked Abbie to book Jesse, happy with whatever fee he demanded (luckily for her, the only payment he wanted was Abbie), and set about finding the right designer for her dress, but less than a week later, whilst discussing wedding plans on the phone, she'd literally stumbled across a young man on the street, breaking two of his fingers and badly bruising his arm. She discovered he was homeless as she drove him to the hospital and the expense of the day suddenly hit her as hard as she'd hit poor

Brad. Paying for him to be treated privately, she decided to rent him a flat and, as Fate waved her mysterious hand, discovered he was a very natural and talented cook. A local restaurateur owed her a favour and took Brad under his wing, whilst she used her wedding budget to fund his evening tuition. After eighteen months of sheer bloody hard work, he was able to branch out on his own, and it was his company, not hers, that was providing the catering today, and she insisted on paying. Her generosity amazed Danny, but he totally got her; he understood exactly what she stood for and was proud of all she had achieved. Abbie couldn't think of a couple more suited or more in sync. Frankie, as straight-talking as her mother, had her father's softer edge and was passionate about her local community, and Danny was awed by her.

Abbie watched him chatting and smiling with the guests and wondered how it must feel to find 'the one'; she and Pete had just kind of happened, and only because he was the first opportunity she'd had to get away from her father. With rumours about her dad always familiar, she'd ignored them until he turned his attention to her. He'd never touched her, but he didn't need to: making her strip to her underwear and dance provocatively while he wanked was enough to make her scrub herself with bleach, night after night, in a desperate bid to remove the filth that, although not visible, could be felt on every inch of her body. With no mother or sibling to trust, and too scared to confide in her friends, the shame she felt ruled her existence, and she'd kept her dirty secret until she met Pete, and when she'd finally scrapped together enough courage to uncover that festering wound, she knew instantly she'd misplaced her trust. Once he knew, he beat her daily, blaming her, not only for what he was doing but what her father had done, delighting, seemingly, in prolonging her suffering. She thought she'd loved him once, despite the punches, and assumed he must have loved her, but seeing Danny and Frankie, she laughed at her naivety. Rose and

Michael had been together for twenty-nine years, but they, too, would admit they didn't quite have what the happy couple had. What the hell was their secret? She wasn't the jealous type, but she had to concede to a tiny bit of envy. She'd had many partners since Pete but nothing serious; the older guys were too serious, and thankfully, very few, expecting her to be responsible and demure; the younger ones...well, they were just too young, though somewhat more exciting. She wondered what could have happened if she'd found Danny before Frankie...

"Who are you smiling at?" Eddie startled her. "I've just seen Rose trying to be polite – she can't do it. She made me swear you'd find her after the ceremony. Don't show me up again, Mum!" He knew they were a lethal combination, but he found their behaviour amusing, though he would never tell his mother. Besides, he was hardly saintly himself and, although she was party to only a fraction of his antics, she accepted him as he was, with no reproach.

"Loud and clear, Ed! Do I embarrass you as much as my beloved son, Joe?"

"Nope. You do what you like, Abbie. In fact, if it's going to humiliate Eddie, you have my total backing; I could fill you in on a few of our evenings out recently, if you like. What happened at The Well last week, mate...?"

Joe loved having a hold over his friend. He could understand Eddie's need for extremes: his own behaviour was somewhat egregious but always controlled; his partner in crime, however, less so, but...well, he was just Eddie, love him or hate him. It made for some very interesting evenings: girls – lots of girls – usually drunk or stoned, different positions, locations and occasionally the odd toy or two – it gave him a lot of ammunition! He, unlike his friend, was generally a little more discreet...though there would always be the odd moment...

"Yeah, yeah, whatever! How's the poker going, Joe?!" Eddie knew his friend would never reveal his secrets, nor he Joe's, and he was eternally grateful. He wasn't ashamed, but there were some things his mother didn't need to know – he would hate to disappoint her.

As the room suddenly hushed, the music began and Frankie and Michael walked in to a room full of standing smiles. She would command the room quite naturally at any time, with no effort on her part, but today, no one else stood a chance. And a single, collective thought emanated from the men in the room: *Lucky bastard!*

2

A short and simple ceremony paved the way for a lavish and luscious breakfast, jubilant toasts and crisp, honed, perfectly-timed speeches. Now the partying could begin in earnest, with no restrictions and no questions asked. Tomorrow's hang-overs were a given and quite possible a condition of each invitation, but anything else would be a bonus.

As Eddie dragged Joe to the bar, Abbie went to rescue Rose and she surveyed the room to assess the attitude and competition. Jesse would be here later and she knew that would bring its own storm...but then there was Joe – woe betide anyone that went near Joe.

"Right, Ms Dawson, this is now my time! I have a glass, I have a bottle, and now, I have my best friend – behave like it and get pissed with me!"

"Yes, Mrs Wells. Pop that cork and top me up." They chinked glasses and Abbie praised her friend. "Well done. You survived the service without blood-shed – I knew you could do it."

"Yeah, well, luckily I only have the one child so I won't have to repeat the ordeal again."

Abbie laughed. "They can't all be that bad..."

"Yeah, they can...and they are; just look at them. Michael's sister's the worst – just watch the way she looks down her nose at everyone. Mind you, she's got to have pretty good neck muscles – look at the size of it!" Rose's forced geniality could now be packed away for another time.

Abbie allowed her confidante to dissect every aspect of her family and in-laws until finally, exhausted from hysteria, she thanked her for her counsel and for not stooping to the levels of her relatives.

Sipping her wine, Abbie tried her best to avoid Rose's eye. "So, what time's the band arriving?"

"You mean: what time's Jesse arriving! You're terrible, my dear friend, terrible. They'll be here in about half an hour or so. Are you going to sneak him back in the boot of Joe's car?" Rose was amazed at the effect Abbie had on young men.

She giggled. "I don't think Eddie would approve if he found out."

"I'll have him then, I'm sure Michael wouldn't mind, especially after my generosity today… I don't know how you do it. How long have you known him now – it's got to be six years, surely?"

"Yeah, something like that." Abbie raised her glass and smiled mischievously. "Six wonderful, mouth-watering years…!"

Rose laughed. "How's his mother these days?"

"I know! I feel awful when I speak to her: she's so sweet and she always thanks me for 'discovering' him…she just doesn't know how much of him I've discovered!" She buried her face in her hands as Rose roared. "She clearly has no idea that her little boy's talents aren't just limited to his music!" She sighed dramatically. "And he's not such a little boy either…"

Rose raised her hand. "That's enough, thanks." She reflected on how many of Abbie's affairs remained a mystery. "Was Jesse the first…one?"

Abbie feigned ignorance "The 'first one'…?"

"What: you want me to spell it out? The first guy barely out of nappies that you decided to f—"

"OK, OK…but that's a little unfair, Rose…"

"Really; how would you describe them, then?"

Abbie's smile spread. "Well…I'd say they were pretty delicious…willing to learn…"

"That's enough!"

"You asked…"

"Yes, and I also asked if Jesse was the first, but as you're deliberately avoiding the question, I'll ask again: was Jesse the first guy barely out of nappies that you decided…"

"Shh! Keep your voice down." Abbie's concern was rather amusing. "No…that was Carl." She felt her face flush.

"Carl…do I know Carl?"

"No, I don't think so." She sincerely hoped not.

"And how old was Carl?"

"C'mon, Rose, what does that matter? Can't we just continue discussing the day so far and slagging off your relatives?"

"We'll get to that. It doesn't matter, I just want to know."

Abbie sighed in protest. "Twenty-one."

"Abbie!"

"But I was only thirty-four…" *Only…*

"Oh, that's alright then. Was Jesse the youngest then?"

She bit her lip. "No…that was Matt…"

Rose poured the wine. "What, *Matt?* Abbie! And how old was he? Please tell me he was legal…though, to be fair…"

Abbie feigned shock. "Rose! Don't you judge me when you're thinking the same!"

Laughing loudly, she looked at her friend. "Yeah, the difference is, my darling, I only think about it; you, however, are happy to act upon it."

"You have a wicked tongue!" Ignoring the lack of subtlety, she had to concede: her friend was right.

Although she adored Abbie, Rose couldn't resist teasing her about her…interests. "Well, you may well be right…but yours is rather more celebrated…"

"ROSE!" What had she heard?

"I'm joking, I'm joking. So come on then, how old was Matt? Hang on, do the boys know?"

"Eighteen…and no, they don't know."

Because of her father's penchant for young flesh, Abbie had avoided anyone under the age of eighteen and, besides, what would she tell the boys? Her partners may have been young, but they were adult and only too happy to accommodate her; she had never expected them to do anything they weren't comfortable with, but it would seem they were comfortable with…well, pretty much anything.

"That's shocking, why did I not know? I need time to digest this, Abbie, it could have a major impact on our friendship."

"I know, I'm sorry. But I didn't force them – they were very willing, Rose, *very* willing, and, well, I didn't want to appear rude…"

Rose was amused. "Well, that's very honourable of you!"

Joe joined them for a while, and joked about Eddie's attempts to impress not one, but two of Frankie's bridesmaids, aware that Abbie was completely ignorant to his preference for multiple partners. "There should be enough room in the car for both of them. More wine, ladies?"

Rose waited until he was far enough away. "So, what about Joe?"

Abbie looked at her friend. "What do you mean, 'What about Joe?'"

"What about Joe, where does he fit in?" She'd had suspicions about them for years but was reluctant to probe…until now.

"Well…he…Rose: what do you mean?"

"What? C'mon, Abbie: he's fucking you in his head every time he looks at you!" But the response she received made her laugh. "Oh, my God: you didn't know? That's hilarious! Abbie, wake up!"

Whilst she wasn't sure either way, she had at least hoped, but couldn't bring herself to share that. Now, with Rose's observation as confirmation, things could very well change…and not before time. She smiled at the implications.

"I assumed you'd been screwing for years but just kept

it quiet. Christ, what's taken you so long? He's gorgeous! He's sexy, he's young – sorry – he's charming…he's dirty – haven't you heard? God, I'm jealous! There's something quite sinister in those eyes…I wouldn't mind finding out what that's all about…"

Abbie giggled. She may have been in total agreement with her friend, but she had no desire to betray her interest…for now. She trusted Rose with everything, but Joe was different…very different: she wasn't sure she'd understand.

On cue, he arrived with another bottle and Rose couldn't resist: "So, Joe, if Eddie's taking care of two of the bridesmaids that leaves two more – either of them any good? Be a shame to miss out…"

He chuckled. "Thank you, Rosie. I'm touched by your concern. Who would you recommend?"

She looked at Abbie. "Well, Ella's the brunette – I think she'd be more suitable, but she's thirty, I think… Are you fond of older women?" Abbie gently kicked her under the table.

"You know I am, Rosie, but I thought you and Michael were very happy…"

She smiled. "We are, my darling, but you know there's always a place for you."

He took her hand, kissed it gently and smiled. "Believe me, Rosie, I know. Just let me know when." Another kick went undetected.

Eddie sauntered over, a little worse for wear. "What you up to, mate? Just been trying to get you in there."

"Thanks, Ed, but maybe not tonight. I need to make sure you get home safely, my friend." Drunken girls really weren't his style, but Eddie couldn't quite understand that.

"Fine, mate. If you want to be gay, you be gay. I don't have a problem with that."

"Well thanks, man, that means a lot!"

Rose looked up and saw Jesse walk in. "Yay, Jesse's here! Wow, he's early…I wonder why that is…?" She stood up and waved him over. "Hiya, gorgeous. How the hell are you?"

The change is Joe's manner did not go unnoticed; Abbie's relationship with Jesse was something she never openly discussed, but he knew, as did her son, though Eddie was less concerned. Joe, however, found it hard to hide his contempt, a fact Jesse was well aware of, and rather amused by. Abbie looked forward to seeing how the evening progressed.

As she stood up, Jesse hugged her tight. "Hi, Abbie, you look amazing. How are you?" Aside from his obvious beauty, he had an enchanting air that he could easily abuse – as could she – if he were so inclined. He endeared himself to everyone, except Joe, and seemed to know which metaphorical buttons to press.

"I'm great, Jesse, thank you. So excited you're here. How are you, how's the family?"

He smiled. "Yeah, they're good thanks; Mum sends her love." Not a whiff of irony. Abbie ignored Rose's elaborate choking. Although she adored his mother, it wasn't quite enough to leave him alone. "Hi, Joe, how's it going?" Jesse shook his hand and Joe managed to smile. "All good, Jesse."

"Where's Eddie? EDDIE! Hey, man, how's it going?"

Eddie walked back to the table. Unlike his friend, he was fond of Jesse, but more so after a little self-indulgence. He hugged him and shook his hand. "Fantastic, mate, couldn't be better. How's things with you? Can't believe you're everywhere, man. I'm getting sick of seeing your face."

Jesse laughed. "I know, me too, but good job I don't look like you, aye?!"

Despite his on-going affair with Abbie, he and Eddie got along well; it was never mentioned and Jesse respected them both enough to keep it private. They knew it would be short-lived, but so long as Jesse treated his mum well, Eddie was happy.

"Right, let's get you a drink and you can tell me everything that's going on." Abbie took his arm and marched him to the bar.

As Eddie wandered off back to his bridesmaids, Joe watched Abbie and Jesse intently, trying to gauge their conversation.

Fuck! He'd forgotten about Jesse; that could fuck things up a little. Why hadn't he thought of that? Although he knew their history, until now, he hadn't seen them together – he could have survived without that little gem – but being party to their flirting was, at best, nauseating, at worst, fucking infuriating! He breathed deeply to calm his rising anger: Jesse was no threat. He could see the attraction: he was a pleasure to look at, and he'd be tempted himself if he hadn't been so desperate for Abbie, but he was nothing more than a temporary distraction.

"Are you OK, Joe…?" Rose had seen his face.

He smiled – charm restored. "Absolutely."

"Looks like she's spoiled for choice…"

Realising she'd recognised his intentions he was momentarily thrown but quickly recovered his façade. "But you know I'd never cheat on you, Rosie."

She laughed. "Yeah, celibacy comes so naturally to you, Joe."

He held her gaze. "There are some things that come more naturally to me – would you like me to show you?"

Rose shook her head. "Oh, I think that would be a very bad idea."

Walking back, arm in arm, laughing as Jesse talked about his work, Abbie knew Joe would be watching. "Make sure you come and find me when you break, Jesse. You owe me a dance…"

"Just a dance…?"

As they sat down, Joe excused himself and went to get some air – a little too much Jesse, and a little too much familiarity from Abbie. Hopefully, it wouldn't be too long until the band started and his competition would fade into the background.

Seeing Ella, he watched her: she wasn't bad – not Abbie, of course, but Rose had chosen well. What did he have to lose? As he approached her, she smiled provocatively and it was clear there was no need for introductions: she knew who he was and made no attempt to conceal her admiration.

"Have you had a good day, Joe?"

"Yes, I have thank you, but I generally find the evenings are more fun at weddings...you never know what's going to happen."

She smiled. "Mmm...all those endless possibilities. I think weddings bring out the romance in most people."

Joe erred more on the side of pragmatism. "Romance? I was thinking weddings bring out the drunk in most people..." He smiled at his own asperity, but he was nothing if not honest. Romance was never part of his agenda, and he never pretended it was; sex, however, was top of the bill. With his acerbity wasted on Ella, he lowered his expectations.

"Have you seen the gardens, Joe?"

"Yes, many times. I spent a lot of time here when I was younger..." *with Abbie.*

"Have you seen the 'hidden garden' at the back of the courtyard?" She started to walk away, confident he would follow.

"No, I don't believe I have." Smiling, he played her game. Accustomed to the attention he attracted, he was unfazed, although it certainly had its advantages. Sex always came easy – which was just as well given his appetite – and he was happy to relinquish control, so long as he reaped the rewards. Whenever he was horny, he could find any number of women happy to indulge him at the local bar, but occasionally, just occasionally, he would treat himself to a wank, for the sheer hell of it.

Ella led him round the outside of the house to the courtyard on the other side where it was quieter, and in the far corner a gap in the wall led to a fairly large, formal garden, not visible from the house, and in amongst the maze of box hedges was a concealed wooden bench, surrounded by lavender and delphiniums.

"See." She bit her lip. "A 'hidden garden.'" She led Joe to the bench.

"So how do you know about this?" He imagined this wasn't her first visit.

"I've been to a few weddings here."

Smiling, he sat down, and, joining him, Ella leaned forward and kissed him softly. Whilst never a surprise, it amused him to see how quickly women revealed their intentions, but it made his life a whole lot easier, so he felt no need to complain. The expectation of more could be a tricky issue and, no doubt, she too would idealise her charms and their ability to hook him. Disappointment was a hard, but very necessary, lesson.

She slowly unbuttoned his shirt. "You have quite a reputation, Joe. I was interested to see what all the fuss was about…"

"Really? How interested?"

She kissed his chest as her hands moved down to unbuckle his belt and as she quickly unbuttoned his trousers, pleased at her own directness and initiative, she was keen to prove her proficiency. His wry smile gave way to a gasp as she nuzzled her face deep in his crotch, unaware, despite her knowledge of him, that she'd be nothing more than a pleasant memory. This was what he preferred: his cock deeply imbedded in an eager mouth. Sex could be tricky at times, although he always managed to find a way. Abbie would, of course, feature, and low-lighting helped; in fact, anything that could facilitate his illusion of her, so observing the manipulation of his dick from above was always welcome. The only exception had been Molly – *Oh God, Molly*. Barely fifteen when he met her, she'd just turned seventeen and her cousin, Freddie, lived a few doors along from Abbie's. The three boys had grown up together, though Eddie had got on infinitely better with Fred than Joe, but when Molly came to stay for a week in the holidays, his life changed immediately and irrevocably. There had been an instant spark between them and a silent acknowledgement of where it would lead, and to his delight, Molly slipped out every night to meet him in Swallow Lane Park. The gates would be locked at eight o'clock, so they would sneak down to Shadow Lane, at the back of the park, and climb a couple of trees to get in.

Heading to the far end, where the foliage was denser, she had endowed him with a week he would never forget. With complete domination, initially, she'd demonstrated her expertise, and he was keen to learn, but by the end of the week, he'd developed a contumacious, insatiable taste that would change him dramatically. Confident and demanding, she'd communicated her requirements succinctly, and naturally he'd obliged and with her propensity for pain, masturbation and experimentation, she'd whet his appetite, and his palate was transformed. Needing more and seeing her lust for sex and discomfort, he'd pushed boundaries he was previously oblivious to and the excitement he'd experienced was like nothing he'd felt before, and she'd happily relinquished control and indulged his every whim.

His new-found confidence and loss of all inhibition had furthered his desires and the week had shown him a world he would continue to explore, but sadly, without her. Used to servicing many of the local females, he'd always played by their rules, but Molly had none, and his own gratification had become his priority, though her satisfaction had come primarily from his appetence for the extremities, and the ease with which his hands, his tongue and his cock could affect her was an education he was happy to foster. It was a sad day when she returned home, but the transformation in Joe was incontrovertible.

Now, as Ella attempted to demonstrate her attributes, he had to close his eyes and visualise Abbie. Calling her name had caused a few awkward moments over the years, but he could control that now…just…unless, of course, it provided an easy exit from a potentially expectant situation that would otherwise drag on; in which case, it was a blessing.

She sucked hard and groaned; she appeared to be enjoying herself more than Joe, but despite her efforts, he'd had better and with attempts to focus on the positives – or Abbie, instead – finally, he came, pleased it was over quickly. Raising her head, Ella ran her tongue over his stomach and up to his chest, playing with his nipples, hoping for a reaction, but he was finished. As she redressed him, she watched him, trying unsuccessfully to read his face and as she kissed him again, he held her gaze.

She got up, smiling. "I'd better go back." She felt sure she'd left her mark. "But come and find me later."

She mistook his smirk for sincerity. "I'll see what I can do."

Enjoying the quiet, he sat for a moment and his thoughts returned to Abbie. Jesse wasn't an issue; she saw him once a year at most, but Joe was always there and she clearly had no issue with younger men...and he'd waited long enough.

He laughed as he thanked Ella. She'd calmed his thoughts with her generous mouth and allowed clarity to win out, but she'd never know, and he was certain she'd prefer not to.

Making his way to the gents', he washed away all the evidence: he didn't want to be smelling of somebody else's perfume when he finally had Abbie to himself. Danny walked in. "You got lucky already, Joe? Christ, it's my wedding day and I've got to wait 'til tonight!" He was amused, though not surprised, at Joe's speed.

"Yeah, but you got it on tap now, my friend."

"You're right. Thanks, mate, much appreciated!"

"Anytime. Right, next..." He knew Danny was discreet, and was grateful; he couldn't risk exposure, although Abbie, too, was well aware of his reputation, and was, in fact, not so different herself.

As he wandered back to the reception, he felt the weight of Ella's glare but managed to avoid it. Abbie was still with Jesse and Rose, but she was looking a little concerned. "Joe! Where have you been?"

"In the gardens. Why, what's up?"

"I think Ed's had a little too much to drink; he needs to ease up a bit. He won't listen to me, but do you think you could have a word with him? Sorry, but he's not usually this bad."

Oh yes he is! "Yeah, it's alright, I'll find him." As he gently touched her arm, Jesse, for the first time, noticed the spark. *Wow, where did that come from?* He hadn't seen much of Joe over the years but couldn't believe he'd missed that. The animosity had been clear for a number of years, but he'd put it down to Joe's ego, dented by missing an opportunity Jesse had secured; never once had he considered that Abbie may be pursuing her own prospect. *Shit.* That could seriously impact on his evening.

Eddie was sat next to the pond when Joe found him, looking like he'd seen water for the first time. "Alright, buddy?"

"Joe! Where have you been, man? Got some good stuff here, you want some?"

"No, you're alright, Ed. And maybe you should ease up a bit, mate. If you want to play nicely with those bridesmaids later, you might want to calm it down a bit."

"Yeah, good point, good point. You're always so clever, Joe, always know the answers. No wonder all the girls want your cock." He grabbed at Joe's crotch. "Maybe I should have a go." He giggled like a child.

"Nah, I'm not your type, Ed; I don't drink enough. Let's get you to the car, you can lie down for a bit."

"Is that how you do it, man, take 'em for a lie down in your car?!" Eddie amused himself.

"No, mate, I don't need the car. C'mon."

Dragging his friend to the car-park, Joe eased back the seats in the car and gave him a bucket from the boot. "I'll come back in half an hour to check you're still alive."

Eddie unzipped his trousers. "I'll be waiting…"

Unimpressed, Joe slammed the door and shook his head: why did he do this to himself? Maybe he'd been conditioned by a drunken father, but Joe rarely drank to excess. He could drink, no doubts there, but as soon as that fog descended, he quit. Yet, despite his own father's addiction, Eddie was happy to try anything if it enhanced his evening – always amused at Joe's refusal to indulge – unaware that, with no ability to moderate his enjoyment, it generally had the opposite effect and for Joe, safeguarding his friend had become a regular feature of their evenings – what the hell would happen if he wasn't there? Maybe he should let Eddie sort himself out...but he cared too much for him, and his mother, to leave him be.

Back with Abbie – thankfully, she was without Jesse – he reassured her that Eddie would be OK, knowing she was unaware of her son's habit, but he couldn't bring himself to tell her; not a line he was prepared to cross.

Abbie sighed with relief. "Thanks, Joe. I really appreciate it." She squeezed his hand, and held on a little too long. "He wouldn't want to miss the evening."

"Is Jesse about to start then?"

"Yep, they start at seven, I think; the girls should be here soon."

3

'The girls' were a group of disparate friends Abbie had enjoyed for years, ever since the boys were at grammar school when, with more free time, she'd joined a book group who, without her prior knowledge, focussed on more adult literature and, despite the initial surprise and reticence, they'd entertained her with their amusing, albeit indelicate, interpretations and observations, fuelled by the requisite supply of alcohol – during the day – and frequent hysteria that followed each comment, and, at a time when she felt quite isolated, they'd welcomed her and forged an unlikely bond that, to this day, was imbued with indecent behaviour, regardless of their sophisticated appearance. Rose had reluctantly tagged along, but she too had found a place where her unbiased critique of the world was welcomed and encouraged.

They were a rowdy bunch who enjoyed gossiping as much as drinking and were well known by the boys. Many a party at Abbie's house consisted of the girls, obscene quantities of alcohol and outrageous conversations, whilst their husbands discussed business and sport. Josie, the loudest, was conscious of Joe's reputation and had made it very clear, when he was about seventeen, that she was available to him. Generally the centre of attention, she took very good care of herself and was confident with the results, and he'd taken her up on her offer only once, but they never spoke about it and he was sure he wasn't the first, or indeed the last, aware too that she'd made a play for Eddie because she'd suggested that maybe the two of them would like to arrive together. Joe saw no problem, but Ed wasn't so keen. Instead, Joe asked if she might like to invite a friend and the following week, he was greeted by her and said friend at Josie's house, and practically dragged to the bedroom. The house was pretty much as expected: large and contemporary, with very lavish furnishings and far enough from the neighbours that noise and visitors were never an issue. The master bedroom was elegantly finished and he was struck by the irony of the refined surroundings being the backdrop to the salacious activities he was hoping for.

With the experience of a man several years older, he was nonetheless astounded at the events that followed: on their insistence, he'd hand-cuffed them to the bed, close enough to ensure ease and he'd watched as they kissed and licked and writhed around, instinctively showing his appreciation by masturbating and coming over their bodies, watching in awe as they proceeded to lick his cum off each other, and, as they finished, he'd buried his face in Josie's pussy, teasing her with his tongue and forcing his hand inside her, riveted by the satisfaction she displayed, but she'd come quickly, minimising his own pleasure. But his disappointment was short-lived: with barely enough time to catch his breath, he was pulled on top of her nameless friend, as she grabbed his swelling cock, encouraging more rigidity and, when satisfied with its magnitude, pushed it deep inside her. Honouring her request for a little rough treatment, and wondering if Abbie would be so demanding, he'd hammered hard, sighing deeply as he witnessed Josie's mouth devour her counterpart's breasts; he reached for Josie's in return and marvelled at the scene playing out before him, silently commiserating Eddie on his decision. With endless possibilities dancing around his mind, and too many sensations in his hands and dick, his breathing became erratic and he came easily, uncuffing his accomplices when he'd recovered and watching them entertain themselves and, indeed, him once more, whilst he waited patiently for the next erection, confident, with the support of the performance provided for him, it wouldn't be long. Soon enough, his patience was rewarded and he'd forced Josie's face in her friend's pussy whilst he fucked her from behind, hard and fast, enjoying his vantage point, appreciating the sights and sounds that stimulated his prurient tastes, grateful for the commitment of his hosts and their apparent lack of inhibition. As Josie sated her friend, Joe closed his eyes, allowing her rasping breaths to entice his climax, conceding control, totally, embracing the iniquity that he would continue to pursue. It had been a very satisfying afternoon for all concerned and his only regret was that he hadn't thought to record their activities: replaying them would have been a sheer delight if sex ever became thin on the ground...*if.*

Next, was Philippa. She'd been a little more persistent and, having dropped hints for years, she'd tried many times, unsuccessfully, to inebriate Joe enough to coax him into a compromising position, but had finally cornered him in the bathroom at Abbie's house the previous year. Before he'd managed to zip up his trousers, she'd grabbed his cock and wanked him. Nothing was said, but she'd turned him round to watch his face in the mirror, and he'd closed his eyes, thinking of Abbie, hoping it would be over quickly. Whilst Philippa may have been lost on him, he'd take a free wank any day, and he had to concede, she was pretty good at it. As he visualised Abbie's mouth covering his dick, he came over her hand and she casually rubbed his cum over her breasts, kissed him on the cheek and left. Remaining momentarily, he'd smiled at himself in the mirror and thanked Abbie for the major role she played in his sex life. A knock on the door prompted him to wash his hands, and as he opened the door, he wished he'd remained partially dressed as his saviour greeted him with a smile. "All OK, Joe?"

He smiled devilishly. "Not bad, but it would be a whole lot better if you'd let me stay in here with you..."

Sorely tempted, Abbie hesitated: Eddie was too close. She smiled seductively. "Not the most romantic of venues…"

He held her gaze. "Who said anything about romance?" He backed away as she watched him, wishing she'd locked the door before he'd left.

Philippa had often suggested a replay, but he'd convinced her that her husband's reaction, if he ever found out, would be catastrophic and she eventually turned her attention to some other poor soul.

And then there was Lizzie. She was the quiet one and by far the prettiest but very small and very slight, and Joe felt sure he would break her if he fucked her. She'd never propositioned him as Josie and Philippa had, but her eyes said more than she did, and she was the one he felt would be the most delightful. Now, however, with Abbie so close, he didn't want to take a chance… but if things didn't work out…

Lastly, Jackie, and she just wanted to drink and have fun. It was clear she loved her husband, but Joe was sure he could seduce her if he were so inclined, though being the warmest of the group, he was happy to engage in light banter, rather than direct innuendo…for now…

Husbands followed shortly after, with strong hand-shakes and the obligatory slaps on the back. They all liked Joe, but then they had no reason not to; at twenty-three, he was just a boy and had a lot to learn, unaware he had already learned, and mostly from their wives. With no knowledge of their beloveds' surreptitious activities, he had no desire to enlighten them. They worked hard, drank loads and constantly changed their cars; there were bound to be mistresses along the way, but everyone kept their secrets secret and nobody asked too many questions, though if he suddenly felt it necessary to unburden, he suspected his life would be in danger.

***

With greetings dutifully administered, Joe went to check on Eddie. He was snoring loudly with his hand down his trousers, but he hadn't thrown up and he was still alive. He left the sleeping beauty for a while longer and went back to report to Abbie.

"Stephen, honey, you may as well get three or four bottles to start us off – red, ladies?"

Stephen knew he was lucky to have Josie so was usually pretty agreeable and, although oblivious to her penchant for younger men…or, indeed, her close friends, he undoubtedly benefitted so a happy man had no suspicions.

As the wine was poured, the gossip began and, whilst enjoying their conversation far more than their husbands', Joe never heard such vulgarity when he was out with the boys, but these women had no shame, and he had no problem with that.

"Oh my God, Rose, you never mentioned Jesse would be back for the wedding – you dark horse!"

Rose smiled. "I wanted to keep it a surprise, Phil – I know how much you all love him." She winked at Abbie.

"Ooh…is he alone? I may have to fight you for him, Abbie. Joe, I never thought I'd see the day when you had competition, but Jesse's looking pretty damn good." Philippa was almost salivating.

Joe laughed, watching Abbie's face flush, though he had to agree, Jesse and his voice had an inexplicable effect on women, but so long as her stayed away from his target, he was unconcerned. With any luck, his adversary would be inundated with offers and leave her alone.

Josie was in total agreement with her friend. "You know, if I was a doctor, I would insist that all men between the ages of eighteen and thirty be checked monthly for testicular cancer; there's a job I could do!" The girls laughed at her complete lack of censorship.

"But they wouldn't all look like Jesse. What about the dirty ones – by dirty, I mean unclean – would you really want to?" Jackie was less convinced.

"I could wear gloves for those!" The girls erupted.

"Just let me know if you need any help with your research there, Josie. Only too happy to help…" Joe held her gaze as he smiled broadly, watching her blush ever so slightly.

"Woohoo!" The collective response made him laugh.

"You're top of my list, Joe. Always." Taking her hand, he kissed it, lingering a little too long.

This was his domain, surrounded by the women he preferred: confident, mature, worldly-wise, and never afraid to speak their minds…and their minds were usually somewhere close to the gutter. None would ever surpass Abbie, but they were a welcome substitute: sex was far more adventurous and intense, and they were insatiable – always a bonus. AND, they couldn't get enough of him.

He went to check on Eddie and was surprised to see he'd faired pretty well. "How you feeling, man?"

"A little fucked, but not too bad. How long was I out for?" He didn't want to miss the fun.

"About half an hour, but the band's just about to start. The girls are here and they're on form. Come on, let's go inside."

Eddie was immediately besieged by the group. Being Abbie's son, they were slightly more reserved, but there was no mistaking their subtle innuendoes and, as the alcohol flowed freely, they bitched about the distinct lack of clothing covering the younger girls, encouraging a debate with him. Joe, in total agreement, entertained them with his observations and suggestions, keeping Abbie well within view. Eventually, when they took to the dancefloor they controlled it, but Joe's eyes were still on Abbie. As innocent as her movements appeared, she was never one to be ignored and he was certain she was aware of the effect she had, not least on him, and he longed for a private performance, with a slow, provocative removal of the seductive clothes adorning her body, confident the bulge in his trousers would fit quite comfortably inside her. Looking up, she smiled when she caught sight of his supervision and whilst he mentally pursued his plans, he spotted an irritating lad sidling up to her, believing she needed support. Tempted to push him away, Abbie chose, instead, to play along, if for no other reason than to antagonise Joe, but he was a little too close and a little too much, and as the song ended and another started, he was still there, squirming around her.

"Who's that prick, Rosie? He's a little too familiar, wouldn't you say?"

"Oh, that's Danny's cousin, Dom. Yeah, he's always trying to get off with one of the girls; you'd think someone would tell him. Feel free, Joe. You'll be doing us all a favour."

Well if it would help... He watched Dom eventually leave the dancefloor and head for the gents' and followed, strolling in behind him and locking the door, confusing the hell out of him.

"Alright, mate?"

"Yes, Dom, I'm well, thank you." He paused, prolonging the poor man's discomfort. "Can I ask you a question, Dom – man to man? Have you ever been fucked in the arse, my friend?" He enjoyed the fear in his victim's eyes. "No? Well I suggest you leave the ladies alone, otherwise there's a strong chance it could happen. They don't like your attention – it's not pleasant to watch – so I think it's best you dance alone…or I'm happy to come back next time you visit the gents' and show you what two men do when they're alone in a public convenience – is that OK?"

Dom stood motionless. Slowly, he nodded his head.

"Thank you, Dom. I really appreciate it; enjoy the rest of the evening."

Unlocking the door, Joe walked out, amused by the fact that men were more terrified of being fucked than beaten up. He, however, felt differently. Nothing, and no one, was off limits and he struggled to understand how anyone could be so narrow-minded, recalling, with a smile, his natural, curious transition to same-sex stimulus. In a state of permanent arousal in the years following his discovery of Abbie, the girls he'd inveigled were unimaginative – despite their assurances and confidence in their limited aptitude – and only searching for a trophy to impress their friends, but with Molly still evoking a lurid greed, the hunt for her successor was fruitless. During the Christmas festivities following her departure, he and Eddie had been to a party locally, and once the alcohol flowed, Eddie was lost. Surveying the room, Joe looked for any female willing to participate in some seasonal cheer, but they were all drunk and spreading themselves around: uninviting and unoriginal. He chatted to a few friends, smoked a couple of cigarettes and soon became aware of a familiar, yet unknown face watching him, and with no viable distraction to exploit, he sauntered over and introduced himself. Carl, unsurprisingly, knew his name – everyone knew Joe – and was surprised at his suggestion to get some air. With Joe's reputation undeniably heterosexual, any deviatory assumptions were farcical, but with a few drinks refuting the copious rumours, Carl took a chance, following readily as he was led away from the party to a secluded field behind the church. Stopping behind a large oak tree, with minimal light, Joe turned and kissed him passionately, relieved to channel his unrequited hunger and keen to experience a new prospect, delighting, if not startling his admirer, and with Carl unwilling to waste time, he unbuttoned Joe's trousers and dropped to his knees. Surprised at Carl's proficiency, equalling that of Molly and surpassing that of any other female at that time, it wasn't long before he came, exhilarated by the notion of a man's mouth around his cock and filling it, undeterred, with his cum. Carl lingered, savouring the taste of him, not ready to part company and as his hands and tongue explored Joe's body, he was eager to encourage further empirical investigations. Facing Joe, he'd kissed him gently, hands still wandering until they rested, massaging his crotch. "I need you inside me."

Smiling before returning his kiss, Joe's hands found their way inside his partner's trousers and with a rejuvenated excitement, he manipulated his dick, mesmerised by the sound of Carl's breathing – desperate and deep, controlled by anticipation and lubricity – and pushing himself against him, he continued to play, relishing in Carl's uncensored felicity, fuelling his own. With escalating fervour, he kissed him aggressively, excited by his reciprocation, still grasping his cock whilst his free hand examined the contours of Carl's body beneath his shirt, taut and smooth, reflecting his own much-celebrated form. As Carl carefully and skilfully engaged in exhorting the means to further his gratification, Joe felt the inevitable stirring that would feed his inherent libidinous curiosity and foster its success, allowing Carl to secure his request. Squeezing his companion's hand, Joe contemplated the ecstasy that would reward him as he exploited the desperation emanating from his prey. Turning him round, his heart pounded and he struggled to control the intensifying concupiscence but, closing his eyes, he steadied his breathing enough to regain his composure and as he penetrated Carl, he sighed deeply, allowing salacity to guide him, leading him to a state of euphoria he had neither expected nor previously experienced. This was good sex, stimulating an urgency to reach a violent consummation and, with no protests from his partner, he plunged deeper and faster inside him, encapsulated in a sublime fantasy of, as yet, unknown magnitude but immense repletion, indomitable and unrelenting, fixed on nurturing his own pleasure for as long as he could. As each thrust propelled him closer to his goal, he welcomed his orgasm, engulfing him in a blanket of delirium, warming him as he stood for a while wallowing in the aftermath of self-indulgence, eventually extracting himself and pulling up his trousers. Carl, blissfully subdued, was satisfied with Joe's work and asked when he could see him again.

Joe, unused and indifferent to repeat performances was happy to part company. "Mmm…unfortunately, Carl, I'm just fifteen and you're what, twenty-one? I don't think that's legal so maybe we should just leave it here…" Watching the change in his expression, Joe thanked him for the experience and left without looking back.

Having assured Abbie he wouldn't be long and that he would visit his father afterwards, he decided to get that pleasure out of the way whilst still on a high but as his father had clearly been waiting for his annual bottle of scotch, the abuse started immediately. "You're late – where the fuck do you think you've been?" He despised his father with a vehemence that was deserved and he chose to ignore the greeting, but his permanently inebriated abuser was looking for a fight. "I said, where the fuck have you been?"

Turning to face his father, he moved closer and, with a low voice, told him what he wanted to hear. "You want to know, really want to know? I've just fucked a man, *Dad*, and it was good – really good: he sucked my dick and I came in his mouth and then, when he'd wanked me enough, I fucked him; you should've heard him when I came inside him… You should try it…but I doubt you're man enough to even get a hard-on."

He recoiled, speechless, scared of what he'd just heard and the venomous way his son's words were delivered. Joe sneered: that was it! He'd beaten his father, finally. No more fear, no more abuse and no more visits – he'd won. He returned to the party to retrieve Eddie and walking back to Abbie's, he was a different boy to the one that had left: his control of Carl and now his father was intoxicating, something he could well get used to. It was an important day and although the only time he'd had sex with a man, a memorable night a couple of years ago, with his dick in the mouth of a married salesman, staying locally during a one-stop commute to an important client, sustained his appreciation of homosexual encounters.

***

When Joe returned from the gents', the tempo had changed somewhat so he took Abbie's hand and led her back to the dancefloor, impeding any attempts by Jesse. He held her tight and breathed deeply; that scent…

"What's their secret, do you think, Joe? Frankie and Danny's? They fascinate me."

"Sex." What else would it be?

Abbie laughed. "Is that it, just sex? No love; no respect; no history? That's a little cynical…"

"I'm a man, what would you expect me to say? It's always about sex, but whilst it will always be that way for a man, the novelty wears off for women and that's when it all goes sour… What?" Whilst there was humour in his tone, Abbie could see the truth in his words.

"Said by the guy who's never had a relationship!"

"Yeah…they get in the way of my…interests."

Abbie smiled. "You won't be rushing into marriage then?" Ever hopeful.

"What makes you say that?" His aversion to matrimony was no secret.

"So, who could tempt you, Joe – one of these lovely young ladies? I can always stay here with Jesse if I'm going to be in the way…"

"'One' Abbie? I'm insulted. Not a lot of point unless there are at least two of them."

She laughed loudly. "OK, which two then?"

"None of them. Not my type: too drunk; too silly; too needy. Not for me."

"Who is for you then? Come on, I've known you for what, eleven years…?"

"Twelve." He'd been counting since day one.

"OK, but I've never seen you with a girl more than once and I can't remember the last time you went on a date."

He laughed. "Not always necessary, Abbie… And why

see someone more than once when there are so many to get through?"

"So it is just about sex? Don't you want a proper relationship?" Surely, at some point even he would want the security...but not before she'd had her way.

"Do you, Abbie? I don't remember seeing any lasting relationships in your life..."

She smiled and looked deep in his eyes. "Maybe we're more alike than you think..."

"You may well be right but, unlike you, I don't see the need to revisit old territory, whereas you fuck Jesse every time he's back. I'd be tempted myself if you didn't have such a hold on him." It was true: although he didn't like the man, he wouldn't turn him down.

Shocked, and visibly so, as his words resonated, that changed somewhat. Joe...and Jesse – now that was a powerful image. Her voice was low when she replied. "But you don't like Jesse...but that's irrelevant. He's a man, in case you hadn't noticed, Joe. Are you...?"

"Gay?" He laughed. "No, I'm not, but I'd rather fuck him than these silly girls in their irritating, drunken state, completely unaware of what they're doing or who they're with. I don't want to wake up tomorrow and be accused of rape."

Taking a little time to respond, Abbie enquired further. "And is that something you're guilty of?" She thought it unlikely, given the endless stream of females offering themselves to him...but he seemed to have no boundaries.

His eyes sparkled dangerously and he whispered in her ear, "Only when I've been asked to..."

Uncomfortably aroused, she avoided his gaze, unable to offer a suitable response, praying her blushes avoided detection, but Joe smiled knowingly, sensing her uneasiness, and banked her reaction for another time. "So what's so special about him, Abbie? Feel free to spare me the details, but it's been going on a long time."

She was relieved to revert to safer ground and turned the tables. "He's very good with his hands, Joe...in fact, it's not just his hands..." Feeling him tense, she laughed. "Come on, you know he's no danger to you..."

But before he could request an elaboration, the song finished and Jesse announced a short break. He kissed her cheek and led her back to their table and, although he'd missed one opportunity, he was determined to forge ahead with another. "Who do you dance for, Abbie? You know you're good, but who's it for?"

She smiled – *why limit yourself?* "Everyone."

Eddie was embroiled in entertaining the girls and Abbie was pleased that he'd slowed down a little. With any luck, he'd enjoy their attention enough to sober up.

"Is it my turn next, Joe?" Josie, more brazen with several glasses of wine, looked at him with innocent eyes and a wicked smile.

"To dance...or did you have something else in mind?" He detected Abbie's annoyance so wanted to see how far he could push Josie.

She felt her face warm slightly. "I don't mind..."

"But her husband might!" Jackie was oblivious to their history so happily joked at their expense. Whilst the others laughed, Joe smiled and watched Josie as the colour increased in her face.

Unfortunately for her, Eddie noticed. "Feeling a little flushed there, Josie? Perhaps it's the wine...or...is there something else...?" And as he smiled into his glass, all eyes turned to her. Joe looked away, enjoying Eddie's taunts and Josie's embarrassment, but as the attention inevitably shifted in his direction, he looked back at her and winked, slightly aggrieved when Jesse's return halted any questions.

Jesse was immediately passed around like a new baby, with kisses from all and hugs that were a little too tight, but like Joe, he was used to it…and Josie was immensely grateful for his unintentional intervention.

"How long are you back for, Jesse?" Philippa, having given up on Joe, thought she might try her hand elsewhere.

"About a week or so. It's back-to-back festivals this time of year, but I turned one down to do this gig so I've got a little time off."

"So what are you doing with your time?" A little too eager and a little too obvious, but Jesse smiled sweetly.

He looked at Abbie. "I'm going to try to do some writing and catch up with a few old friends."

"Hands off, Phil, he's way too young for you!" Lizzie was used to her friend's indiscretions but very guarded about her own affairs; none of the girls knew if she'd ever been unfaithful but, conscious of Jesse's many charms, she could always make an exception.

"Never stopped Abbie!" Realising she'd vocalised what should have been an amusing silent reflection, Philippa looked apologetically at her friend for her unintended insult, but she wasn't offended: she knew Phil and her wine too well.

"Anyway…" Rose chipped in. "Food's ready."

As the girls headed for the buffet, Eddie excused himself. Joe, party to his intentions was determined to dissuade him, but as he followed his friend, Ella caught up with him, indignant and unwavering. "What's your game, Joe, are you playing me? You haven't spoken to me since we came back and I saw you dancing with that woman; what is she, your mother?"

He swallowed the anger and gave her a sympathetic smile. "As I recall Ella, it was you who led me to the hidden garden; you who undressed me and you who put my dick in your mouth. If anything, you played me, but I'm not complaining…"

As she raised a hand to slap his face, he stopped her and held her arm firm until she winced. Releasing his grip, he watched her storm back to the house and grinned, rather pleased that little hurdle had been dealt with so early.

Eddie, safely locked in a cubicle, jumped as Joe hammered on the door.

"Hey, this one's taken, man…" He wasn't too pleased at the interruption.

"Eddie, open up."

"Joe, how's it going, mate. What's up?"

"Come on, Ed, open up. I know what you're doing…" Somewhat relieved, if not a little surprised at hearing the door open, he was tired of the stupidity. "Just leave it, man, you don't need it. Let's go back and play with the girls."

Eddie laughed. "Joe, you're sounding more like my mother every day! What's happened to you, when did you become old?"

"I just don't think you need that shit. Come back and have another drink. You've got two bridesmaids waiting back there; too much more of that and you won't remember where your dick goes or where you left it."

He agreed, surprisingly, though Joe knew it was a temporary delay; there was as much chance of him leaving his habit in his pocket as Joe leaving his dick in his trousers.

Returning to the house, he was greeted with the sight of Jesse dancing with Abbie. *Shit – thanks, Ed!* The girls, now in full party mode, grabbed the boys and sat them down between them, continuing their lewd conversations with Abbie out of ear-shot, and whilst Eddie happily encouraged them, Joe was slightly more concerned with his view of the dancefloor.

Conscious of his glare, Jesse was intrigued. "He's a little intense, Abbie." He looked in Joe's direction. "What's that all about?"

"He's harmless, just a little serious sometimes."

"Yeah, I can see that. Be careful, yeah? Not sure I trust him." The evening had demonstrated that no matter what she felt for him, Joe had a hold that she either couldn't or wouldn't escape, and as he kissed her softly on the cheek, he sensed that once Joe had her, he wouldn't let her anywhere near him.

As he returned to the stage, Abbie re-joined the group and sitting on Joe's lap, she caught him off guard and as she wriggled to get comfortable he became instantly hard. He battled with the instinct to gratify himself now, giving the guests a story to recount in the years to come, but with Eddie present, prudence prevailed. With any luck, the party would die down over the next hour or so and he could get her home, lose his friend and… enjoy her company…alone.

With Jesse performing once more, the girls dragged Abbie and Rose back to the dancefloor, singing loudly, gesticulating perversely in his direction and wolf-whistling every time a song ended, and, with no Dom in sight, Joe congratulated himself, though still aware of the potential complication of Jesse. Watching for a while, he was amused by the girls' uninhibited behaviour: by no means indecorous, but close enough to warrant a second glance. Focussing on Abbie and the way her body swayed, he slowly undressed her with his mind, creating his own rhythm and as he considered a trip to the gents' for some instant relief he became aware of Eddie's absence once more. Irritated by the interruption to his contemplation, he finished his drink and went in search of him, finding him sat at a picnic bench, openly enjoying yet another indulgence.

"Eddie, what the fuck's wrong with you? What the fuck are you doing?"

"It's OK, Joe. I've got some more if you want it."

Grabbing the joint, Joe threw it to the floor, extinguishing it with his foot.

"What you doing? Fuck off!" He tried pitifully to push him away.

"Ed, you're wasted!"

"Yeah, I know – I could have been so much more!" His amusement was unappreciated.

"EDDIE, for fuck's sake! You can't keep doing this. You need to sort yourself out, man. Listen to me: sort it out, Ed, you're fucked up!" Despite his anger, Joe's obligation prevented the realisation of his instincts and he kept his hands low. From the age of eighteen, when Eddie first discovered the joy of illegal substances, he'd tried to minimise the damage from his friend's excesses, failing to understand the attraction, but unable to persuade him to stop, and with the passing years, it had become decidedly worse. Dragging him out of view, Joe went in search of some water. "You stay there and don't move!"

"Yes, Mum!"

The temptation to tell Abbie had never been greater, but what would he say? Eddie was her baby and he would surely be implicated in some way, and blah, blah, blah… He walked back to the house, not only irritated, but now acutely frustrated.

"You OK, Joe?" Abbie could see he was tense.

He smiled. "Yeah, just need a drink. Any wine left or shall I get some more?" He headed to the bar to replenish supplies and get Eddie some water, vowing it would be the last time. He made his excuses and headed back to his friend.

"Get up – you can go back to the car." He marched his patient back like a policeman, which amused Eddie no end.

"Here, drink. Stay there 'til you sober up and drink the water. I'll come back in about half an hour and if you're no better, I'm taking you home, Ed. Drink!"

Slamming the car door, he strode back to the house, hovering outside to avoid elaborating on his mood, but the sudden appearance of Ella, walking back from the ladies' gave him the opportunity to vent his frustration.

"I'm sorry, Ella, I was very rude; you caught me at a bad time."

"Really, Joe? What could possibly have been so bad after you'd shot your load in my mouth?!"

He smiled at her candour and gently touched her arm. "You're right, please forgive me. It was appalling behaviour and I have no excuses."

She softened; he was too gorgeous to be angry with and those eyes...

"Have you seen the hidden garden at night?" Taking her hand, he led her back to the courtyard and guided her through the gap in the wall, before pressing her against it. Kissing her softly, he took her hand and placed it on his crotch, slowly lifted her dress and was pleasantly surprised to find no underwear.

He whispered, "I like that."

She released his cock with ill-concealed haste, betraying her desperation once more, satisfied her persistence had finally rewarded her, but as Joe pushed inside her, he felt nothing but contempt for her naivety. As he thrust harder, the wall rubbed her back and though wincing, her pain went unnoticed. This was what she wanted and through arrogant obduracy, he was further aroused by, but completely indifferent to her discomfort, smiling in the darkness until the sound of her scream made him come.

"Happy now?" Swiftly removing himself from her, he readjusted his clothing and, shocked by his tone, Ella silently pulled her dress down. "Thanks, Ella – just what I needed. Good luck walking back to the ladies' with cum dripping down your legs." Sauntering back to the party, leaving both her and the garden behind, with his anger abated, he reasoned she'd been worth it.

Eddie had found his way back to the reception, clutching a half-empty bottle of what looked like vodka and Abbie was worried.

"Joe, I think we need to get him home; I don't know how much he's had, but he's not looking good." She was disappointed in him and to be leaving so early.

"Yeah, OK. Give me a minute." A final visit to the gents'

was necessary to remove all traces of Ella; she wasn't worth jeopardising the rest of the evening.

Back at the Manor, Joe found Abbie saying her goodbyes and caught up as she reached Jesse. A hug was exchanged and a kiss on the cheek, but he was reluctant to let her go. Rolling his eyes, Joe couldn't resist a triumphant smirk.

"Good to see you, Abbie…but I was hoping to see a little more of you…" His disappointment was clear.

"I know. I'm sorry, but Ed's in a real state and…" She shrugged the remains of her apology.

"OK, take care." Convinced she would end the evening with him, he fought to supress thoughts of what he knew Joe had in mind. "See ya, Joe. Look after her."

"Oh I will, Jesse: no need to worry."

"Give me a call towards the end of the week, Jesse, and we'll do lunch." She couldn't let him go completely.

"Sounds good." But not to Joe.

Having found Eddie, they man-handled him back to the car and Abbie opted to sit in the back with him to supervise. Despite the distractions to the evening, Joe was somewhat comforted by the prospect of no interruptions once they were back home.

4

Driving quickly, Joe had to stop en route to ensure Eddie wouldn't throw up. With a slower journey more conducive to his friend's fragile state, he eased up a little, consoling himself with the promise of a suitably vitiated end to the day. Finally, pulling up outside the house, he shook Eddie hard to rouse him: he wanted to conserve his energy for more rewarding activities and carrying a snoring man inside was not what he had in mind.

"Alright, Joe. I'm awake." He was still clutching his bottle and was in no rush to relinquish it.

"Ed, let me take that; if you fall, it's going to go everywhere…"

In his drunken stupor, he was taking no chances. "No, no. I know what you're doing…I'll keep hold of it, thanks." And with Joe as a crutch, he staggered through the door and collapsed on the sofa.

Abbie, concerned about logistical issues, was hopeful for some assistance. "Sorry, Joe, would you mind helping me get him into bed? I don't want to hold you up, but I'm not sure I'll manage on my own."

"Sure. Let me get him some water and we'll sort him out."

Eddie giggled as Joe forced him up the stairs and having finally released the vodka to Abbie's care, she placed it out of reach as he fell onto the bed, retreating to hunt for a bucket, leaving Joe to strip her son to his underwear. "Come on, Joe. Let's see what all the fuss is about!" He pushed his friend's face into his crotch and for a moment, Joe was tempted to grab his cock to see how he would react, but as his looked at him, Eddie seemed to sense his thoughts and backed down, feeling confused. Relieved at his mother's return, he obeyed her instructions to drink the water and sleep it off, confirming the location of the bucket, should he feel the need to use it, and closing the door, Abbie finally relaxed.

Alone at last, Joe could feel the atmosphere change to a more palatable level, assured that the day had, inadvertently, worked to his advantage and would, indeed, end fortuitously.

Back downstairs, Abbie was grateful for his help. "Thanks, Joe." She gently touched his arm. "Do you fancy a glass of wine? I know you've been good all day so one won't hurt. You're welcome to stay if you want to…"

What a charming idea! "Well, if you're sure…"

"Of course! Grab a bottle and I'll get some glasses… What's Ed done with the glasses?" Searching the cupboards, she cursed her son silently. "Why the hell did he put them up there?!"

"Trying to tell you something, maybe?" If Eddie had a problem with his mother's proclivity towards alcoholic palliation, he needed to do some serious soul-searching.

Stretching wasn't quite enough, even in her heels, and the glasses remained elusive, but whilst she considered the availability of other vessels, Joe, watching the silhouette of her body, moved in close behind and pressed against her, located the source of her irritation and placed them next to the open bottle. With the feeling of his unexpected erection on her lower back, Abbie gasped, a little apprehensive but disinclined to allow its hindrance with such possibilities within reach and she slowly turned round, her heart pounding and her pussy throbbing. He leaned closer and kissed her tenderly and, concerned the expectation threatened to overwhelm her, Abbie closed her mind to thought, allowing instinct to reign, and as he kissed her again she unbuttoned his shirt and gently stroked his chest, slowly moving her hands over his stomach and down to his belt, unable to resist examining his hard cock through his trousers. Regaining her composure, she released it from its incarceration and sighed deeply, clasping tightly, longing to sink her nails in, kissing him hastily, whilst squeezing her prize repeatedly. Her mouth watered and for a moment, she was struck by another dilemma: drop to her knees and suck him hard until he filled her mouth, or let him ram her repeatedly until she came. Such decisions...

But not for to her to make. Smiling to himself, Joe enjoyed the softness of Abbie's hand surrounding the hardness of his dick and he gently lifted her onto the worktop, slowly raised her dress and teased her with his fingers as he moved her underwear to one side, listening to her breathing whilst his delicate touch tortured her skin, and, stepping just close enough to allow his cock to gently brush her pussy, he faltered briefly, closed his eyes and savoured the moment; the realisation of his fantasy, his dream – every dream – was now imminent and although the long, long wait seemed incomprehensible now, it had to be worthwhile, for there was every chance this would be an isolated occurrence. With Abbie's hands coercing his senses, he wanted to sustain her torment, ferment her desperation and make her beg him to fuck her, and his taunting fingers provoked the mania he coveted. "Joe, please..." His jaw tightened and he kissed her aggressively, driving his cock deep inside her as she clutched him tight, her breathing heavy and rapid, and she responded with her mouth, finding his tongue with hers. Slowing down, he thrust gently and casually, watching her face intently, enjoying her frustration.

"I've waited a long time, Abbie..." His words superfluous, he licked her tongue before stroking her neck with his lips and, as her attention refocussed, he whispered in her ear, "But it'll be worth it when I watch you come..." His voice, almost threatening, excited her and as he held her tight, he could feel her diminutive frame against his body. "So...how do you want this, Abbie...?" Composed and controlled, he traced her lips, barely touching her, enhancing her arousal, and he hoped his assessment of her predilections was accurate. "Slow and gentle, like it's your first time..." He looked in her eyes and listened to her breathing, hands on her hips, anticipating her response. "Or hard...like it's not?" Her face revealed her inclination. "That's what I thought." With a triumphant smile, he pushed harder, incited by her congruence and the recognition that the reality of being inside her surpassed even his most embellished fantasies and he resolved to effect a reoccurrence, no matter what. Finding her mouth, he filled it with his tongue, his breathing matching hers, recalling the image of her in the bathroom in her underwear when he was twelve, and he took her hand and cupped her breast with it, squeezing, encouraging independent inspiration. Stimulated by his view, he continued his pace, whispering again. "Is that hard enough, Abbie? Am I fucking you hard enough...or do you need it harder?"

The peremptory menace in his eyes directed her response. "Yes." Her voice was barely audible.

"Yes?" He wanted to hear it again.

"Yes."

"Yes? Then say it...say it, Abbie – SAY IT!" His composure wavered, enhancing his appeal.

"Fuck me harder, Joe."

The context in which she said his name excited him. "Again."

"Fuck me harder, Joe."

Responding to her request, he wanted more from her. "Is that hard enough?" He held her tight, certain, and hoping, he would hurt her, confident too it was what she wanted, but the sound of her wince hit him abruptly and he had to fight to control his climax, no longer able to hide the aggression in his voice. "Is that hard enough, Abbie?"

"Yes."

"Yes?"

"Yes!"

She screamed as she came, breathless and elated, each ripple of ecstasy, more powerful than the last, and as her pussy pumped hard around his cock, she held him tight, anticipating his orgasm, willing it with a provocative, knowing smile and, as she kissed him softly, he relinquished control, engulfing her mouth with his, coming violently, thrusting deeper inside her, paralysed by the agonisingly lavish apogee that refused to end, hurtling through him like a tsunami. He stood motionless, his head resting on hers, sweat dripping from his face, and trembling as his cock throbbed inside her. Kissing him again, she pulled gently at his nipples as she wrapped her legs around him.

As his energy gradually returned, he pulled her head back to look in her eyes. With a triumphant smile, she remained silent and he held her gaze as he kissed her before grudgingly pulling away to dress himself.

She slid off the worktop, readjusted her clothing and sighed. "And I thought you just wanted a glass of wine."

He laughed: that was one of many things he wanted from her.

As she left for the bathroom, he poured the wine and headed for the sofa, content his waning patience had been so pleasantly rewarded; as Abbie returned, she sat down close and stroked his stomach.

"A pleasant surprise, Joe..."

He chuckled. "Surprise? Surprised because it wasn't Jesse...?"

She smiled. "You don't strike me as the jealous type. Jesse's sweet but..." She leaned forward to kiss him; he was satisfied. "Well, you have another notch, another name to add to your list..." Not naïve enough to expect a marriage proposal, she hoped she was slightly above most in his extensive collection of partners.

"I don't have a list, Abbie, and, no, you're not another notch... is that what you want?" He was uncomfortable discussing previous victories with anyone but especially with her.

She smiled mischievously and ran a finger along his waist and down towards his crotch. "I'll be whatever you want…" Smiling, he let her continue; her touch exhilarated him and he wasn't finished with her yet. She kissed him, still tracing his body with her finger.

"I could ask you the same question…" Without judgement, he knew she had her own portfolio, which, although not as substantial as his, was still pretty generous.

She laughed. "Touché!" Pausing momentarily, she watched her hand on his body. "The others were just…available…when you weren't…"

As much as he wanted to, he wasn't sure he believed her. "And Jesse? What was he?"

"Ah, Jesse! He was a little different…there's just something about him…come on, Joe; all those girls you've had, there must have been one that you couldn't let go?" If she was more than just another conquest, she knew he'd expect her to forget Jesse, but it would difficult – Jesse was just…divine.

Joe thought for a while. "Nope, not a single one; it was just sex, Abbie. Molly was the most memorable, but she was only here for a week…Carl, maybe, but he was a little too desperate…"

As his words settled on her, she looked at him, astonished. "Carl? Carl who? But…you said you're not gay?"

He laughed. "Carl Banford, and I'm not gay! But he was rather keen and it was something different, so I thought I'd give it a try…"

"Carl Banford?" She smiled. "Well, there's a surprise…" Her mind was suddenly filled with Joe and Carl…and it was pleasantly engaging… She kissed him, maintaining eye-contact, and rubbed his crotch. "I had a thing with Carl a few years ago, but had I known about the two of you, I would have invited you to join us…" She sucked his lip, resisting the urge to bite hard. "Did you like it, Joe?" *Yes. Please say yes…*

He smiled devilishly. "Yes I did, very much so." Shuddering

involuntarily, erotic images taunted Abbie, but they weren't quite enough, and sensing her thoughts, he took advantage. "I'm sure there'll be somebody else…" He grabbed her hand and pushed down harder on his cock. "When's Jesse free…?" Watching her face, he waited. This would be interesting…

She sighed deeply; having toyed with that idea earlier, now, with Joe's provocative interest, previously unimaginable doors were blowing wide open, and kissing him passionately, she allowed her imagination a free rein so long as both Jesse and Joe were included. With her body warmed and her pussy pulsating, she looked at Joe and returned his smile. "I'll find out…" But, right now, there were hormones to satisfy and, to Joe's surprise, she got up. "More wine?"

Mystified by her sudden divergence, he abstained from disappointment…at least momentarily. "Yeah, OK."

She filled their glasses and placed the bottle back on the side, and, returning to Joe, knelt down behind the sofa and spoke very softly in his ear. "Now it's my turn…" Her words implied auspicious delights and he smiled, feeling the tightening of his cock and Abbie's hand running very slowly across his chest, playing with his nipple whilst she softly nibbled his ear. Kissing the side of his face, her hand continued its exploration, down his chest to his stomach and inside his trousers, evoking a quivering sigh from an expectant Joe. Now, on very unfamiliar ground, he had little control over his responses, but it wasn't an entirely unwelcome feeling; on the contrary, he was finding her touch and command intoxicating and he closed his eyes to enhance his appreciation.

With his dick in her hand once more, she squeezed, awed by her reverent vantage point and, as his breaths mirrored her own, she whispered, "I'm going to fuck you with my hand, Joe…" Her euphonic language elicited a deeper yearning and as she gently rubbed his cock, she smiled, enjoying his unexpectedly passive reaction, accelerating her own exigency. Compelled to escalate progress, she continued in a low voice. "And when you come over my hand...I'm going to lick your cum and swallow it..." Tensing, unaccustomed, as he was, to such an assenting position, he was, however, content to countenance the consequences, open to any proposition, especially if his cock was the beneficiary, and Abbie's beguiling narrative was serving a rather pleasant and a rather inevitable objective – an essentiality she was quite possibly ignorant to...for now, and as her hand intensified its exertion, she persevered with her stimulus. "And then, I'm going to kiss you, Joe...so hard, you can taste it." A previously unexplored concept sounded increasingly more attractive with her guidance and with her proficient manipulation, it was a concept that was creeping ever-closer to effectuation...and she seemed well aware of it.

Excited by her own influence, Abbie was eager to conclude her efforts, impatient to fulfil her promise and, squeezing his dick harder, she had to fight the urge – the need – to inflict pain, and though convinced he had no aversion to a little suffering, the bounty in her hand was quite possibly the wrong outlet for it. Kissing his neck again, she worked her magic. "C'mon, Joe, c'mon. Let it go..."

Within minutes, he succumbed to her inducement, exploding in her hand, grasping it tight to exacerbate the intensity of the orgasm palpitating through him with an unprecedented force, providing a formidable model that would be difficult to surpass, but an obligatory challenge that he would strive to overcome. In achieving her initial aim, Abbie had created a voracious thirst for more and without losing grip of Joe, she gradually moved around the sofa, lowered her head and licked her hand, whilst he watched in fascination. Reluctantly releasing her hold, she straddled him, writhing around on his crotch and although he needed a little longer to reload, he embraced her methods and her tenacity. She leaned forward and kissed him hard. "Can you taste that, Joe?" A rhetorical question, but an explicit need. "Can you? Can you taste it?" Forcing her tongue down his throat to affect the desired outcome, she asked again. "Can you, Joe?" His response was essential.

Relishing her need for gratification, he was only too willing to assist her. "Yes."

"Yes?"

He kissed her again, playing with her tongue before whispering her need, "I can taste it, Abbie."

Thrilled by his reply, she ground her crotch into his and, closing her eyes, she called his name as she came over him, holding her breath to inhibit any possible diversions, momentarily detached from everything but the storm pounding her immediate existence. Joe watched closely, mesmerised by his view, assured now of a diminished wait for further deeds.

Abbie sat motionless, allowing her body to recover from its achievements and as she regained a semblance of sanity, she opened her eyes to look at Joe. He was pleasing sight at all times but particularly now, with a new perspective; a dominant Joe would be worthy pursuit, but then so, too, would a submissive one and she wondered if he'd be so compliant again…an investigation was clearly necessary.

She kissed him softly and removed herself. "I'm going to freshen up."

Once in the bathroom, she looked in the mirror and was pleased with what she saw; glowing and looking at ease, she felt pretty good. She finished up and sauntered back to Joe. He, too, looked contented and pulled her to him, passing her a glass and kissing her neck, but she interrupted his attempts. "I need to check Eddie."

He groaned. "No! I need you here…"

"Joe…!"

He sighed dramatically "C'mon, Abbie, really? He's a grown man!"

"I know, but he's still my son. I'll be quick so you better be ready…"

With a disgruntled look, he let her go, watching her arse as she walked away – he wanted that. He drank his wine and closed his eyes, feeling her roaming hands on his crotch. Her touch had been sublime – imagine how her mouth would feel... But as he settled for a few moments of anticipative reflection, his musings were crudely interrupted.

"JOE!"

5

Fuck! What was that about? Hearing the scream, Joe buttoned his trousers and ran up the stairs to find Abbie shaking and lost between concern and hysteria, her colour drained and her voice, a contradictory fragility that reverberated around the room. "He's not waking up, Joe; I can't wake him…Joe: why won't he wake up? Joe?" *He would know, surely; he'd have the answers.* "Help me, please. Wake him up. Please, Joe, please wake him up." Unsure whether to touch her son, the panic emerged. "Eddie? Eddie, darling, it's me. Wake up, darling, c'mon… Joe, why isn't he waking up? JOE!" Now frantic and confused, she felt the betrayal of her sanity.

Waiting for his call to be answered, Joe avoided her imploration. "Ambulance, yeah. I need you here now; my friend's not waking up." He tried to steady Abbie as he talked on the phone. "Yes, we've been to a wedding so he's been drinking all day. I-I'm not sure. I think…maybe, yes. Possibly some cannabis…"

"No, Joe! What are you doing? That's not Eddie! Joe, what are you doing?"

His attempts to pacify her were wasted and she pushed him away. "I-I think…it's possible…"

"What; what's possible? Joe, what the fuck are you saying?" With a feverish irascibility, she looked pitiful. "JOE, DO SOMETHING!"

Ending the call, he tried to console her. "Let's go and wait for the paramedics, Abbie. They'll be here very soon."

"No! EDDIE'S NOT WAKING UP! I CAN'T JUST LEAVE HIM!" She knelt beside him, wanting to touch him but scared of what she would feel.

With the ambulance taking way too long, Joe's ambivalence was crippling. He found a pulse, but barely and Eddie's colour told him more than he needed to know. When at last he heard the sirens, he bounded down the stairs, buttoning his shirt, and opened the front door wide. "He's upstairs, but his pulse is weak."

As the paramedics walked into Eddie's room, Abbie jumped up. "Please, wake him up; I can't wake him and that's not like him."

"Are you his mother?"

"Yes."

"What's your name, my love?"

"Abbie."

"And what's your name, sir?"

"Joe."

"OK, I'm Tracey; can you tell me how old Eddie is, please?"

"Yes…he's twenty-three."

Tracey surveyed the room as her colleague assessed Eddie. "Thank you. Could you tell me also, my love, if he has any medical conditions that could affect his treatment and if he's on any medication: we need to make sure we treat him correctly."

Abbie knew the answers, but her mind was clouded with indecision. "Er…no…I don't think so…" She looked to Joe for confirmation.

"No, he's fit; there's nothing wrong with him, nothing that would cause this."

"Thank you. Now, Abbie, it would be better if you waited outside. Go with Joe, we'll look after Eddie, but we need as much room as possible – is that alright?" Tracey looked at Joe.

"Yeah, that's fine. Come on, Abbie, let's give them some space. We can wait right outside." Guiding her out, he tried to control her shaking.

"He's going to be OK, Joe, isn't he? They're going to wake him up?" Her search for confirmation was fruitless. "Joe? I can't lose him – he's all I've got." The reality of what she'd witnessed suddenly registered and she sobbed uncontrollably, with Joe holding her tight, helpless and scared: this wasn't supposed to happen.

Finally, the paramedics appeared with Eddie on a stretcher. "Can you follow behind?"

"Yeah, of course. Let's go, Abbie."

Steering her downstairs, he grabbed their shoes and jackets, but she was unresponsive. "Come on, Abbie, we need to get to the hospital."

She looked at him and suddenly snapped back. "Yeah… yeah, OK. Thanks, Joe."

The silent journey seemed endless and although Joe managed to keep up with the ambulance, it was still too slow. Finally at the hospital, he abandoned the car and escorted Abbie inside where they were taken to a family room and questioned about Eddie's condition: Joe was consumed by an implacable fear.

"Hello, I'm Doctor Bartup and I just need to ask a few questions so we can give Eddie the right treatment. Have you been with him all day?"

Abbie faltered, reluctant for him to see her failings. Joe, sensing her hesitation steeled himself for the inquisition. "Yeah…pretty much. We've been to a wedding for most of the day."

"OK, and how did he seem the last time you saw him?"

Joe recalled those final moments, filled with irritation at his friend, but with hope for what lie ahead. "Well…he was pretty wasted; we had to get him undressed and put him to bed, but he was awake."

"Thank you, Joe. When you say 'wasted', do you mean he was drunk?"

"Yes...very." Joe avoided Abbie's eyes, knowing his revelations were about to become more damning.

"OK. Can you please tell me exactly what Eddie may have had during the day?" The doctor was firm but kind.

"Uh...he's been drinking for most of it. He started on beer and maybe had two or three of those..."

"Bottles or pints?"

"Bottles. He had a couple of G and T's, I think. Can you remember, Abbie?"

"Yeah...yeah, I think you're right." She wanted the doctor with him. Surely the questions could wait until later. "What are they doing with Eddie?"

"They're doing everything they possibly can, but we need to establish what's happened and by analysing what Eddie may have taken, we can treat him appropriately; what else?"

Avoiding the obvious, Joe knew the question would come. "He had a couple glasses of champagne and then spent the rest of the day drinking wine...red wine."

"And how much red wine did he have?"

Under scrutiny now, the details seemed quite damaging. "Probably a bottle...maybe a bottle and a half, but that's not unusual for Eddie – he's used to it...but as we left, he was carrying a bottle of vodka."

"Was it empty?"

"No, he'd probably had half."

"And what's he eaten?"

"Um...we had beef and salmon...but I'm not sure which he had...but he doesn't have any allergies and I think we would have known if there was a problem with the food; there was a buffet in the evening but I couldn't tell you what he had – sorry."

"That's OK; I'm just covering all angles. What about drugs?" Sensing Joe's reluctance, the doctor wanted to reassure him. "It's very important that you tell me everything Eddie's taken:

it could save his life. I'm not here to judge, I'm merely trying to assess what treatment he needs."

"Eddie doesn't take drugs." Abbie was adamant.

"Are you absolutely sure? It will make a huge difference to the way he's treated…"

"Yes, absolut—"

"Abbie, he's been smoking pot…for years."

She looked at Joe as if he'd struck her. "What, wh-why didn't you tell me?"

"I'm sorry, Ms Dawson, but I need to know what I'm dealing with. Joe, do you know what he's had?"

"Yeah, he's had a few joints throughout the day…" He could feel Abbie's glare but avoided it; he'd have to face that trial later.

"Do you know how many?"

"Er…four, I think…maybe five…"

Her shock was evident and its roots lay predominantly in Joe's apparent duplicity and Eddie's betrayal. She'd thought he was sensible, that his father's death had been enough of an education but clearly not. Why had she been so stupid…and how could she not have known?

"Anything else you can think of, Joe? I really need to know."

"No…but it's not unusual for him to drink like that or smoke a few joints…"

"OK, thank you. That's a great help." Dr Bartup promised to report back as soon as he could and left them alone.

As the door closed, Abbie turned to Joe. "Why didn't you tell me? Why the fuck didn't you tell me what he was doing?"

"How? How could I tell you? He knew you'd be upset and he made me swear not to tell you…but Christ, Abbie, wasn't it obvious?"

"Well, clearly not! You should have told me…you should have told me."

"I couldn't. I told him to stop or tell you himself, but… he just kept telling me he'd do it some other time." Joe felt cornered. "I'm sorry, Abbie, I didn't know what to do." As his voice cracked, he looked away. He'd held back for her sake, but unlike her, he was certain Eddie wouldn't recover and the thought of losing his best friend and now, quite possibly, Abbie, weighed heavily.

She sat down and sobbed quietly and as he tried to comfort her, she began to shiver, lost in her own thoughts, unaware of his presence.

"I'm going to call Rose." No response.

Searching his phone for her number, his hands shook. "Rose? Hi..."

Still full of wedding joy, her voice reflected her day until she registered the irregularity. "Hey, Joe, what's up? What's the time? Are you OK?"

"No, we're at the hospital. Eddie's in a coma..." Although reluctant to spoil her day, he was relieved to share the burden.

"OH MY GOD! What the fuck happened?"

"Abbie checked in on him earlier and couldn't wake him, but I don't know any more than that – we're still waiting for news."

"Oh God, Joe, that's awful. How the fuck's Abbie?" She grabbed her keys and signalled to Michael.

"Not good." His voice tremored. "I'm sorry, Rose: I didn't know what else to do."

"No, don't worry; don't worry, my darling. I'll be there as quick as I can. Look after her, Joe. See you in a bit."

Comforted slightly, he tried to calculate her journey time: he rarely lost control, but his mother had died in this very hospital as he sat by her side and it was a difficult memory to shake; the only time he'd returned was when Frankie had broken her arm. With only negative associations at hand, he struggled to subdue the cynicism that tugged at his emotions, but for Abbie's sake, he would have to simulate optimism.

"Abbie?" He crouched down and took her hands. "Can I get you anything? A drink, a cigarette? Rose is on her way."

She slowly looked up. "This is our fault, Joe. I should have checked him sooner but I was…with you and…" Finishing her sentence was unnecessary; the absence of words was more powerful.

"Don't do that, Abbie. Let's just wait and see what happens." *Come on, Rose. Please!* "I'll see if I can find someone, find out what's happening."

"NO! I don't want to be on my own." Her rising antipathy was overshadowed by her fear.

"OK, OK, I'll stay. It's alright…it's alright." Holding her close, he could feel the tension in her body; the same body that, an hour ago, delighted in his touch. Now, it was clearly uneasy at such close proximity and the repercussions were too severe to fully comprehend.

As the clock ticked, the hands hardly moved. Abbie removed herself from Joe's arms and wandered around the room, trance-like, lost in a world where he wasn't welcome and he wasn't sure if it was deliberate or otherwise. Now and again, she would cry and she'd sit down and bury her face, alienating him further. Putting aside the obvious distance she'd put between them, he had nothing to offer; he couldn't promise Eddie would be OK because to him, it was already clear there would be no happy ending.

The door opened and Rose walked in, and although Abbie looked up, she proffered no greeting. "Oh my God, Abbie, I'm so sorry." Her voice sparked a response and as her friend attempted a smile, she embraced her, with Joe watching and trying to stem the rumblings of resentment; what the fuck had he done wrong?

Her body shook as she cried in Rose's arms and Rose looked at Joe apologetically, sensing his mood and desperation.

"What have they said, my darling?"

For a while she couldn't speak, all energies focussed on retaining the merest semblance of equanimity, but eventually she stammered a reply. "Nothing yet. They asked…loads of questions…about Eddie and…Joe seems to think he was using. I can't believe it, Rose…after what happened to his father." Her strength depleted, she cried again.

"I know, I know…but I can't say it's a complete shock, given the state he was in today." Whilst keen to soften the rift that's Joe's revelation had clearly caused, she knew she was walking a perilous path.

Abbie stopped crying and looked at her friend. "What? Why didn't you say? Why didn't you tell me, Rose? Am I the only one who didn't know? For fuck's sake – you're my best friend!" Rose understood her need vent.

"I didn't know for sure, but I assumed you did. I'm sorry."

Shaking her head, Abbie held her hand. "I know, I'm sorry. I'm so scared I'm going to lose him." She hugged her friend again.

"Let me get you something – a drink…or something to eat. Have you had anything, Joe?"

"No, I was going to get something earlier but didn't want to leave Abbie alone."

"I'll get something; back in a minute."

Without Rose, Joe was struck by the silence; he hadn't noticed it before, but now it was inescapable. "Abbie…I'm so sorry. I thought he had it under control, but if I'd thought this would happen, I would have told you, I promise. I didn't want this; he's the only family I've got…and you." Overwhelmed, suddenly, by the enormity of the situation, he sat down feeling unsteady and exposed.

Abbie looked at him sadly, torn between anger and pity. She could never hate him, but she hated the deception…and now, every time she looked at him she could see the decision she'd made; the decision to put sex before her child, her only child, her world…and was it a price worth paying, now, waiting to hear if Eddie was alive or dead? Joe wasn't to blame – he'd hardly forced her – but his presence was a punishment, a reminder of the sort of mother she was…a reminder that she was her father's daughter.

Sitting next to him, she put her arm around his shoulders and, burying his face in her neck, he was unsure whether to cry or kiss her. It was clear he was as worried about losing her as he was Eddie, but at this time, there could be no reassurances… and there was no guarantee that there would ever be. With the memories still too vivid, she had to consider the possibility that, should she leave the hospital without her son, the association with Joe would torture her for the rest of her days…and he'd be best forgotten. She couldn't tell him now; the strength or, indeed, the stomach for such a denouement was currently out of reach.

Steadying himself, he looked at her. "I'm truly sorry."

"I know."

As Rose returned, Abbie got up and helped herself to a drink, dismissing the snacks, but grateful for her support, and as the silence prevailed, a knock at the door made them jump up. Dr Bartup walked in, flanked by a nurse. "Ms Dawson, would you like to sit down?" Abbie obeyed and looked at him expectantly; Joe recoiled, covered his ears and blocked out the room.

"Abbie, the team did everything they possibly could and have given Eddie the best treatment, but there is nothing more we can do; I'm so very sorry, but he died a few minutes ago."

Her scream pierced the walls as she lurched towards the doctor, unwilling to accept she'd lost her world. "NO! There must be something else you can do…he's young…and he's strong… please, don't give up on him…"

Holding her firm, the doctor spoke softly. "Abbie, we've tried everything, I promise you…I'm sorry." Beating her hands on his chest, she screamed again, her face contorted in the agony bestowed on her for her own conduct. "Abbie, this is Judy and she's going to stay here with you…" But she wasn't listening; her mind forced her to acknowledge the tragedy that she had caused, that could have been avoided, had she taken care of her son rather than herself. As her understanding deepened she could feel the accusers in her head stabbing at her with their critical theories, condemning her to her rightful punishment, and confusion took hold.

Judy stepped forward, observing the turmoil in Abbie's face. "Abbie? Abbie, can you hear me?"

Yes she could, but she needed clarification; she could hear voices and she could hear her name, but what exactly were they saying to her? What did they mean? She looked at Rose, unable to speak, unable to move, not sure what to do. Rose rushed to her side but she didn't respond. Breathing erratically and struggling to focus, she dropped to the floor and scrabbled around, trying to escape, without knowing what she was escaping from; the room slowly turned and it stole her concentration. Aware of being held but not entirely sure by whom, there was someone else in the corner, pacing, and she wondered if it was Eddie. She hadn't seen Eddie for a while – *why was that?* No…it wasn't Eddie… didn't look like Eddie: *who was it?* Joe – it was Joe! Smiling, she tried to move but nothing worked; she tried to speak but didn't hear her voice, but she could feel herself floating and smiled again – sleep: that's what she needed, sleep, and she welcomed the respite that banished the blame temporarily.

Rose caught her as she blacked out and laid her on the sofa.

"ABBIE!" Joe leapt across the room. "What's wrong with her?"

Judy was calm as she assessed the patient. "She's in shock, which is completely natural. We'll just keep an eye her; she'll come back round soon. Is there anyone I can call for her?"

"No." Joe looked to Rose and she shook her head.

"Can I get either of you a cup of tea? You could be here for a little while…"

"No, thank you."

"OK. Would you like me to wait until Abbie wakes up?"

Joe preferred a little privacy. "No...thank you."

"Well, I'll be right outside so if Abbie stirs or if there is anything you need, come and get me." She smiled warmly as she and the doctor left the room, leaving Rose and Joe to nurse their grief.

Rose sat back down and watched Joe; he looked like shit. Eddie's death would hit him hard, but Abbie in this state was just as cruel, and though there was no doubt he was strong, these were the only two people he cared about and they seemed to be disappearing very quickly. Taking his hand, she squeezed it tight and he looked at her, comforted by her touch. She'd always been good to him, despite knowing a great deal more about him than most, possibly even Abbie, and at this moment, she was all he had.

With Abbie stable, they waited. She would want to see Eddie when she woke and they debated her reaction when reality kicked in.

"Joe, do you want to go home and get some sleep? You look dreadful, my love. I'm happy to wait here 'til she wakes up, and I'll let you know as soon as she does." It was an undeniably futile suggestion, Rose knew that, but it could save a lot of upset.

"Thanks, Rose, but I'm not going to sleep: I need to know she's OK." When she woke, he wanted her to see he was there supporting her, not absconding at the first possible opportunity, and pacing the room, in the hope it would make time move quicker, he willed Abbie to wake up. "How long do you think it's going to be, Rose? This is agony."

"I know, but she's tough, Joe. She'll be OK." Her attempts to reassure him belied her own consternation but diverted her despair to a more productive course. Certain they had a significant wait, she was keen to learn the details of Eddie's death, but with no desire to distress Joe any further, to question Abbie so soon would be insensitive and she would have enough questions herself. "Joe, what happened? I'm sorry, sweetheart, but I need to know and I don't know when Abbie will want to talk. I'm sorry, my darling."

"It's OK." Taking a deep breath, and in need of some alcohol, he reluctantly shared those painful moments. "We put him straight to bed when we got back, gave him some water, and when Abbie checked on him about forty-five minutes later...he looked like death and wouldn't wake up."

"Oh God, that's awful!" She began to cry. "My dear Eddie; what are we going to do without him?" Smiling sadly at Joe, she hunted for a tissue. "So was it drugs? It looked like it this afternoon. Was he awake when you put him to bed?" If losing him wasn't enough, Abbie would be crushed by the circumstances of his death.

"Yes, and acting up, as usual." He smiled, recalling his friend's lighter side. "I undressed him and he was joking, though completely wasted." He shook his head. "Didn't expect...this. I would never have left him alone if I thought this would happen. Christ, I spent most of the day making sure he was OK...but, I always do. Abbie has no idea that this is what he does...did... but, he'd always sleep it off and be OK."

"Well, she's not the only one. It seemed pretty obvious today, but I can't say I've noticed it before."

"No, because you just saw him as Eddie – you didn't have to deal with the fallout or constantly watch to make sure he was safe, like I did...but...he really pissed me off today, and for a moment, I thought about leaving him to it, just to see what happened...but I couldn't do it. And when I finally did..." His eyes filled and he looked to the floor.

"Don't do that, my darling. If he's never suffered before, how could you know? You can't be completely responsible for someone else, Joe, you know that."

"Yeah...but..."

"I know, but it's not your fault, sweetheart." Rose's compassion, whilst welcome only exacerbated his state and he sobbed quietly. "Come here, my love." She hugged him tight, stifling her own tears as her body absorbed the sobs shaking his. "She's going to need you, Joe – you know that, don't you?"

He wiped his face and nose. "I'm not so sure now…"

"Don't be ridiculous! She's in shock, but when that subsides and the reality hits her, you're Ed's best friend and she's going to need that. And, she phoned you, didn't she – what does that tell you? Christ, you're going to need each other."

For a moment, he considered the pretence, but he had neither the strength, nor the inclination to lie. "She didn't phone me, Rose…I was already there."

"Oh sorry, darling, I assumed you'd gone… So why were you still there…?" Slowly, his words and tone registered and her eyes widened. "You didn't…?"

He laughed – she was like a teenager! "Yes, we did."

"Well about bloody time…lucky lady!"

"Oh, c'mon, Rosie. You know you're the only one for me, but you have a husband."

Chuckling, she was pleased to see a spark of Joe return. "If only that were true! As tempting as it sounds, I fear you would kill me, Joe…but what a lovely way to go! Sorry, that's a little insensitive."

He smiled. "Don't worry, I'm not the sensitive type."

"Mmm…I've heard…" She imagined that most of the rumours were rather embellished – but hoped that some weren't – and she was too fond of him to gossip. "Well, there you go, even more reason for her to rely on you."

"Maybe…but she said it was our fault; that if we hadn't… been screwing, she would have checked Ed sooner. She's going to need someone to blame and I think it's going to be me…"

"No – if you hadn't been there, she would have gone to bed and wouldn't have found him 'til the morning…and he might have died in the house, and she would've been alone. Christ, that would be even worse. Don't worry, darling, I'll talk to her…"

Their conversation was halted by Abbie stirring, whispering Eddie's name.

"Joe, get the nurse."

Judy quickly arrived and Rose and Joe stepped back, nervous but somewhat relieved. Abbie looked around the unfamiliar room, devoid of comprehension and troubled by her companions. Rose was there, and Joe, but not Eddie. Why? Where was Eddie? He should be there…but where was 'there'?

"Where am I? What's going on? Joe, where's Eddie?" Looking to him for answers, she gasped as her memories caught up – memories of her indulgence in him, memories of her neglect of her son – and her agony emanated from her like a haunted dream. "NO!" Her attempts to get up were controlled by the restraint of the nurse.

Joe moved towards her. "Abbie…"

"NO!" She shook her head as she sobbed. "Eddie…"

With his forced impassivity waning, Rose held his hand tight, signalling temperance, yet weeping silently, frustrated by her spectatorial position.

Exhausted by her fight, Abbie complied with Judy's compassionate demands and Rose hugged her. "My darling, Abbie, I'm so sorry. I'm so, so sorry."

Although unable to speak, she was more accepting of her grief, for now, but her body ached for a return to a more halcyon time. Watching pitifully, Joe was scared: a life on hold for this woman and although his intentions were far from honourable, they had mirrored hers, but the balance had now shifted irreversibly and he had no alternative diversion. What the fuck was he going to do? Another day and she may have turned to him for comfort, but now the comfort he'd provided was the very instrument she would use to repudiate him…and he didn't take too kindly to rejection.

Assuming a more positive demeanour, he walked over to the

sofa and sat down. "Abbie, I'm so sorry, but I'm going to be right here. If you need anything, just let me know." No response, but he persevered. "I'm going to have a chat to the doctor to see when you can go home. Can I get you anything?"

Looking at him, she slowly shook her head: progress.

He left with Judy and was gone for so long, Rose wondered if he'd gone home and given his mood, it was a distinct possibility. She prayed she was mistaken, but with Abbie drifting in and out of sleep, she was happy: less stressful for all and a necessary tool for her friend's recovery.

With a confident air, steeped in authority, Joe came back and, seeing Abbie dozing, he spoke quietly to Rose. "OK, they're happy for her to go home, but only if one of us stays with her; I'm happy to, but I understand if you want to." He sat down next to her, choosing his words carefully. "I went to see Eddie – I couldn't leave without saying good-bye. He looked so different... but I expected that... I don't know if Abbie will want to see him or if it would be better to come back another day...I'll see what she says. Can I get you anything, Rose?"

She was impressed by his transformation. "Just a hug. Thank you for doing this; I'm not sure I could do it on my own." Holding her gently, he kissed her hair, needing as much reassurance as she did and, waiting until Abbie stirred again, they reminisced about Eddie, generating guilty laughter and many more tears.

As Abbie slowly opened her eyes, Joe took her hand. "Abbie?" His voice tender, he looked for recognition. "Abbie, you can go home if you want to. They're happy for you to go, but only if it's what you want; I can get your things if you want to stay."

She tried hard to focus. "What?" She hadn't quite understood what he'd said.

"Do you want to go home now, Abbie? The doctor's happy for you to leave, but I can get you a bag if you prefer to stay here for the night."

"Abbie, can you hear Joe?"

A little encouragement from Rose triggered a reaction. "Yes...yes...I want to go home...I want to go home."

"Ok, I'll go and speak to the doctor. Rose – could you get her stuff together?"

As he left, Abbie turned to her friend. "I need to see Eddie, I don't want to leave him here..." A lamentable plea from a disconsolate woman and as Rose held Abbie's hand, her stomach churned.

"Of course, my darling. Let's wait for Joe to come back and we can talk about it, OK?"

"No. I don't want to talk about it, I want to see him!"

Rose chastised her choice of words. "I know, I didn't mean... sorry, Abbie, of course."

The doctor returned with Joe and confirmed his statement. "You're free to go, Abbie, but I'd like you to see your own GP tomorrow, just to make sure you're OK; I'll just finish the paperwork." He gently touched her hand.

"I want to see my son, please."

"Of course. When, Abbie? I'll arrange it for you."

"Now. I don't want to leave without seeing him."

"OK, just hang on here for a bit; I'll see what I can do."

Uneasy, Joe looked at Rose. "Abbie, are you sure you want to do this now, are you sure you're up to it?"

"He's my son, Joe, I can't just leave."

"I know, I know...I just..." He shrugged his shoulders.

Within minutes, the doctor was back. "OK, Abbie, they're ready for you." As he led her out, Rose held her hand and Joe carried her coat and bag. Stopping outside the doors, Dr Bartup took a moment to inform her of the experience that lay ahead, but having seen her husband here, she was prepared; seeing his soulless body, however, had signified an end to her suffering, but on this occasion, it would very much symbolised the beginning and, seeing her baby now, she considered that this was perhaps the reparation for her previous transgression and for that, justified or not, her contrition would be endless.

"Do you want me to come with you, Abbie?" Despite her offer, Rose preferred to remain outside.

"No…thank you; I want to go on my own."

Watching her, however discreet, was torturous, and whilst Joe could understand her need to be alone with her son, his efforts to appease the mounting resentment were ineffectual and he bowed his head.

As her perpetual tears fell unnoticed, Abbie studied the beautiful face before her; the child she'd nurtured and watched, proudly, grow into a man, free from the paternal influence that could so easily have destroyed the essence of his gentle soul, acutely aware that she'd ultimately failed him and that would be her abiding retribution. She knew she had to leave him, but the agony of that decision was intense, debilitating, and she remained, immobilised, until Rose appeared by her side. Words were unnecessary, but as she took her friend's hand, Abbie reluctantly blew Eddie a final kiss before leaving her heart behind. She left the hospital silently, without tears and, with Rose's arm linked through hers, the three of them carried their sadness to the car-park.

"Joe's going to stay with you tonight, Abbie, but I can stay too if you want me to." Rose would sleep on the roof if she thought it would help her friend.

"I think I'd rather be alone…" Her eyes remained downcast. "I'm sorry, Joe, but I need to be on my own…"

His jaw tightened, but he controlled his response. "But the doctor said…"

"I don't care what he said, he hasn't just allowed his son to die."

"Of course…if that's what you want, but are you sure it's a good idea? I can sleep on the sofa…on the floor, if it helps; I'll stay out of your way…"

"Thank you, but I'll be fine. I'm grateful for all that you've done, but please…just let me do this."

Fuck, fuck! "OK…OK, let's get you home."

There were hugs and condolences all round before they walked Rose to her car and left for home. The journey back, conversely, was too quick, but still silent, and as Joe parked up, he lingered in the car in a vain attempt to prolong his time with Abbie but, with nothing to gain, he gathered himself and finally got out, opening her door. Walking towards the house, he waited as she fiddled with the lock and as he stepped forward she stopped him, and this time, she looked him in the eye. "Thanks again, Joe, but I need to be alone."

"Abbie…"

"I know, I know, but I need to deal with this and I need to do that on my own." She touched his cheek. "I'm sorry." He stared at her; if he left, he was afraid he'd lose her and she sensed that. "Let me go, please." She turned, opened the door and disappeared inside.

'Let me go' – *fuck!* 'Let me go'?! Eleven years of waiting and now 'let me go'?! He raced home, fuelled by anger: anger at Abbie, anger at Eddie, anger at the whole fucking situation. Abandoning the car, he opened his front door, and for the first time since leaving the wedding, he looked at the time. Four-thirty. *Fuck!* Too late to find a bar, he grabbed a bottle of wine, sat down and drank; no point in sleeping now.

6

Closing the door, Abbie heard Joe's car screech out of the drive and, closing her eyes, she fell to the floor and wept...and wept, her body contorted in the worst pain she'd ever experienced; she heard unfamiliar sounds, loud sounds, that seemed very close, and after considerable time, realised they were emanating from her. Frozen, incapable of movement, her body struggled to manage the agony coursing through it and the sobs that wracked it continuously, leaving her gasping for breath, her brain unable to cope with another task. Finally, freeing itself from its oppressive burden, it allowed the hysteria to subside long enough for its host to draw breath and move to a more comfortable setting. Wiping her face, Abbie grabbed a glass and the half-filled bottle of wine, ignoring the significance of what its opening had preceded, and sat on the sofa, breathing deeply, knowing it wouldn't be long before the assault began again. Sipping slowly, her mind struggled to keep pace with the images battering it, the memories flashing brightly, noisily, and she willed the clock hands, after centuries of forward motion, to change direction, just for a few hours, to change her fate, promising to learn from the experience and be a better person, but they refused her imploration. And then came the alternatives, the 'what-ifs', the 'maybe-they've-got it-wrongs', and the sudden spark that told her they must have missed something that had her reaching for her phone to call the hospital, just as the tiny, remaining speck of sanity removed the phone from her hand, placing it carefully on the coffee table, allowing a moment's grace before the next wave of grief attacked, with little warning or concern for the wreck it sought to destroy. Abbie knew this process would continue for the night and chose to allow it to take its course unchallenged, for what would be the point? Aside from the inevitable failure, she had no energy or will to fight, nor for anything else right now. As the tears flowed freely, and her body continued to shake uncontrollably, her mind remained a writhing mass of tormented thoughts and she continued to drink in the sincere hope it would, at worst, send her to sleep, or at best, send her to Eddie; she could hope for nothing more now, because nothing else mattered.

***

The wine helped Joe somewhat but had, indeed, sent him to sleep and he'd dreamed about Abbie with his cock in her mouth. When he woke just after ten-thirty with a throbbing dick, he'd had to relieve himself in the shower before he could think about breakfast. Now what? He picked up the phone – Rose? Abbie? Abbie…no, Rose. Yep, Rose.

"Hi, Rose. Sorry, have I called too early?"

"No, my darling, it's fine. What time is it?" She mustered as much lucidity as she could.

"Eleven. Did you sleep?"

"Yeah, a little. You?"

"Yeah, a few hours, I think. Have you spoken to Abbie yet?" He was hopeful but unsure exactly what for.

"No, darling, I haven't; I thought I'd leave her a little longer in case she didn't sleep."

He refused to allow his disappointment to surface. "I might drive over to see if she's OK: I can't sit and wait for her to call…" He was concerned the call would never come.

"Oh, Joe. I'm so sorry, my love. Give her a little time – she'll come round."

"Yeah...I don't know, Rose, but I need to talk to her." How could she be so sure?

"OK, call me back if you need anything, yeah?"

"I will, thank you."

"You can thank me later, Joe...in that special way you do..." His diversion from the usual banter was unsettling.

"Anytime."

He steadied his mind and set off for Abbie's. His driving was certainly calmer this morning, but he was conscious of last night's bottle sitting empty in his kitchen; thankfully, it was a short journey. As he pulled up outside, he hesitated for a second. What the fuck was he going to say? Getting out of the car and walking slowly up the path, he was suddenly aware of feeling nervous: the thought of talking to Abbie terrified him...no, the thought of what she had to say terrified him...but delaying it would make little difference.

He knocked on the door, expecting her to be asleep, and was caught unawares when she appeared instantly. As she walked away, he faltered; he wasn't expecting the warmest of welcomes but hadn't anticipated a silent one. Having known Abbie for so many years, he was familiar with her moods, her high and lows, but this was all new, though he reminded himself it was wholly justified.

He followed her in and quietly closed the door. Abbie was on the sofa, arms wrapped round her legs and as he sat down opposite her he studied her face: she looked distant and an absolute wreck, her face almost unrecognisable with swollen eyes and sallow skin. "Did you get any sleep?"

She shook her head. "No, I don't think so. Don't think I'm going to be sleeping much for a while." She smiled pitifully.

"Can I get you a coffee...or some breakfast? Have you eaten anything?"

"No, not yet; not sure I can stomach anything at the moment...but if you want something..."

"Maybe some coffee." He filled the kettle, relieved that she was a little more communicative than the previous night and hoped his presence would soften her stance. Sitting back down, he looked at her. "Is there anyone you need to contact, Abbie? Can I do it for you?"

She sighed. "Er…I don't know. I hadn't thought about that…" Fighting for focus, she closed her eyes – *how hard can it be?* "Maybe…yes…I'll need to let Ed's boss know – God, he adored Eddie." Despite her sense of duty, that was a call she was happy to avoid. "And his friends…do you know all of his friends?"

"Pretty much. Leave it to me, I'll call them, and Frank." *Shit, where's Eddie's phone?* "Do you have Frank's number?" Wincing, he prayed she wouldn't rescind his offer.

"It'll be on Ed's phone. Where is his phone – is it upstairs?"

"It must be – shall I get it?"

"No…it's OK, I'll get it." Disappearing for a short while, she returned, looking at the phone as if expecting a call, but reality eventually mocked her presumption and she started to tremble.

Removing it from her grasp, Joe clasped his hands around hers, and this time, she didn't flinch. She looked at him and attempted to smile. "You're a good boy, Joe…"

But? He disliked the inference and…*boy?* He'd lost that luxury when he was seven but, on balance, he figured now wasn't the time to pick a fight.

"What do I do, Abbie? I'll do anything you want, you know that. I hate this so, please, just tell me what I can do to help. I'll make the calls; I'll make you some coffee and breakfast, but let me in, OK?"

Stroking his face, she said nothing, but her eyes declined.

He kissed her forehead and walked back to make the coffee. "Do you want to freshen up? I can clean up here." Glancing over his shoulder, he saw her crying.

She whispered, as if someone might be listening, "I don't want to go back upstairs."

As he put the coffee down, he held her hands again, desperate to remove the agony she carried. "Then let me go. What do you need?"

He returned with clean clothes, towels and hairdryer. "Take as long as you like and if you need anything else, just shout; I'll start making some calls and when you come out, I'll make you some breakfast…" She protested. "I know, but just try a little something."

Hearing the bathroom door close, he sighed with relief and he thought back to the first time he'd seen her in that bathroom: he was twelve and had wandered into the house unable to find Eddie but desperate for the toilet. Abbie, having seemingly woken a little later than the norm, had just finished showering and, with the bathroom door open, was getting dressed. As he walked in and caught sight of her in her underwear, he'd got a pleasant, if rather unfamiliar, shock. Unable to look away, he became increasingly aware of a strange sensation in his crotch and the huge bulge in his jeans, and he left quickly, heading towards Anna's house. Until then, sex had just been a word to him, one he'd understood but never appreciated and the connotations seemed unpleasant; that changed quickly. Anna, a local girl, acquainted with all the boys, in ways that he was completely unaccustomed to, had teased him endlessly since he hit puberty and had tried, unsuccessfully, to tempt him, but this time, she was in luck. Seeing him at the door, she was delighted that her patience and perseverance had finally been rewarded and she led him to the woods, giving him an experience that would shape his life. The teasing stopped, but the memory remained. Abbie had no idea what happened that day, or that she was the catalyst for the path his life would take, but he'd never forgotten. And so, his obsession began, and with it, a relentless need for gratification, that not only centred on her but proliferated because of her.

Smiling alone, he looked at Eddie's phone and started to

break the news and Frank, as expected, was devastated. Where Abbie had taken Joe under her wing, Frank had done the same for Eddie, though, presumably, not in quite the same way... Having no kids of his own, he'd bonded quickly with Eddie and shown him everything he'd learned himself, proud of his enthusiasm and the effort he'd put in; it hadn't been easy and Frank made no concessions, but his protégé had proved himself a sagacious employee and there were rumours he would hand the business to the him when he retired. What would he do now? Deeply shocked by the news, he thanked Joe for the call and asked that he offer his sincere condolences to Abbie and to be informed of the funeral arrangements.

With quite a substantial group of friends, Joe was unsure where to start – Jamie. Jamie had probably been closer to Eddie than the rest, though less friendly to Joe since he'd refused Jamie's advances. Convinced Joe was gay, albeit to suit his own agenda, and choosing to ignore his formidable reputation, he'd made several attempts to corner him, but Joe had politely declined: he disliked labels, preferring to remain open-minded, but if the opportunity arose, it would be of his own volition... he didn't take too kindly to assumptions. Confident nothing had happened between Jamie and Eddie, he was equally sure that Jamie had been forever hopeful.

Offering to ease the load and make the necessary calls, he'd shown a genuine warmth that was unexpected but very welcome and Joe thanked him sincerely before cautiously scrolling through Eddie's recent calls to gauge the importance of anyone unfamiliar: Ella! Ella? Well...she'd probably hear from Frankie so no need to revisit that chapter...

The hum of Abbie's hairdryer emanated from the bathroom, signalling the need to start breakfast. Joe would rather have wandered in and made good use of her body before she dressed but conceded there'd be little appreciation, and given the tenuity of his current position, the risk was quite possibly indefensible so he settled for eggs…a rather more innocuous option. He started mixing as she walked out.

"Pancakes sound good?"

Abbie faltered. "Joe…thank you, but you being here…it's… Every time I think of Eddie, I see…us and I can't get that out of my head. And all the time you're here…it doesn't stop and I want it to. I want to think of Eddie as he was…not dead because I couldn't keep my hands off you."

"Abbie, you didn't do anything wrong; *we* didn't do anything wrong. Christ, it could have happened at any time, and if it hadn't been for Jesse…it probably would have happened years ago, you know that. What, you'd rather remain celibate in case something bad happens? That's ridiculous!"

"But that's just it, Joe! You…Jesse, and…fuck knows how many others, I was so focussed on getting laid that I didn't pay attention to the only person I've ever cared about. I didn't see what he was doing."

As he absorbed the impact of her candour, Joe's mood darkened. "The only person…?"

"You know what I mean." *Shit!* He'd twisted her words and she attempted to elaborate. "Eddie was…"

Too late: her unintentional insinuation had ultimately, however indirectly, precipitated her initial aim. "Yeah…I got it." He picked up his keys and left.

"JOE!" *Fuck! That went well!* She watched as he sped out of her drive. *Fuck!*

***

Kicking the front door closed, Joe found the empty wine bottle and threw it across the kitchen and, falling back against the fridge, he covered his eyes and yelled. "Fuck! Fuck you, Abbie, fuck you!" Why? Why had he wasted eleven years waiting for her, waiting for somebody else to fuck off out of the way for this?

He grabbed another bottle of wine and a glass, and searched for some cigarettes, and as he sat down, his phone rang.

"Hey, Joe…you OK?" Abbie had called Rose as he'd left and, setting aside her friend's undeniable, and justifiable, grief, Rose was disappointed. Yes, there were seemingly insurmountable issues: Joe was a lot younger than she, though never a previous concern, and, by all accounts, a little twisted…and somewhat controlling, depending on your perspective, of course, but he was not responsible, nor she, for Eddie's death and to punish him in such a manner, having willingly brought him into her life – and now, into her bed – bordered on malevolence, especially given that he was grieving too. She had, however, adopted a more sympathetic tone when speaking to her friend and promised to contact him.

"Hi, Rose. Yeah, I'm good. You've spoken to Abbie…"

"Yes, I have and right now I could slap her…but please don't repeat that! I'm sorry, Joe…but don't take it personally – she'll come round. I'm on my way over there now and I'm going to try to talk some sense in to her."

He chuckled. "Yeah, well good luck with that! I'm going to go across to the bar, have a few drinks and get laid."

"Yeah, well, good luck with that!"

"I don't need luck, Rosie…" Hearing her laugh as she hung up, he wondered whether he should show her how much he appreciated her help but, despite her obvious love for her husband, he honestly felt he might be a little too much for her.

7

Rejecting his wine, Joe wandered across the road. Huge drinking sprees were not really his thing, especially during the day, but he was in an unusual position and, well, he may just find the solace he required.

"Hi, Mike, the usual, please…in fact, make it a double."

"Hi, Joe. It's a little early for you, isn't it?" Very attentive to his regulars, but never too intrusive, Mike rarely saw Joe during the day, but he wasn't about to judge. Besides…it was Joe.

"Yeah, I know. Been a rough day." He was fond of Mike: their relationship was a little more than just landlord/customer and they enjoyed, on occasion, ruminating on the ways of the world and the calibre of the clientele, and if the conversation deepened, Mike would listen intently, interject where necessary and, if the called upon, offer appropriate, circumspect advice that was neither confrontational nor enforced; he never expected too much information…AND, was the epitome of discretion, which was rather fortunate.

The Well had been a hovel when he took it on, but in two years he'd totally transformed it; though not as stylish as the city bars, it was comfortable, nonetheless, and very well contrived: the cubicles in both conveniences were slightly larger than usual to ensure comfort for all and a carefully designed 'back room' was available for a little more privacy, to those deemed worthy enough. Mike knew if he looked after the boys, they'd look after him and whilst fully aware he was taking a risk by allowing the opportunity to nip to the bathroom for a brief 'interlude', it ensured a return to the bar and further spending; if they went home, it cost him money. If anyone complained, he knew he could blag it long enough for the dust to settle, but thankfully, no protests so far, and despite the insalubrious nature of the venue, it had a good reputation and was frequently full to capacity, with an eclectic mix of personalities, not all familiar with its secret agenda.

Poker games, held once a month for a select few were popular and, in the early days, money exchanged hands, but as word spread, a few female regulars, intrigued by these clandestine gatherings, requested inclusion and the rules changed. With no interest in participating in the games, their curiosity lie, simply, in the surreptitious atmosphere and concentration of testosterone, and Mike, unopposed to a little female company had suggested, in jest, they be the ultimate prize, and amazingly, to everyone's approval, they agreed! With higher stakes, the games took on a more serious, and somewhat more urgent tone and the victor was rewarded with exclusive use of the facilities: no one asked any questions and no one was judged. A frequent winner, Joe rarely exercised his rights to exclusivity, choosing, instead, to have his fun in the bar, accentuating his fellow players' losses and, on a particularly lucrative evening, he'd won three times. Saving his winnings until the end of the evening, he'd persuaded two of his prizes to amuse each other whilst he took care of the third, listening to his fellow players groaning behind him as they masturbated in envy. Having achieved his objective, he'd decided to finish what he'd started in the privacy of his apartment, much to the disgust of his male companions, and he'd spent a very gratifying few hours without his audience but deeply engrossed in his trophies: Mike understood his clientele.

"Oh, sorry, mate. Anything I can help with?"

"'No, not this time." Where would he start?

"OK, well, just shout if you need anything."

"Thanks, Mike."

Within minutes, Joe had company. "That's not a happy face. You look like you need cheering up?"

Sighing as he looked to his left, he held up his glass. "I have all I need, thanks."

"Are you sure? I could do a better job than the alcohol…" She was feeling pretty confident.

He turned and looked deep into her eyes. "Well, unless you can bring back my very recently deceased best friend, yes, I'm pretty sure." Holding her gaze, he delighted in her discomfort.

"OK…sorry…" And then she was gone. One down…

Mike returned. "Is she the first? You're slacking, Joe! Another drink?"

He laughed. "Yes, please." Looking around the bar, he noticed he was being watched from the other side and when he caught his admirer's gaze, she smiled and walked away. He paid for his drink and watched Mike wander back to a small group of women and excite them with his cocktail-making skills, speculating how many of them would be pissed by the time it was dark. His admirer was one of the group and seemed equally impressed with Mike, and whilst he wasn't averse to sharing, Mike's stance was unclear. He searched for an alternative to no avail.

Mike walked back with an elaborate glass, full of brightly coloured liquid. "For you, my friend, with the compliments of my lady-friends." He waved a dramatic arm in their direction.

Sighing, Joe accepted the offering. "Thanks, that's exactly what I need. How perceptive of them." To his surprise, however, it tasted better than anticipated.

Mike laughed. "I don't know what you're complaining about; I thought I was in there but, no, they were more interested in you – thanks, mate! If you weren't such a good customer, I'd bar you."

Looking to the crowd of cocktail ladies, Joe was optimistic. "Do you know their names, Mike?"

"Emma, Sarah, Carol...Tina...Marsha and the one with her eye on you is Lila."

Focussing on Lila, he smiled charmingly and as she raised her glass and mouthed 'cheers', he reciprocated.

"Thanks, man." He watched her move away and head towards the ladies' and, smiling at Mike, he followed, catching the door as it swung shut.

"Thank you for my cocktail, Lila."

She turned round, a little surprised at his presence. "Aha! So you know my name. You're most welcome...?"

"Joe." Moving forward, he leaned against a washbasin. "You must allow me to return the favour..."

Smiling with patent intent, she acknowledged his suggestion and stepped into a cubicle and, heeding his cue, he locked the door behind him.

She was very small and, towering above her, he wondered if he might hurt her but reasoned that this probably wasn't the first time she'd had sex and if she were that delicate, she wouldn't be welcoming him into a cubicle. Pushing against her, they heard footsteps outside and she looked worried.

"Is there somewhere a little more private?" Leading her quietly out of the ladies', he headed to the backroom and unlocked the door. "You have a key?"

"I'm a good customer."

Alerted by a silent alarm by the till, Mike left the bar to check his monitor and, seeing Joe, he made his excuses to his staff and watched intently.

"There's a lot of equipment in here, which is your favourite?" Lila was intrigued, if not a little disturbed by what she saw.

"All of it...but the question is, which do you prefer?"

"Well, I'm a novice so maybe you should educate me..."

With a devilish smile, he lied, "I'd better be gentle."

"Why are there cameras?"

"They're for your protection, and mine: you enter this room

at your own risk, but in case anybody decides to cry wolf, there's evidence."

"Or free porn!"

He was impressed by her perception. "Well, that's a chance you're going to have to take. Your choice…"

She studied the space, wondering how regularly and how extensively it was used. "So does this all get cleaned properly?"

"Yes, I can assure you it does; I wouldn't use if it didn't."

"And how often do you use it?"

"When it's necessary…"

She smiled. "It's nice to be 'necessary.'" She sauntered around the room. "No bed…?"

He laughed. "It's not a hotel! This room is designed exclusively for sex. If you're looking for romance, you're in the wrong place."

"Isn't everyone looking for a little romance?"

"No." Holding her gaze, he moved towards her. "So if that's a problem, I suggest you leave now."

She smiled to hide her disappointment. "I didn't say anything about leaving…"

Returning her smile, though with infinitely more satisfaction, he walked her back to a padded post. "Then let's have some fun." Kissing her softly, he ran his hands down her body. "No escape now." He reached for the drawer and removed a vibrator, turned it on and drew it down her chest and stomach, listening to the change in her breathing. "See, here's my dilemma: this little thing wants to go here…" He nestled it in her crotch, watching her face carefully. "But that leaves no room for me, so I'm going to have to go here…" Dragging it round to her arse, he could feel her tense. "Just relax and it'll be easier for us both. I promise you'll enjoy it."

He kissed her eagerly – she tasted unexpectedly sweet – and his hands worked their way down to her skirt, disappeared underneath and gently stroked her thighs. With his mouth exploring her neck, she sighed deeply, pushing her body closer before finding his belt and unzipping his jeans, her hands investigating their contents ardently and, savouring their inspection, confident of a satisfactory analysis, he permitted their continuation until he felt the softness of her clothing against his cock. He raised her arms above her head and closed the cuffs around her wrists.

She faltered. "I don't know…that's not what I had in mind…"

"Now that's a shame, because I gave you the chance to leave…"

"I know, but…"

"Shh…" Slowly raising her skirt, he turned her round, sliding his toy into her underwear and manoeuvring it deep inside her, feeling her tension abate. "Isn't that better?" Securing it in place, he pushed against her, holding her hips, sharing the erection she'd freed. "It would be a shame to miss out…" Rubbing his cock against her bare skin and nuzzling her hair, he sighed. "That's better."

Pulling her back to provide an easier penetration, he pushed cautiously but deep inside her, stepping forward to afford a more advantageous position, and he enjoyed his view as he pushed harder and harder, smiling at her easy acquiescence, given her initial protests. She'd wanted an education and he'd most certainly honoured that, but she may not be quite so keen on the finals. She was good and he could feel her relax…but she wasn't Abbie. *Fuck!* He didn't want to lose his erection and closed his eyes to facilitate a more vivid picture of the woman he would rather be engrossed in. With the image of her in his mind, he felt her hands on his chest, and it was she he could hear gasp as his dick probed forcefully, unrelenting and purposeful, seeking deliverance from the transgression that had embodied the last twelve hours. He kissed her again, harder, and he could taste his cum in her mouth as he had the night before when the slightest intimation had effected her immediate climax, writhing around on his lap. Feeling her, smelling her and seeing her come over his crotch was enough and he erupted inside Lila as she welcomed her own orgasm, stimulated by the simultaneous motion of both Joe and his accomplice. Still embroiled in Abbie, he took a while to compose himself and find his way back to the present.

As he removed himself from Lila, she smiled broadly. "You were right, but you could've just bought me a drink…"

Uncuffing her and buckling his belt, he replied without eye-contact. "Yeah, but I would have had to pay for that."

She was unnerved by his tone and expression. "Thanks!"

"No, thank you, Lila. Could you close the door on your way out? You can keep your gift." Unlocking the door, he strolled out without looking back, leaving her rather dishevelled and feeling rather uncomfortable.

As he walked back to his drink, his phone rang. "Hey, Rosie, perfect timing! Just had my first course, do you want to be the main?"

"Hi, Joe. How much have you had to drink?" She wasn't feeling as playful as he.

"Not much. Don't worry, it won't affect my performance."

His customary approach, whilst decidedly absent earlier, was now unwelcome. "Joe, focus!"

"Always focussed, Rosie, but sometimes it's a little more rewarding." He walked outside to continue their conversation without distraction.

"Joe…I've just come back from Abbie's and…"

"Hey, did you give her my love? Ooh, now there's a thought… did you…? Did you record it, Rosie? Mmm…just the thought of it makes me hard…"

"Joe! I need to talk to you about Abbie…"

"Rose, there's nothing to say. Short of kidnapping her, and you'd be a fool to think I hadn't considered it, there's nothing I can do. She fucked me last night and…do you want to what we did, Rosie; huh? Is that why you're calling, you want me to show you?" As he heard her sigh in protest he laughed bitterly. "But now she's fucked me completely! I waited eleven fucking years for her; for what? To get laid and told to fuck off! It's not my fault Eddie fucking killed himself; it's not my fault and it's not her fault. He did it Rose, but she won't see it. She won't blame him because he's the only person she ever cared about...but me? I'm just another name on her CV. I didn't force her last night: she wanted me to fuck her and she has for years, but she led me on and on and now she's got what she wanted. She won't get a second chance..."

Tired and tense, she interrupted his rant. "Joe...listen to me: we need to talk, but clearly now isn't time so have a few more drinks, get a good night's sleep and I'll call you tomorrow, OK?"

His tirade had served its purpose and he calmed down. "Yeah, OK...unless you want to come over now...?"

"*Joe!*"

He wandered back inside, happy to find his drink.

"Are you OK, Joe? You look like shit!" Mike was genuinely concerned.

"Yeah." He downed the last of his drink and slowly turned the glass. "Eddie died last night."

"*What?!* Fuck! Christ, Joe, I'm so sorry! What...how...what the fuck happened?" He was stunned; he was fond of Eddie and his drunken antics. "Why didn't you say anything earlier?"

"I don't know...it's not the best way to greet someone." He sighed, fighting the tears he'd avoided all morning. "They think he OD'd, but they'll need to do a post-mortem to be sure."

"Shit, I'm sorry, mate. I don't know what to say. Drinks are on the house...and I'll join you."

"Thanks, Mike, but that's OK..."

"Joe, they're on the house. Christ, Eddie was my best customer."

He laughed. "Yeah, I'm not surprised."

After a couple more drinks, he started to feel the effects of the previous night's drama and, thanking Mike, he left for home, disappointed at the lack of suitable females, but figured they'd probably do little to placate him right now, and there was always tomorrow.

***

Joe's dreams returned to Abbie, but they were not as pleasant as before: she was taunting him with Jesse, laughing at him, calling his name as she fucked Jesse. Waking early was a relief of sorts, but his head was slightly muzzy – a rather unfamiliar and unwelcome feeling. Why did people do this voluntarily? He looked at his phone: *seven-thirty – better phone work.* Having toyed with the idea of taking just the one day, the impact of the weekend was slowly creeping up on him and he opted to take a week. He rarely used his holiday allocation, so now would be a good time.

Speaking to his PA, he was touched by her concern, battling the emotion that her kind words induced and promising to call her should he need anything at all, amused when she corrected herself in case he saw fit to misinterpret her intention. He thanked her and apologised again, and assured her he would return the following week.

Next: Abbie. Before he could dial her number, his phone rang. "Hi, Rosie, you're early." Slowly, he recalled a rather heated conversation with her, or, rather, an angry, monologic lecture. "Did you call me last night, or did I dream it? I think my dreams of you would be a little more exciting…"

Ignoring his customary theme, she tried to be gentle. "Yes, I called you last night, but you weren't really in a talking mood. Actually, you were very much in a talking mood, just not in a listening one." She paused nervously, unwilling to worry herself further by anticipating his response. "Joe…Abbie's gone…" She winced as she waited for the blast.

"What do you mean she's 'gone'? Gone where? Where is she, Rose?" Feeling a little uncomfortable, he hoped it was the remnants of his alcoholic extravagance.

"She's gone. She said she couldn't stay in the house with all the memories and..."

"Bitch!" He threw the phone on the sofa and grabbed some clothes from his bedroom. Collecting his phone on the way out, he jumped in the car and sped off.

"Shit!" Rose was scared; after yesterday's session, he really shouldn't be driving, at least not at that speed, and she grabbed her bag, heading over to his apartment, to await his return from Abbie's.

***

Arriving at the house, Joe hammered on the door. "ABBIE!" No answer. *Fuck!* He looked through the windows but no sign. Whilst he had no reason to doubt Rose, he didn't think Abbie would be so selfish as to add to everyone's woes with an unnecessary departure. Picking up a rock, he stopped just short of smashing the window: no sense in being arrested for attempted burglary as well as driving under the influence. What the fuck was she thinking? Was she the only one grieving, the only one involved here? And did she seriously think this was all going to disappear because she'd run away? Well, true to form, she'd only thought about Abbie. Maybe she should have considered the consequences before she started fucking every bloke under the age of twenty-five! *Fuck you, Abbie!*

Driving home, he was unable to calm his racing mind. He pulled up outside his apartment, opened the front door and kicked it shut, but Rose stopped it before it slammed, although with an endless supply of objects on which to vent his rage, it went unnoticed. Grabbing a photo of Eddie and himself, he threw it across the room before striding into the kitchen, seizing whatever cups he could find and subjecting them to the same fate, but with no alleviation, he picked up a chair and smashed it across the table, and as he looked up, he saw Rose at the door. His lip trembled, but he refused to cry and as she walked towards him, he threw his arms round her and held her tight, afraid that if he let go, he'd have to face the nightmare that was unfolding. After a considerable period, he pulled away and looked at her, searching for an answer, an explanation, anything that would elucidate Abbie's behaviour. Rose placed her hands gently on his face. "I'm so sorry, Joe."

Covering her hands, his wrath took a different course and he slowly moved in to kiss her, and with no resistance, he pulled her close, moving his hands down her back and running his fingers along her belt, unbuckling it before unfastening his jeans. "Joe…" Rose whispered, but he wasn't listening. Loosening his jeans, he worked on hers, determined and proficient. "Joe, stop!" He pushed her against the fridge and as he tugged at her underwear, pressing hard against her, she faltered, momentarily tempted by the intensity of his proximity and his mood, but pulled from under him as she finally came to her senses. She adjusted her clothing before turning on him. "Joe, don't…"

He spun round and, putting his dick away, walked towards her, smiling irresistibly: he wouldn't be beaten. "C'mon, Rosie, you know how much I want you. Why do you always turn me down – who's going to know?" He cornered her and pushed against her again, placing her hand on his crotch. "C'mon, I promise I'll be gentle…" *There's always a first time…*

"Joe, I said stop!" She pushed him off and held out her hands.

Throwing back his head, he sighed. "What's the problem, Rosie? I know you think about me when you fuck Michael…" She looked away and he smiled, moving close enough for her hands to touch his chest. "What does he do to you, Rosie, does he make you come?" He pulled her hands down to his waist and whispered, "Tell me what he does…" Kissing her neck, he guided her hands to his unbuttoned fly, breathing deeply, anticipating her accession. "Tell me what you want me to do… you know I'll do it…and next time you fuck your husband and think of me, this is what you'll remember – no more guessing." With hungry fingers, he pulled at her jeans, edging closer to his goal, vehemently resolute she would not deny him again, unaware that, whilst her rationale was blinded by the emotive circumstances of their convergence, and the temptation for capitulatory alleviation was compelling, the fallout from such a decision would be catastrophic, and the choice between a repined and resentful Joe, or a betrayed and distrustful Abbie and Michael would prove an easy one. Removing herself carefully from his grasp, she walked into the lounge and sat down, feeling frustrated but infinitely safer. Joe reluctantly fastened his jeans and sauntered in behind her.

"You'll regret it, Rosie…" With his anger ill-concealed, he sat down opposite, crossed his legs and looked at her with an air of arrogance. "If you're not going to indulge me, then I'll satisfy myself…" He watched her face as he slowly unbuttoned his jeans, revelling in her discomfort and her struggle to avert her eyes. Seldom was he refused sex and his patience with the day so far was wearing dangerously thin, so his proposal wasn't entirely unreasonable and, whilst he would prefer her participation, he wasn't opposed to her spectating, with or without her approval.

"Joe, come on…don't do this…" Forcing her eyes to the floor, she ignored the sounds that told her he wasn't listening. "If you're not going to talk to me, I'll go…"

He smiled. "If you had any intention of leaving, Rosie, you would have gone already…"

"For fuck's sake, Joe!" She got up and headed for the door, but he grabbed her wrist.

"OK, you win…" Moving closer, he kept his eyes fixed on hers, tenacious and deliberately ominous. "But I won't be so understanding next time…and there will be a next time; I can see it in your eyes." As he released his grip, he buttoned his jeans in defeat. "Do you want a coffee?" He turned towards the kitchen.

"Do you have any mugs left…?"

***

With a coffee in his hand, Joe leaned back with a smile. "OK, I'm all yours."

"Firstly, I don't think of you when I fuck my husband…"

"Liar. What's next?"

Rose laughed as she shook her head. "How do you suppose Abbie would react if she found out, if I'd let you continue? Have you spoken to her?" Whilst relieved the tension had subsided, she wasn't entirely sure this conversation would be any better.

Joe's mood changed. "Of course I haven't, she's not fucking there!"

"I know, but have you called her?"

"No – what would be the point? She didn't tell me she was going; why would I call her?"

"You can't just leave it, Joe. Don't you want her back?" She started to question her loyalty.

With irascibility beckoning, he smiled sarcastically, dropping his eyes as he deliberated his response, endeavouring to steady his tone. Raising his eyes, he kept his voice low as he replied, "She has played me for far too long, Rose, and now she's fucked off without a word. I'm not going to beg her to come back. I don't beg; I don't have to. There are plenty more where she came from. Don't worry, I'll be alright – I fuck very well." He watched, waiting for her to cower and he smirked as she looked away.

She was torn: she felt for him – his anger was somewhat justified, if a little misdirected – but she could equally understand Abbie's need to escape; communicating her thoughts to them both, however, and expecting Joe to keep his dick in his trousers whilst doing so, was quite an undertaking and, right now, she was feeling less and less inclined to try. "OK. Well, you seem to have it all figured out so there's not an awful lot of point in my being here; I'll leave you both to behave like children and get myself a decent night's sleep." She stood up, heading once more towards the door.

"Whoa!" Taking the bait, Joe was by her side before she could leave. "Don't include me in that, Rose. Abbie ran away like a spoiled teenager! I tried to help, I tried to talk to her, but she wouldn't listen. What the fuck was I supposed to do?"

"She's just lost her son, Joe: do you know how that feels? I don't and don't ever want to. She doesn't know what she wants; she doesn't know what to do. Cut her a little slack, for Christ's sake!"

But with his position unchanged, his expression hardened. "Running away won't change that."

He was right. "I know...I know." She gently touched his arm. "She should hear from the coroner in three or four weeks and then she can sort out the funeral. I'll let you know what they say." She nervously kissed his cheek, but this time he didn't proposition her.

Watching her drive away, he closed the door and looked at the mess in his apartment that, a few minutes ago, went unnoticed. *Better clean it up.*

✼✼✼

With lunch well and truly overdue, Joe fancied a change of scene and, surprisingly, as little female company as possible. Avoiding The Well, he wandered down the street for inspiration. Stopping at a burger bar, he collected his order and took it to the park, where thoughts of Molly – not in this park, but not too far away – came flooding back. She'd opened his eyes and his mind to experiences that he'd since developed and relished, and that had governed his life ever since, and he wondered whether his own predilection was ineluctable or influenced by his early encounters. She hadn't been the first, and his years of pandering to the whims of the local female population had already stimulated a desideration that was almost unquenchable, but she'd channelled it and demonstrated that he should command his precedencies to give him the ultimate gratification. Had he propositioned Abbie then and she'd rejected him, maybe he could have laughed it off as teenage jinks, but she would have registered his interest and things may have been different; he had decided, however, that experience was key and that, as most of her lovers had, indeed, been young, he wanted his maturity to distinguish him from them. But then there was Jesse, less puerile, himself, than the rest, and Joe pondered his hatred of him – was it just because he'd screwed Abbie…or was it simply because he quite fancied Jesse himself? With thoughts of a threesome pervading his mind, he smiled mischievously. Abbie had seemed keen, but it was unclear where Jesse's preferences lie… Aware of his burgeoning erection, he looked around but found no one to share it with…perhaps The Well would have been a better option. He finished his lunch and wandered back home to freshen up. Relieving himself in the shower, he was on unfamiliar territory: two rejections and two huge erections in one day, with only his right hand for comfort. Rose wouldn't get away next time.

Once dressed, he checked his phone; Mark had called and left a message so he returned his call. "Hey, man, how are you?"

"Hey, Joe, how the fuck are you? Sorry, I meant to call you yesterday but you know…" He'd preferred to air his grief in private.

"Yeah, I know, don't worry."

"So how are you doing? Do you know what happened yet?" Mark's battle with incredulity continued.

"No, it'll be a few weeks before we know anything. Did Jamie get in touch with everyone?"

"Yeah, I think so. I still can't believe it – I only spoke to Eddie

Friday night. How's Abbie?" She'd been good to all the boys' friends...some more than others, but no one was exactly sure who.

"Not good. She's gone away for a bit; needs to get away from the house, I think."

"I'm not surprised. I'm so sorry, mate. Do you want to go for a drink? Kinda feel we owe it to Eddie really."

"Yeah, absolutely; you free tonight?" It would be good to have some different company.

"Yeah! Where do you want to go, The Well?"

"It's easy for me..."

"Yeah, no worries; see you there around eight?"

"Great. I'm going there shortly so I'll be pretty oiled by the time you get there!" One more night would be OK.

"OK, man. I'll try to get there a little earlier. You take it easy, yeah? See you later."

"Yep, see you later."

"Oh, Joe?"

"Yeah?"

"Shall I see if I can get some of the guys to come along?"

"Yeah, good idea. Thanks, Mark."

"No worries. See you later."

Joe hadn't seen the boys for a few days and, of course, the last time had been with Eddie so it would be a little odd, but it was just what he needed. So long as he could get some positive female company today, he didn't mind – the boys didn't usually cramp his style. He stopped to think about his friend for the first time since he'd left the hospital: he missed him badly. The last few days would have been spent with him, this evening too, and whilst he was happy with his own company, he was rarely alone because there was always Eddie, with or without Abbie, or some willing female: two out of the three were now missing.

With time to kill, he opened a bottle of wine and, sitting in his lounge, he finally allowed himself to think about the impact of the last two days. Until now, functionality had ruled his days, dealing with the issues that Abbie's behaviour had caused and not focussing on the significance of his own loss. Eddie had given him a life by just being his friend and he truly loved him. Losing his mother had completely overwhelmed him and being an only child, she was his world. Having no particular bond with his father, he was sensible to the jealousy that existed because of her love for her son and when she died protecting him, Joe was the inevitable target for his rage. At seven, he'd lost his mother, whatever relationship he had with his father and his innocence overnight. Enduring his father's abuse for four years, he'd contemplated, despite his tender age, joining his mother… but then he'd met Eddie and for the first time in as long as he could remember, he'd laughed. Eddie made him laugh and wanted to be with him, and, though, at first, he tried to avoid him, unwilling to trust anyone, Eddie had persevered and he'd succumbed to his kindness, and put his morbid intentions on hold until they were no longer a necessary consideration. Abbie, familiar with his troubled past but not the detail, never enquired about his life: she just took care of him. She'd fed him, loved him, nursed him and educated him. She'd shown him his worth and taught him that only he could control his life and his mind – no one else. An avid pupil, he eventually found a way to control others and the supremacy his father held would never torment him again.

As his hostility towards her lost its reasoning, he pulled his phone from his pocket and dialled; it rang and rang and eventually went to voicemail. "Abbie…hi. I won't trouble you again, but I just wanted to say thank you. If it weren't for you and Eddie, I wouldn't be here now; I would probably have taken my own life, or my excuse for a father would have taken it for me. I never thanked Eddie, but I think…I hope, he knew, but I can thank you. You have given so much to me, which I have mostly taken for granted and I took for granted that you would always be here. I hope you'll be happy, Abbie, and I hope that eventually you'll be able to forgive me."

Reluctantly ending the call, he stared at his phone for a while and, as he drank his wine, he cried: he cried for Eddie; cried for Abbie and he cried for the mother stolen from him too soon, and for the child he wasn't allowed to be. He was alone again like he was at seven but no longer scared, no longer vulnerable and no longer broken, and for that he was forever grateful – Abbie had transformed his thinking and transformed his life at a time when everything was slipping away so at the very least, she deserved his understanding. He drank some more and welcomed the repose that followed before washing his face, and with a calmer mind he looked hard into the mirror and slowly smiled: he may have lost the only woman he ever really wanted, but the image he saw would always serve him well.

Feeling lighter, he crossed the road and entered The Well, looking forward to seeing Mark and whoever else he managed to bring. "Hey, Mike. How's it going?"

"Hey, Joe, how are you? You look better today. The usual?"

"Yes please, but I better stick to singles. Are you cooking tonight? I need to keep my strength up…" With such a bad start to the day, he was hoping it ended better.

Mike laughed. "This is a fucking bar, Joe, not a health food shop…or a brothel!"

"You sure about that? I'll have chicken, please."

8

Feeling more settled with a full stomach, Joe was pleased to see it wasn't long before the bar started to buzz. No sign of Mark or the boys, but there were a few ladies who could possibly kill some time and he strolled to the gents, to freshen up. As he dried his hands, the door opened and in the mirror, he saw one such candidate saunter in. "I'm sorry, you've got a little lost; this is the gents." Turning round, he smiled innocently.

"No mistake; I watched you walk in…"

Although quite young – though, hopefully legal – she was very confident and that impressed Joe. He walked towards her but stopped far enough away that she had to make a move. "So are you going to watch me walk out?"

"Not just yet…" Stepping forward, she pulled him to her and he was taken with her directness: no introductions – why waste time? Her kisses were surprisingly aggressive, and whilst a little surprised, he felt no immediate compulsion to complain. Picking her up, he carried her into a cubicle, but as his hands wandered under her dress, she wriggled free, dropped to her knees and unbuckled his belt. At last! He watched her continue, unaided, and waited patiently to feel her tongue on his dick. Closing his eyes, he smiled as he felt her mouth close around his erection, gently moving her head around, savouring every second, and he groaned softly as she moved faster, visualising once more the woman who fed his imagination, uncertain, though unconcerned, given the inactivity of the day, how long he would last. Feeling the building of his climax, he enjoyed the steady rise, forcing himself deep in her mouth, grateful that this orgasm was shared and not the solitary experience that had characterised the day. He held her still, allowing his cock to finish throbbing, eventually releasing his grip, and as she rose, she looked at him with a smile. "You owe me…"

He returned her smile and moved in close, and after buttoning his jeans, he removed his wallet from his pocket. "How much?"

"Bastard!"

"You're welcome." He walked out satisfied and ready for the boys. *Should have been you, Rosie…*

Mike laughed as he returned. "You know, those cubicles are not just for you, Joe…"

"Really, who else needs them? Get me a drink, barman!"

***

Mark was the first to arrive. He hugged Joe tight and insisted on buying another drink. "I was expecting you to be a little worse for wear – you OK? Hi, Mike."

"He's just been entertained in the gents' so I'm guessing that's helped! You alright, Mark?"

"Yeah, I'm fine, thanks. Do you want a drink?"

"Maybe later, but thanks, mate."

"So who was she – anyone I know?" Mark was a little envious of his friend, if not a little disapproving of his promiscuity. Preferring a relationship to a constant stream of impersonal coquetry, he wouldn't mind, however, the occasional indulgence during the dry spells, but with Joe around the odds were severely diminished.

"I don't think so; I don't know who she was and she had my dick in her mouth for the best part of ten minutes!"

"You're disgraceful, Joe, do you know that?"

"Yes, I do, but I'm the one getting laid, my friend!"

"Fair point."

Before they'd finished their drinks, Jamie walked in with Matt and Andy. Handshakes and back-slaps all round, followed by heart-felt condolences.

"Such a shock! Did you know about the drugs, Joe?" Andy was a sweet guy, if a little naïve. Always seeing the best in people and the first to lend a hand, Eddie's death would haunt him, but his would be the shoulder should anyone require consolation.

"I did…kind of. I tried talking to him, but you know what he was like; he didn't take me seriously, just wanted to have a good time."

"Did Abbie know? She must be in a dreadful state." Joe knew they'd all be concerned about her, but something about Matt's interest disturbed him.

"Yeah, of course she is. She didn't know, no, so she's in a pretty bad way."

"Give her our love, Joe, and when the others get here, I think we should have a drink to Eddie. Do you know when the funeral is?"

"No, we've got to wait for the post-mortem first…but thanks, Andy – appreciate that."

"OK. Well, let us know as soon as you hear, would you?"

"Yeah, of course."

"Right, I'm getting thirsty, chaps. What are we drinking?" Jamie was ready to start the merriment.

"What time are the others getting here?"

With a derisive smile, Matt shared his theory. "They shouldn't be too long. I think James had to go and see his girlfriend before he was allowed out!" Something his pride would oppose.

"You're just jealous, man – when was the last time you had a girlfriend?" Joe laughed at him; he'd been single a little too long.

"Yeah, funny, Joe! Tell me, how many girlfriends have you had?"

"How long have you got?"

Matt shook his head. "A quick fuck doesn't constitute a relationship, mate!"

"Well, there's definitely a relationship between my dick and her..."

"OK." With a swift intervention from Mark, the evening continued in a more jovial tone and when Miles and James finally arrived, they were all joking about Eddie's misdemeanours.

"What have we missed?" James joined the rowdiness whilst Miles bought drinks.

"Quite a lot, it would seem! Did you know about Eddie and the lesbians?" Being the only homosexual in the group, Jamie was intrigued, and despite his steadfast allegiance to his gay community, he allowed sentiment to overrule his instinctive response.

"No, what happened?" They laughed loudly as Joe retold the story and Miles, catching the tale-end, choked on his drink.

When the hysteria subsided, James enquired about Joe's bond with his best friend. "So how long have you known Eddie, mate?" The last to join their clique, he was unclear of the details. He'd worked with Joe for a very short time, but they'd hit it off immediately and when they'd gone to The Well for drinks after work one evening, giving Joe a chance to gauge his inclination, the rest of the boys had descended upon them unexpectedly and he was promptly included. A little disappointed he may have missed an opportunity, Joe was a little relieved when shortly after James had introduced his new girlfriend and they were now very settled. He was the oldest at twenty-seven and the only one with commitments.

"About twelve years – I met him at school."

"Didn't you move in soon afterwards?" Matt had detected vibes between Abbie and Joe when he'd first met them, but it had never been clear where it had led, though given his own experience with her and Joe's reputation, it seemed inevitable that he'd enjoyed rather more than just her cooking.

"Yes I did."

"Sorry, Joe, but where were your parents?" Careful not to offend, Andy was struggling with missing detail.

He replied impassively. "My mum died when I was seven and my dad was a drunk; he died a couple of years ago, I think."

"Christ! Sorry, mate."

"That's OK."

"Is that why you never get pissed?" Miles was impressed at Joe's capacity for drinking but more so his ability to stay sober.

He laughed. "No, he wasn't important enough to have that much influence! I just prefer to be in control; I like to know where I am; what I'm doing…and who…"

"Even if you don't know her name…" Mark smiled; no matter what he said, he knew Joe had no shame.

"Not always necessary, Mark."

"How long did you live at Eddie's?" James was suddenly aware of how little he and the others knew about each other.

"About seven years, I think."

"Don't tell me you didn't bone Abbie!" The temptation was too strong and Matt's audacity was fuelled by the free-flowing alcohol.

Joe's expression changed and he stared at him. "Have a little respect, prick!"

"Come on, I'm just saying – I would have done." Looking to the others for validation and with his instincts clouded, he misjudged Joe's humour. Lunging towards him, Joe grabbed his shirt.

"You wouldn't stand a fucking chance, Matt, cos your mouth's too big and your dick's too small!"

"Whoa, Joe. Easy, man." Mark held him before he could do Matt any harm.

Keen to prevent an unnecessary disturbance, Mike wandered over to set some ground-rules. "That's enough, guys. Take it outside if it's going to get heated."

"It's alright, Mike, sorry, mate." Mark looked to Joe for an apology, but he was reluctant to relinquish his hold on Matt's shirt.

With silent accession, he finally removed his hand but maintained eye-contact. "Sorry, Mike."

Satisfied, Mike returned to the bar, but Matt remained uneasy. "Sorry, Joe, I didn't mean…" Shrugging his shoulders, he concluded, given Joe's unexpected reaction, he'd escaped lightly, and, unaccustomed to such behaviour from his friend, he figured the truth was probably better left unspoken.

"OK, it's been a tough few days…" Whilst the tension may have been diffused, Matt's words remained stagnant in his mind.

"Let's sit down, guys, before it gets too busy." Miles led them to a large table in the middle of the bar giving them the best vantage point, and Mark separated the hostiles. After Joe, Miles was the most popular of the group, with a very easy manner and boyish smile that met with great approval, and if Joe was occupied, he took up the slack.

With more drinks ordered, the atmosphere returned to a more playful mode and when a small group of women arrived, sitting at the next table, the boys exchanged brief glances and proceeded to turn and introduce themselves. Joe watched Matt intently: he'd homed in on one of the girls and she was seemingly captivated by his attention. Tempted to interject, he decided to monitor proceedings.

Despite the brief altercation, the evening was rather successful: they drank to Eddie with great cheers and told the adjacent females amusing anecdotes for the rest of the night, unashamedly exploiting the note of sympathy. Mike called last orders and offered a lock-in, but three of them had scored and the rest had work in the morning, leaving Joe, and he was in no rush.

"Same again, Mike, please. That's the last time I invite the boys over here; I didn't expect to be alone tonight."

Mike took the glass and topped it up and, glancing over his shoulder, he caught Joe's eye. "The night's not over yet…" Putting the glass down, he went to call time as Joe, analysing the interpretation of his insinuation, watched in utter amazement. Did Mike just come onto him? Mike? He picked up his glass and took a swig, looking at his host for substantiation, but as he was happily charming the last of the ladies who were hopelessly trying to persuade him to let them stay, he rationalised his judgement had been unusually shrouded by alcohol.

As the bar slowly emptied Mike's admirers were refusing to leave. "Why's he still here?"

"He's staff and I need to reprimand him tonight so keep your voice down." Joe smiled; he was convincing.

When, finally, they left, Mike locked the door.

He poured himself a drink and joined Joe at the bar. "You look like you had a good night; I think you probably deserved it."

"Yeah, it was good. Sorry about Matt – that guy needs to grow some balls."

Mike laughed. "That's OK, don't worry. You not working tomorrow?"

"Nope, taken the week off. Thought it was probably a good time; there's too much going on to face work."

Mike sipped his drink and with an unfaltering gaze, took a bold chance. "Have you seen Abbie?"

Slightly unnerved, Joe looked away. Did Mike know? "No, not today; she's gone away for a while and I'm not entirely sure when, or, indeed, if she'll be back."

"Sorry, Joe…but she'll come back."

Studying Mike's face, he searched for something that would endorse his erstwhile musings. His perception was typically flawless, but Mike's approach had challenged his discernment and that was troubling, but as he turned to face him, deliberating his sagacity, his suspicions were confirmed and he slowly smiled.

Sipping his drink, he contemplated the inexorability of his assured delectation. Mike, at thirty, was in good shape and it was easy to see why he was never short of female admiration, and, like Joe, he was inclined to ambiguity regarding his intimate avocations, never openly discussing them, choosing, instead, to generalise, avoiding disloyalty to his partners and, quite possibly, the occasional irate boyfriend. Until now, however, he had no reason to question Mike's propensity... but Mike's confirmation of his erroneous assumptions were proving advantageous and, as his cock responded, he stood up and walked towards him, kissing him passionately. Mike pulled Joe closer to demonstrate the consequences of his presence and as Joe's dick started to throb, he forced his tongue further into Mike's mouth. Equally aroused but somewhat less patient, he slowly unbuttoned Joe's shirt, running his hands across his chest, caressing every slight curve, before moving down to his belt whilst his anticipative companion willed him to persist. Adhering to his unspoken command, Mike released Joe's expectant cock and rubbed with one hand as the other moved seductively down his back and hovered just below his waist, prolonging the torment as he returned his kiss, dilatorily brushing his skin before moving his fingers lower and forcing them way inside Joe, momentarily paralysing him with euphoria and longing. With his senses heightened and his desire augmented, Joe loosened Mike's jeans, pulled them down and responded with reciprocal masturbation. As his hand moved faster, Mike breathed heavily, and silently deliberating the loss of his fingers, Joe turned him round, consoled by the prospect of fucking him. He faltered slightly as he held onto Mike's hips, centring his focus before thrusting hard inside him and, reminded of Carl, he reflected on the lack of male intimacy and vowed to rectify it, forcing himself further into

Mike, enjoying every movement, every sound, and, revelling in self-congratulations, he was thrilled by this sheer, unbridled debauchery that he craved but rarely found with the opposite sex – no rules, no boundaries and no inhibitions – and closing his eyes, lost in a world of shameless exuberance, he could see Jesse…and Mike…and endless debased possibilities. Groaning deeply, incapable of any level of restraint, he felt that familiar climatic sensation, unable to prevent its rise, easing him closer to the exhilaration that influenced his every waking hour, compelling his search for his next fix, and when it lashed his body mercilessly, wondrously, he yelled out, allowing the transfixion to prolong his orgasm as long as it could, remaining still as his cock throbbed hard long after. Finally, he removed himself and pulled up his jeans.

When Mike turned round, Joe, intent on maximising the evening's entertainment, wrapped his hand around Mike's cock and resumed his mission, confidently holding his gaze, unashamedly complicit in anything his partner had to offer. Closing his hand around Joe's, Mike squeezed it tighter, not only relieved his insinuation had been realised but feverishly incited by results so far. He'd wanted to fuck Joe the first time he saw him, but as he became a regular, he soon became aware of his patron's prowess with the ladies and resigned himself to the fact that unless he was prepared to pay for some pretty serious surgery, the man was off limits. Tonight, however, feeling reckless and knowing Joe was horny with no outlet, his subtle suggestion that had, fortuitously, had favourable consequences, could just as easily have been refuted if his esteemed client really had no interest in a little homoerotic indulgence. Now, standing with that client's hand clasped around his dick, lost in a delirious trance, he wondered why he hadn't propositioned him sooner, although, something told him his friend wouldn't take too kindly to an ostensibly blunt proposal. He closed his eyes to savour Joe's seductive touch, but Joe wanted his full attention: "Look at me." Excited by the aggression in his voice, Mike complied, and in doing so, he came quicker than expected, with Joe watching his face closely. Moving his hand to catch the full ejaculation, Joe pulled his hand away and licked it clean, appreciating his first taste of another man's cum, as Mike fell silent.

After a quick visit to the gents' to freshen up and a provocative sip of his drink, Joe leaned in to kiss him, unbuttoning his shirt and stepping close enough to gently graze Mike's chest with his own. Very much acquainted with the appreciation of all those who experienced his cock, his body was equally celebrated, and, it would seem, this victim was not immune. Pulling away and licking Joe's nipples, whilst simultaneously rubbing his crotch, Mike hoped to instigate further arousal, and, willingly collaborative, Joe's permissiveness encouraged him to lick, suck and squeeze, and feel the gradual swelling that promised additional rewards.

"I watched you in the backroom earlier…"

Joe smiled. "Yeah? Did you learn anything?"

Returning his smile, Mike spoke honestly. "Only how dangerous you can be."

Looking deep into his eyes, he put a hand on Mike's shoulder, gently pushing him to his knees, still studying his face as he pushed his cock deep into his mouth and, closing his eyes, he sighed deeply, swaying slowly, seeking the most salutary position. His jaw tightened as he rammed his groin into Mike's face, no longer complacent but obdurate in his quest for intemperate decadence, and Mike obeying readily, sucked hard, steadying his movements with fingers deep inside him. Urging more from Mike's hand, Joe embraced the rapture transporting him to the felicitous moment that would furnish him with his condign splendour, and as the intensity grew, he became oblivious to Mike's presence, only his mouth and the licentious dream that claimed his surrender, escalating his orgasm. Shuddering violently, he erupted in Mike's mouth, his cock pumping as he continued to sway, light-headed but elated in a way he had never before experienced – numb yet totally alive – and when his body had finally expended all the cum it had to give, he stood, blissfully waiting for the throbbing to stop. Putting his dick away, he secured the support of the barstool until the trembling subsided, and as Mike slowly rose, pleased with his achievement, he kissed Joe, allowing his cum to trickle in to his mouth, holding him firm as Joe tried to resist; when his mouth was empty, he stood back and smiled, watching his companion's face. Refusing his initial antipathy, Joe licked his lips provocatively and sat down on the stool, enjoying Mike's appreciation of his state of undress. He finished his drink and raised his glass for a refill.

Mike responded, refreshed his own drink and sat down, running a hand over Joe's nipple. "I've heard so many rumours about you."

Unimpressed, Joe concentrated on his glass. "Yeah?" He didn't gossip and didn't understand the need.

"Yeah – most say you're a pussy man; a couple have said you don't mind a little male company, although no one seems to have any proof…but I never thought of you as gay."

"I'm not gay, Mike."

"OK, bisexual…"

"Look, Mike, I like to fuck…a lot, and I do. It makes little difference to me who it is so long as it's good; it just so happens there are a lot of women happy to eat my dick." He was slightly annoyed at Mike's intrusion.

"OK, man…it's OK. I don't care; I'm not judging, I was just surprised, that's all." Joe sipped his drink and buttoned his shirt and jeans. Mike, unable to hide his disappointment, was annoyed at his own indiscretion. "Sorry, I didn't mean to piss you off, Joe." Mike was genuinely unconcerned, just… pleasantly surprised.

Acknowledging his apology, Joe waved a hand and steered the conversation away from his own interests. "Weren't you married?"

"Yeah, for about five years."

"So what happened?" He couldn't remember if he'd already been told.

Mike laughed. "She decided she was a lesbian and ran off with someone at work!"

Nope, this he would have remembered! Joe stared at him in utter disbelief. "Seriously? So, what, you thought, 'if you can't beat 'em...'" He laughed at the absurdity.

"No. I've always fancied men...just fancied women more..."

"Thanks, mate!"

Mike smiled. "I thought all blokes did so it wasn't a problem. But after we separated, I got quite close to one of our neighbours – he was really supportive and just really friendly...overly-friendly – and I could have sworn he was giving me signals... but it turns out I was wrong!"

"No! What did you do?"

With a couple of drinks under his belt, Mike struggled to control the hysteria. "We had a boys' night at my house – his idea; drinking, X-box, a little porn. We watched about half an hour or so, and I had a huge hard-on so I put my hand on his dick and started to squeeze it, but he leapt off the sofa, screaming at me! I was shocked cos I was so convinced he was up for it. So, I sold up and moved here."

Laughing like children, neither could speak, but when they finally settled down, Mike looked seriously at Joe. "Look, Joe, thanks for tonight. If you're ever at a loose end, let me know." Sensing a shift in Joe's mood, he was quick to pacify him. "Don't worry, I'm not going to pester you and I'm not the jealous type... OK?"

"OK...but you know I won't."

"I know, but if you change your mind..."

Joe smiled and finished his drink, kissed Mike seductively and left.

As he locked the door behind him, Mike sighed and drained his glass. "Fuck! He's good…"

***

Waking late, with his head worse than before, Joe made a rather large breakfast and headed to the shower, trying to remember how much he'd had. As the water flowed over his body, he thought of his evening with Mike – didn't see that coming! Mike was a pleasant distraction, but his interest had escaped Joe and he wasn't sure if he'd been caught up in the emotion of the last few days or the alcohol had numbed his perspicacity; either way, it was a risky position and it was probably best to put a stop to the drinking…or maybe just ease up a little. As he washed his cock, the memory of being in Mike's mouth aroused him and he started to masturbate, recalling Mike's transference of his cum into his mouth, and he smiled at the thought. He came quickly and as he did, he caught his ejaculation in his hand and slowly licked it off. That was worth remembering…

9

Finally stirring from a disturbed night, Abbie rose late. Despite the after effects, it was certainly preferable as she could close her mind to Joe when she was awake and avoid the pain of her memories; asleep, she dreamed of him in vivid, exquisite detail. Christ, she wanted him! She ached for him…his touch, his smell, his cock, his tongue. She could feel her pussy throb – *Shit, Joe!* Walking to the bathroom, she looked in the mirror, hoping to find some answers, but got nothing – what the fuck was she supposed to do? She'd been away for, what, two nights? She was desperate to get home, but he'd be there and although she wanted to see him – *God, she wanted to see him* – she couldn't look at him without seeing Eddie lying still and unresponsive. She was angry; angry at losing her son and angry at losing Joe. They could have fucked at any time – *any time* – and there wouldn't have been a problem, and she'd be at home now, with him there to comfort her, and he would have made everything easier, but now, alone, the pain was corrosive, debilitating and constant, and it was going nowhere soon. So what now? She wiped her tears. Eddie was her baby, always, and her heart lurched when she thought of him. Yes, she'd learn to live with the loss – she knew that – but he was all she had, and Joe…and she'd fucked that up by leaving like she did. She regretted it now, leaving so quickly, but it was the easy option and she always favoured the easy option. The consequences were hers to face, but she was getting good at that. And now, with just the bare necessities, desperate to see Eddie's face, she had to make do with the few, meagre photos on her phone, most of which were rendered next to useless as he had tried hard to avoid the camera. With a single decent picture of the boys together, she trembled as she looked at it. Touching his smile, as her tears hit the screen, it wasn't nearly enough: she couldn't hold him or ruffle his hair or stroke his face when he smiled at her; there'd be no more quick hugs when he was trying to get out of the door; no laughing hysterically at the neighbours when they rowed again in their garden and no more gentle, guilty kisses on her forehead when he sneaked in later than expected and found her asleep on the sofa, waiting for his safe return.

She wandered aimlessly out of the bathroom and sat back down on the bed, staring at nothing, and she saw a younger Eddie. He was an extremely happy child, but the loss of his father put a stop to that, and weeping silently for months, almost continuously, she'd held him many nights as he cried himself to sleep. Noting one day that she wasn't crying, he was concerned. "Mummy, if you feel you need to talk to me about Daddy or you want me to cuddle you when you cry, I will. Please don't pretend you're happy if you're really sad." She wasn't sad; on the contrary, she was extremely relieved that Pete was no longer around – she'd suffered enough from his persistent abuse – but Eddie's words had pierced her heart and she'd cried…and he'd hugged her so tight, she thought he would break. She would sometimes think of that day and when he noticed her crying, he would hold her tight again, convinced he was assisting her recovery, which, in turn, healed his wounds.

Three years later, when he met Joe, he was almost back to his old self and sensing Joe's unhappiness, he did all he could to make him happy, and he came home from school, so animated. "Mummy! I've got a new friend. He's called Joe and I met him today, and he looked really sad. He wasn't crying or anything, but I'm sure he was really sad, so I talked to him and made him laugh! And he doesn't look sad anymore. Can he come for tea tomorrow?"

Whoa, what a change! She nearly burst with pride. "Well, he needs to ask his mummy so why don't you talk to him tomorrow and see if he *wants* to come for tea; if he does, ask him to ask his mummy…or I can ask her tomorrow when I drop you off, if you point them out to me."

"I don't think his mummy takes him to school. I think he walks on his own." Having debated allowing Eddie to go to school on his own, she postponed the decision as he hadn't complained, but if Joe lived nearby, perhaps they could walk together.

"Let's have a chat to him tomorrow. Right, homework time!"

The following morning, Eddie wanted to wait for his friend at the school gates, but it was getting a little late and Abbie was about to suggest they walk slowly in when he came around the corner. *Wow, what a stunning child!* "How old is Joe, Ed?"

"The same age as me, but I'm a little bit older." He smiled and ran towards his friend.

Without prior knowledge, she would have sworn he was at least fourteen: he had a beautiful face, long lashes, bright blue eyes, with dark hair and olive skin. Taller than Eddie, with broad shoulders and a slim waist, she had to remind herself he was just a child. As he moved closer, she could see the sadness Eddie had noticed and felt instantly drawn to this young boy, but he looked a disgrace: his clothes were badly worn and way too small, though he seemed resigned to it. He smiled when he saw Eddie, but his expression changed at the sight of Abbie. Was she waiting to tell him off? Had Eddie told her he'd done something wrong?

Smiling as her son introduced her, she was keen to reassure him. "This is my mum, Joe, and she said you can come over for tea if you want to."

His eyes widened and he looked completely shocked. "Really? Can I really come for tea?"

Touched by his response, she wondered if he'd ever been invited anywhere. "Of course you can, sweetheart, but you need to ask your mum first."

His face fell. "I don't have a mum – she died when I was seven and my dad's always drunk so there's no point asking him."

Abbie felt terrible. "Well, why don't you try to ask him tonight...or we can walk home with you and I can ask him for you – is that a good idea?"

The spark returned. "Yes! He might listen to you!"

She smiled, but if what he said was true, she doubted she'd get a better response. "Right, well, let's get you both into school before you get a detention! I'll see you both later. Love you, Ed..." But he didn't hear her; his conversation with his friend was too much of a priority. Joe, however, looked back and waved, smiling like it was Christmas.

Wandering slowly home, she was overwhelmed by sadness: poor Joe! She'd known him for less than five minutes but felt impelled to protect him – what the hell had he been through? Eddie's bond with him seemed inevitable now and, in all probability, mutually beneficial, but as she tried to concentrate on her day, her thoughts kept returning to him. She wanted to ease the burden and the dreadful sadness he appeared to weather unquestionably. She willed the day away and as she waited outside the gates she fought to contain her excitement... but for what? Eddie's friends were frequent visitors to their home and whilst he flourished with a little company, it made little difference to her. But Joe was different...he needed her help...but a gentle reminder was warranted: *he's an eleven-year-old child...and you are NOT your father.*

As they strolled out together – her son still talking constantly and Joe listening patiently – Abbie's presence delighted them both. Running to her, Eddie threw his arms round her waist.

"Thanks, Mum, for letting Joe come over. His dad's really mean to him and I don't like it." He buried his face in her dress so his friend wouldn't see him cry. As he reached them, Eddie looked at her, pleading with her to keep his secret and she reassured him with a smile.

"Right, Joe, you'd better lead us to your house so I can have a chat with your dad." Eddie held her hand tight, nervous of their meeting, but she comforted him with a little squeeze.

Luckily, the house was only a few minutes from the school, and only twenty minutes from Abbie's, but as Joe unlocked the front door, the smell hit her hard. Christ! How the hell did he survive that? She walked into the living room, looking for the culprit. "Hello?"

A figure appeared from the kitchen, half-dressed, unwashed and reeking of booze: she hid her disgust well.

"What the fuck do you want?" Abbie's expression changed: she never swore around children, especially her own, but she had no control over this excuse for a parent.

"I'm Abbie and my son has asked if Joe could come round for tea one night…maybe tomorrow…?" She glanced at Joe and softened when she saw the hope in his eyes.

"Can I, Dad?" Why was he taking so long to answer?

"Do what the fuck you like! He won't be in my way, so I don't give a shit!"

As the anger rose, she took a deep breath. Whilst his appalling language was deplorable, his blatant disregard for his own son was contemptible, but before she could organise her thoughts, she found herself babbling: "Well, maybe he could come for tea most nights; I'm happy for him to stay over, if that's OK with you Mr…?"

Joe dared to hope – *Really? Did she really say that?* "Er…Mr Francis…Dad?"

His father looked hard at Abbie. "Why do you want my boy at yours every night?"

She paused: honesty would not serve Joe well. "Because it would be company for my son – he's an only child too..." *Please! Just let me take him away from this shithole!*

Looking pleadingly at his father, Joe was immune to his mocking laugh. "Why don't you keep him and then you'll see what a fucking waste of space he is!" He sat down in front of the TV and left them to it.

Slowly absorbing the filth she just witnessed, her shock was indeterminate: was it for the abhorrence she'd just observed... or was it for the smile upon the face of a child quite clearly used to this level of abuse? Her decision, however, was somewhat less equivocal; taking the boys into the hall, she spoke quietly. "Joe, could you go upstairs and pack a bag? You'll need pyjamas, toothbrush, clean clothes for tomorrow and clean underwear. If you have any school books or homework, bring those too, and any toys or special things you don't want to leave behind."

He nodded and raced up the stairs, excited, but scared that if he took too long, his father would have changed his mind by the time he got back downstairs and running back down, two stairs at a time, he beamed. "Can we go now?"

As she opened the front door, both boys ran out and down the path and, closing it quietly behind her, Abbie quickly caught up with them. When they were finally at a safe distance, Eddie started to cry.

"Hey, buddy, what's up?" Settling her own nerves, she hugged him tight to alleviate his fear, but he was unable to speak; too scared to utter a word.

Joe put an arm round his shoulders and spoke so gently. "It's alright, Eddie. Don't worry, I'm going to stay with you now."

As reality called, Abbie chewed her quivering lip. *Shit!* What had she done? What right did she have to remove a child from his home? But it wasn't a home: it was a prison and no child should be subjected to anything remotely analogous to that kind of life. She'd give it a few days and assess the situation...

but if Joe's father sobered up and realised what she'd done, there would be serious repercussions and sending Joe back would be a brutal undertaking. Despite the rapidly increasing anxiety, she resolved to trust Fate and the belief that a drunk is a drunk so sobriety was doubtful. "Joe's right, Eddie, it's all going to be OK. Right, what she we have for tea?"

***

She had never seen a child eat so feverishly. "It's OK, Joe. There's plenty more; don't give yourself a tummy ache."

Slightly embarrassed, he slowed down. "I've never had pizza before. My mum said it was bad for me and my dad doesn't cook. It's lovely, thank you." His gratitude for a cheap convenience meal was genuine.

"We have pizza a lot, Joe."

"OK, thanks, Ed…"

"That's OK, I don't mind." He smiled to ease Abbie's shame.

Acknowledging his attempts but keen to show her better qualities, she shifted the conversation. "Joe, when you've finished, I'll show you your room. If you let me have your clothes from today, I'll wash them for you."

He looked worried. "But I'll need them for tomorrow…"

"Oh, I thought you got some clean ones for tomorrow…"

As his face flushed, he dropped his eyes. "I don't have any more."

Annoyed at her intrusion, she played it down. "Oh, well that's fine. You've saved me a job. Don't worry, we'll sort something out."

***

Abbie took the boys to school the following day and asked to see their tutor. Thankfully, she was on very good terms with Mrs

Hamilton, and she hoped she would see sense: the last thing Joe needed was to be referred to the authorities and taken into care.

"Thank you for seeing me at such short-notice; I wasn't sure what else to do." She breathed deeply to steady her bubbling nerves. "Eddie has become good friends with Joe Francis and I met his father last night – are you familiar with Mr Francis?"

Mrs Hamilton smiled. "Yes, I am."

"Well, I know you can't comment but…" She paused to compose herself. "Anyway, we went to his house last night to ask if Joe could come for tea and he was extremely abusive, especially to Joe, and suggested, in that inimitable style of his, that I should keep him, so, I told Joe to grab what he could and come home with me. But now, I'm not really sure what to do. He was so happy and relieved to be with us and that's surely not right, but if I send him back home he's got to deal with that…monster of a man, and if he stays with me, I'm concerned that the authorities will find out and he'll be taken into care. He's had a tough life already, Amanda, and I think he just needs some love and some fun, and some stability. I'm going to give it the week and see how things go, but can you please not notify anyone? He's such a sweet boy, and so polite: he just needs some normality. And he and Eddie seem so close already…"

Amanda thought for a while before responding. "You're right, I can't say too much, but we are well aware of Joe's background. When he started here three weeks ago, he was a quiet, sullen child, but when he met Eddie, he seemed to change overnight and, funnily enough, I was going to have a chat with you to see if, maybe, you could invite him round to play, or stay for tea. He hadn't smiled or even spoken to anyone in the time he'd been here, but Eddie started chatting to him and…well, he was a different child. I am duty-bound to report any suspected abuse, and I have…but I don't have to report kindness. Come and see me at the end of next week and let's see how things are then." She smiled warmly. "You've done a very good thing, Abbie. Thank you."

She sighed with relief. "Oh God, thank you, Amanda. I was so worried you'd have to report me. Thank you so much. I'll see you next Friday and let you know how we're all getting along." Holding the teacher's hands, she smiled brightly. "Thanks again, Amanda. Thank you *so* much."

As she left the school, Mrs Hamilton walked back into her classroom and looked at Joe, but his face was full of concern. Did she know? Was she going to send him back home? But her smile told him he had no need to worry; he needed Abbie, and he needed Eddie.

Walking home lighter, Abbie was grateful for Mrs Hamilton's honesty and approach, and she jumped in the car and headed into town. A new school uniform was necessary; she couldn't let Joe go to school wearing the same clothes he'd probably worn for the last two years and, although she was reluctant to pry, she felt sure his own clothes were minimal but decided she'd take the boys shopping at the weekend and let them choose a new wardrobe and, maybe, go out for dinner so they could dress up. For now, a couple of t-shirts and a pair of jeans would suffice. Sizing was difficult, but she reasoned he couldn't look any worse – shoes would have to wait. At home, she was excited to see his face and she counted the minutes until she returned to school.

As the boys came out, Joe's face was full of relief, though he was still slightly wary: the frown had disappeared and he looked like a child should, but trust would be a slow progression. As she watched them laughing and joking, jostling and playing, the depth of her decision was already visible, and, although confident she was justified, the long-term consequences would, no doubt, demonstrate the validity of her actions and she prayed her judgement was prudent. But, for now, he was safe and Eddie was happy, and that was all that mattered.

Back at home, she handed several bags to Joe, and, unaccustomed to receiving anything, he was puzzled, but as he slowly pulled out every item of clothing she'd bought, he felt the sting of tears. His father had bought him nothing since his mother died, barely stretching to food, and relying on hand-me-downs from well-meaning neighbours, expectations were a distant memory. Now, with new things that were solely for him, he wasn't entirely sure what to do and, folding every item neatly and placing each one back in its bag, he sat staring at them. Eddie looked at his mum, confused, but she shook her head and after several minutes, Joe broke the silence. "Thank you, Mrs Dawson. Thank you very, very much." His bottom lip quivered and a single tear trickled down his cheek.

Crouching in front of him, she took his hands, deeply moved by his reaction but determined he wouldn't see her cry. "Joe, you are safe here and you are now part of this family. You will have whatever we have and you can stay here as long as you want to. This is your home if you want it to be and you can treat it that way. I know it will take you a little while to feel comfortable, but we are here for you, OK? You are very welcome."

Placing the bags carefully on the floor, he threw himself at her and sobbed in her arms, clinging to her as if he would never let go, and, watching the scene before him, Eddie was proud of what his mother had done for his new friend. With no more tears to shed, Joe let her go, somewhat embarrassed at his emotional display. Conscious of the immense transition for this young boy, in a mere twenty-four hours, Abbie immediately dismissed it.

"Right, what's for tea?"

Exchanging a quick glance, the decision was mutual: "Pizza!"

"OK, but that's the last time this week! Oh, and I thought, maybe at the weekend, we could go into town and buy you boys a whole new wardrobe, come home, get dressed up and go out for dinner – what do you think?"

"Yeah!" Eddie looked at Joe.

"Really? But you've just bought me new clothes…"

"Oh, that's just so you had something for now; you'll need more than that and you'll both need some new underwear."

"Mum!" It was Eddie's turn to be embarrassed and Abbie laughed.

"I'll pay you back, Mrs Dawson, I promise."

"That's not necessary, Joe – Eddie's not going to! And while I think of it, it's Abbie, not Mrs Dawson, OK?"

"OK."

***

The week flew by and on Saturday morning Joe was awake at six, eager to go shopping. Excited by the prospect of buying new clothes – in fact, buying new anything – he'd not slept well, but his enthusiasm refused any kind of restraint and, waiting patiently until he heard Abbie in the kitchen, he wandered out of his room.

"Morning, Joe. Did you have a good night?" Struck by her appearance, he'd had little contact with women since his mother died, but Abbie looked as beautiful as his mum had – a stark contrast to his father.

"Yes, thank you, Mrs…Abbie. Did you?"

Wow! Not the response she'd expected. "Yes, Joe, thank you; very well. What would you like for breakfast, my darling?"

He smiled. "I don't mind, whatever you're doing. Can I help?"

Wow! Eddie could learn a thing or two. "Well…if you'd like to make the tea…?"

"Yeah, OK."

Watching discreetly, she smiled in amazement. "Thank you, Joe."

Eddie sauntered in, bleary-eyed and little surprised to see his friend. "I forgot you were here, Joe. What are you doing?"

"Making tea."

"What, why?" That's what his mum did.

"Yes, Eddie, other people can help with breakfast!"

"Mum!"

She laughed. "It's OK, darling…you can do the washing up."

With no excuse to hand, he blew a raspberry.

***

As they headed into town, Abbie could feel the excitement in the car and whilst she allowed the boys to choose exactly where they wanted to go, Joe frequently turned to her for reassurance and confirmation, and though it was clear he enjoyed his freedom and just being with Eddie, she suspected it would be considerable time before he could relax completely. Stopping for lunch – yet another pizza – they replenished their reserves before heading back home. Shutting himself away, Joe laid everything out on his bed, smoothed every crease and looked at what he had. Religion was a mystery to him – people's belief in a higher order – but he stepped back, looked to the heavens and thanked God for Eddie, for Abbie, for his new clothes and for a second chance he would never lose sight of.

Watching TV for a short while, everything was new to him. His father had full control over their own television and it was permanently on sport during the day, or, late at night, another channel that he'd not really understood, but it had scared him so he'd cover his ears and eventually drift off to sleep. Now, riveted by the hilarity of simple cartoons, he laughed unashamedly for the first time in four years and, whilst mindful of the generosity of his hosts, he was ever so slightly disappointed when Abbie signalled time, though too grateful to reveal it.

"Ed, you can use my shower; Joe, do you want to use the bathroom?"

Dragging his heels, Eddie, less appreciative than his friend, voiced his dissatisfaction, but Joe, still acclimatising to the extravagance of showering daily rather than the chore of a stripped-wash once or twice weekly, needed no persuasion, and with his very own toiletries, though no prior experience to draw from, he felt sure this was what a holiday would be like, and aside from the essentials, Abbie had treated them to some aftershave…and he didn't even know what it was, but he liked it! With a father who barely glanced at the bathroom, personal grooming was a curious phenomenon, but he could tell from the scent that aftershave was very grown-up…and he wanted to be grown-up.

After considerable time, and no sign of Joe, Abbie was a little concerned and as she silenced her paranoia, he wandered out and wafted into his bedroom, all clean and shiny and full of smiles, but looking like a young man. With a personal reprimand, she reminded herself, again, that he was, indeed, just a child.

Stunningly dressed and complimenting each other on their choices, the boys strutted around whilst she marvelled at the ease with which they'd made Joe happy. Sure, money wasn't everything, but having none made a little go a long way; Eddie was used to being loved, but although he'd appreciated the unrestrained expense, the impact on Joe was far superior and she hoped there'd be no serious regression from the obvious high. With the help of her son, she vowed to provide the life every child deserved.

Her suggestion of a local pub for dinner, rather than a pizzeria, had met with approval, but faced with a full menu, Joe appeared slightly disheartened. Eddie, unassuming and gracious, had helped and his friend was visibly relieved, and three courses later, the effects of their excesses took hold. Abbie drove them home and suggested a little more TV to allow their tummies to settle, but at nine-thirty, with yawning eyes, they were ordered to bed, amid much protestation from Eddie. Consoled by the promise of some early morning cartoons, he relented and kissed his mum goodnight. Walking away from the stairs, Abbie was surprised to find Joe waiting for her. "Thank you for everything today, Abbie. This has been the best day of my life."

Touched by his sincerity, she smiled warmly. "You're welcome, Joe. I've had as much fun as you have so I should be thanking you and Eddie."

"But I didn't pay for anything. I will pay you back. I'm going to get a job and pay you back for everything you've done…I promise."

"That's very sweet, Joe, but you really don't have to."

"Thank you, but I do…and I will." He kissed her cheek and walked into his room.

Watching as he closed the door, she felt a chill, imagining what sort of life could have driven him to be so grateful for the relative exiguity of courtesy that she'd displayed, and to his conviction to finding work. Unsure what sort of job he was hoping for, allowing him to repay something would provide him with a little of the control he clearly needed over his life, but regardless, she was determined to give him his childhood back, hoping it wasn't too late but fearing it most likely was.

***

Up and about early again in the morning, Joe set about preparing breakfast, having already showered and dressed before Abbie and Eddie surfaced, and when they did, he waited on them like a servant.

"Joe, you don't have to do this." She was concerned he'd been a slave to his father for too long.

"I know, but I want to, and afterwards, I'm going to go and see if people will let me clean their cars or cut their grass." Smiling, he was pleased with his ingenuity.

"Really? That's an excellent idea; Eddie, do you want to go with Joe? It'll be good for you."

"Do I have to?" Having never been without, he couldn't

see the logic in scrubbing cars or mowing lawns to make a few measly quid when his mum would buy him whatever he wanted anyway.

"Well, it would be nice to keep him company..."

He sighed. "OK, OK." There were better ways to spend a Sunday!

Out all morning, knocking on every door in the close, they returned just before lunch, and Joe looked thrilled; Eddie looked fed-up.

Abbie smiled encouragement. "How did you get on?"

"We've got four cars to clean; one of them once a week and the other three are once a month, and three lawns to cut, but once a month for now and they're going to see how it goes. I'm going to work out a timetable so I know what we're doing each week."

"Wow! Did you tell them how much it would cost?"

"Yep! I managed to persuade them to pay us six pounds, which I know we'll have to split, but once we start and if we do a good job, other people might want us to do theirs too." Joe was buzzing with excitement.

"Well, that's fantastic; well done." She turned to her son. "You could be a little more enthusiastic, Ed!"

He faked a smile. "Better?"

Joe laughed at his friend. "He's not used to hard work!" Turning back to Abbie, he felt a little nervous. "Would you mind buying some car cleaning stuff and I'll pay you back when I start getting paid?"

"No, of course not, but you don't have to pay me back. How about you mow my lawn and wash my car, and we call it quits?"

He thought for a moment. "OK, if you're sure... When do you want it done?"

"Whenever you can fit me in, but your customers should come first. The only thing I ask is that you phone me or text me after every customer and again when you're on your way home. I need to know you're both safe."

Eddie looked a little confused. "But we don't have phones, Mum."

"Then we'd better get some quick!" With wide eyes and even wider smiles, the boys jumped like jackpot winners. How cool were they going to be? Their very own phones. "BUT, they are for safety reasons only; you're not taking them to school and you're not calling or texting your friends."

"Thanks, Mum. You're the best!" Eddie hugged her tight.

"Thank you, Abbie."

"And before you say anything, Joe, you're not paying me back this time; it's for my benefit so it's my treat, OK?"

He smiled wider. "OK, thank you." He kissed her cheek and hugged her too.

***

Joe never went back to live with his father. He visited once in a while, mainly at Christmas, to give the bastard a card and a present, getting nothing in return, and his generosity, or, indeed, his absence, was never acknowledged. Years later, the man died in a drunken stupor, clutching a photo of his wife and his son and on the back he'd scribbled 'Sorry'. When the police finally tracked Joe down, he thanked them for their troubles, accepted the photo and quietly closed the door; no tears were shed and he didn't attend the funeral, but the relief was unmistakable.

***

Continuing to wash cars and mow lawns every weekend, Joe, as predicted, secured more customers and consequently earned more money; Eddie, however, lasted about three months, though he assumed control of the itinerary, negotiated better pay and helped manage the finances, albeit with a smaller cut of the profits.

Standing by his word, Joe gave Abbie a third of all he made, despite her objections, but she understood his need and the vehemence in his eyes.

Three years later, she was impressed that, at fourteen, he was still employed by most of the close and spent his free time working but, noticing he was taking a little longer with his clients and earning more money, she hoped he wasn't taking on too much. "Have you had a pay rise, Joe?" Reluctant to intrude, she was surprised at how much cash he seemed to have.

Looking a little uncertain, he was quick to respond. "Yeah... but sometimes they want me to...do favours for them...like odd jobs and things, so it's all extra." He averted her eyes but hoped he'd fooled her.

Reflecting on his explanation, the corollary slowly registered...but who the hell was he doing 'favours' for, and what exactly did those 'favours' consist of? He'd caused a stir in the neighbourhood for quite some time now and she knew it wouldn't be long before he was bringing girlfriends home...but she hadn't expected him to be satisfying the local housewives at fourteen!

A little uneasy and feeling unduly paranoid, the following morning she watched him from her bedroom window as he made his way to his first customer, and, sure enough, he was invited in immediately by a rather under-dressed golf-widow. Checking her watch every few minutes, Abbie was shocked to see him emerge three-quarters of an hour later – no grass cut and no car washed – and she vacillated between tackling these women and reporting them. But Joe, unsurprisingly, seemed untroubled; on the contrary, he was like a breath of fresh air: always pleasant, always smiling, where Eddie was interminably grumpy, and she momentarily contemplated a split in the 'workload' – God, what was she thinking?! The attraction was easy to see: he appeared older than his years, both physically and mentally, but despite his maturity and deceptive looks, he was still only fourteen and that made her uncomfortable.

Confronted by an unfamiliar dilemma, she was unsure how to proceed: discuss her concerns with Joe or turn a blind eye? But his safety was paramount – her discomfort, a by-product – so she opted for the former and as the morning passed slowly, she waited for his final text before sending Eddie to get some milk. As he walked in the door, she chided herself for missing what was now conspicuously evident, for, not only did he reek of perfume, but he had a glow that could only be obtained from exertion not usually synonymous with the use of a lawn-mower, or, indeed, a bucket.

"Good day, Joe?" She watched his face closely.

"Yes, thanks. Worked hard today." As he looked at Abbie, he knew instantly he'd been caught and his face flushed.

"I bet you did!" Amused by his unintentional metaphorical inference, she smiled. "OK, I'm not going to lecture you and I'm not going to judge, but I am responsible for you so I need to know you are safe."

Looking at the floor, he shuffled uncomfortably; discussing sex with Abbie was awkward enough, but he prayed silently she wouldn't guess she was the one he thought about when servicing his customers.

"Firstly, what these women are doing is illegal...and immoral, on so many levels! You're a child, and they're paying you...shall I continue?"

"No!" Why hadn't he been more careful? "I know...but I don't mind..."

"Well...that's irrelevant, Joe. It's wrong and if I reported them, they'd be arrested."

"No! God, please don't...Abbie, *please*... If you do that, they'll take me into care and I don't want to go into care...please."

Shit! The repercussions, in her mind, had revolved around the perpetrators, not the victim...but he was right. *Shit!*

With no defence to offer, she considered alternatives, but there was only one: "OK...OK, but you're going to have to stop.

Now that I know, I can't condone what you're doing; it's wrong... and you're still a child..."

As his face fell, his eyes filled. "But I need the money...and if I say no now, they'll never let me go back to cutting grass and washing cars. They'll hate me...and then they'll just find someone else to...replace me."

"But I can't just ignore it, Joe! I know you want to earn money, but I'll help you find another job. You're older now so it'll be easier to find something else..." She was losing confidence in her own argument.

He laughed derisively, folding his arms in defiance. "What, that's going to pay me as well as they do...?" He detected the doubt in her eyes before she averted them. "Exactly." Demoralised and uneasy about the sudden loss of control, he opened up. "I've been doing it for about eighteen months and you didn't know..."

"What?" Why hadn't she noticed?

"But it's not like they're making me do anything I don't want to... And if they're happy to pay me..."

"But it's wrong, Joe!"

"So was what my father did, but nobody reported him! At least I enjoy...what I'm doing, and I'm getting paid for it...and I have a choice. I didn't have a choice about anything when I lived with him... I didn't have anything then. I'm not stupid, Abbie. They might think I'm their slave, but who's getting the best deal here? I'm not the only fourteen-year-old having sex, but the difference between me and other boys is that I'm getting money for it and I don't have groups of girls calling me names because one of them thinks I'm the love of her life!"

Eddie returned and sensing the palpable tension, felt instantly unnerved. "Everything alright?"

Abbie smiled reassuringly. "Yes, darling, but I need to talk to Joe so would you mind going to your room for a bit? I'll call you when we've finished."

But his fear remained. "He's not going back to his dad, is he?" With pleading eyes, he looked from one to the other.

"No!" She hugged him. "No, darling, of course not; there are just a couple of things that I've...misunderstood and once we've clarified them, you can come back down, OK?"

He reluctantly agreed, unsettled, still, but loath to exacerbate the situation by disregarding her request. "OK."

Once Eddie was upstairs, Abbie looked at Joe and studied his face: aside from the slightly disturbing, albeit, rather accurate psychology he seemed to have mastered, she sympathised and felt her resolve wane, and, having removed him from his home and encouraged him to find work, reasoned that she was, in part, responsible for placing him on temptation's path, and whilst her desire to protect him from any more abuse surpassed anything else, was she not imitating his father by dictating his life? Whilst instinct and propriety screamed at her to reconsider, her conscience prevailed and she capitulated, though somewhat grudgingly; there would, however, be stringent, indisputable rules that would negate her acceptance should they be violated in any way and unless he complied wholeheartedly, there would be no consent.

"Right, as I said, I can't condone what you're doing...but you're right: boys of your age are out having sex with God knows who...so I'd rather know where you are and who you're with..." His scowl slowly eased as he digested the change in her stance. "BUT...that doesn't mean I'm happy about it and there will be rules, and, God help me if you don't adhere to them, Joe, OK?"

"Yes...yes: whatever you say, Abbie." His smile spread as relief swept through him.

"Firstly, these women have husbands and if they find out, they will beat the crap out of you, no matter how young you are, so don't get caught! If I can work out what you're doing, so can others, so change your habits or at least make it look like you're doing the job you're supposed to be doing; secondly, and more importantly, please tell me you're using protection…?" He looked uncertain. "Condoms?"

He suddenly looked very young. "They don't like them…"

"Of course they don't! But, Joe, what happens if you get one of them pregnant?"

"But they've told me they're on the pill."

"OK…good…but, what if you catch something from one of them?" She could see he was puzzled still. "Do you know who else they sleep with?"

"No." Their limited conversations generally revolved around what he did, not anybody else.

"So they could invite the postman in once a week or the window cleaner? If they're sleeping around, which is highly likely as their husbands are never here, they could pick up any number of STI's – tell me you learned about those at school?"

He blushed again. "Yes we did."

"Then you know that some of them can be quite serious. I don't care what they say: use condoms! I'll get you some if you don't want to get them yourself, but I'll need to know…what size…" She could feel the flush in her own cheeks and avoided his gaze.

Smiling, he enjoyed her discomfort: maybe he should show her… "Large, obviously!"

"Joe, it's not funny!"

"I'm not joking…"

She laughed at his cheek, refusing to accept that her intrigue made her no better than the women she condemned. "Right, I'll get a selection on Monday and you make damn sure you use them, OK?"

"OK."

"Next, I still want to know you're safe after every…visit, but if anything happens – like husbands arriving home unexpectedly – you tell me; or, if you notice any rashes, any discomfort, you tell me. I don't care how embarrassed you are, I need to know…

but if anyone finds out, I will deny all knowledge! I'll back you and support you, but I don't know anything about this – are we clear?"

"Yes. Thank you, Abbie…are you're going to tell anybody? I know it's wrong and I agree with everything you said, but they pay me really well…and it's easier than washing cars and mowing lawns." He was deadly serious.

She laughed. "Really?" Returning to a more serious tone, she was keen to reiterate her point. "Look, Joe, I'm more annoyed at them for taking advantage of you, but so long as you're careful and use protection, I'll try to forget about it and, no, I won't tell anyone. It would be naïve to assume that because I disagree with what you're doing, you'd stop – you wouldn't. You'd carry on and lie to me and if the worst happens, you'd have no one to turn to. So, despite my objections, I'd rather know the truth and be prepared…but for Christ's sake, make damn sure you're sensible."

He sighed. "I will…and thank you; it won't be forever…and they're really not taking advantage of me…" Smiling cheekily, he looked a little too pleased with himself. "I'm the one taking advantage – they let me do…"

She put a hand up "Whoa, I don't need to know, thank you!" Feeling a little…protective, she was, however, interested in exactly who the culprits were. "How many of them?"

"Five…"

"Christ, Joe! Two would have been bad enough!"

"I know." He winked as he headed for the bathroom.

"And Joe…" He turned round with his usual carefree composure. "Don't say a word of this to Eddie…or anyone else."

With a devilish smile, he continued on his way.

Sighing deeply, she questioned her actions and care, but with few options at hand, what else could she do? Calling upstairs to Eddie, she wondered if she would have responded differently had he been the subject of her concern. How could they be so different? She viewed her son as a child still, but, despite knowing Joe's escapades, he was still so much more mature and she prayed it was enough to keep him safe.

***

Abbie smiled to herself. They'd been good boys: never in trouble, never impolite, never selfish, and they had both looked after her, as only boys can. Regretting having only one child – although grateful, given her unfortunate marriage – when Joe joined them, he'd filled that gap for both of them and with the relationship between the two boys distinctly brotherly, there'd never been any serious rows, fighting only once…and that, unsurprisingly, was over a girl. Whilst Joe was keeping the village's females satiated from early teens, Eddie paid little attention to the opposite sex until he was nearly seventeen, and although his friend would tease him about it, at that stage, Eddie wasn't aware of the full extent of Joe's exploits, so was completely unperturbed. Meeting Eliza, however, shortly before his seventeenth birthday, he was struck by a deluge of emotions that emerged overnight, alien and unannounced, but he'd harboured his crush, spending almost three months befriending her, defining his strategy, with little comprehension, before Joe swept in, charmed her knickers off and left her dejected. He, as always, was ignorant or, quite possibly indifferent to the devastation he'd caused, but Eliza had confided in Eddie and Abbie had never experienced such rage from her son. Dragging Joe from his room, he'd taken him outside and knocked him to the ground as Joe, shocked and bewildered, tried to defend himself but, despite having a physical advantage, his attempts were futile. Abbie had intervened and helped Joe into the house whilst Eddie screamed at her. "That's typical, take his fucking side! Always defending that piece of shit and he's not even your son, I AM!" He'd marched off, kicking everything within reach, further enraged by his mother's interference.

Having settled Joe with some ice and towels, she set off to find her son, and, relieved he'd not gone too far, persuaded him to come back home. "Get him out of my way first, Mum, cos I'll kill him!"

Rushing back, she'd escorted Joe to his room before Eddie sauntered in. "Right, let's sit down and you can tell me what the hell's going on. That's not like you – what's happened?" Assuming a calm, yet forced, appearance, Abbie was careful not to irritate him any more.

"That prick! He thinks he can go around shagging everyone he likes, not giving a shit about any of them! When have you ever seen him with a girlfriend, Mum? Exactly! He's never had one cos he just fucks them and then fucks off!"

"Could you please ease up on the language a little, Ed? I'm your mother!" His rage may have been warranted but…

"Sorry, but he's really pissed me off!"

"Eddie!"

"Sorry."

"OK, tell me what happened; this has all come out of the blue…"

"He fucked Eliza and now doesn't want anything to do with her…sorry."

Ignoring the invective tone, she sought clarification. "Are you sure? It might not be quite like you think…"

"I've just spoken to her! He's really upset her; he let her think he was interested but, typically, that was just to get her into bed. He's an absolute prick!"

"To be fair Ed, a lot of boys your age want sex without any complications…and, unfortunately, girls do tend to read too much into it…" He had so much to learn, but maybe now wasn't the time.

"So you think she's lying? You're taking his side?"

"No! I just think…" Realising her reasoning was probably eliciting a counter-productive result, she changed focus. "Why are you so concerned, Ed? This probably isn't the first time and I'm pretty sure it won't be the last. I don't think Joe has any plans to become a Catholic priest anytime soon."

"Well, I'm glad you find this all so amusing!" He got up to leave.

"I don't, darling. I'm sorry. Don't go; let's sort this out. Come and sit back down." Reluctantly, he complied. "Why does it matter so much? I don't understand why you're so upset..."

He looked at the floor and considered his response; he sighed heavily. "Because...I liked her before he did, and I didn't get a chance to tell her..." His faced flushed and he looked devastated.

"Oh, Ed! Why didn't you say something? Come here." She hugged him as he sobbed quietly. "Did Joe know how you felt?"

Struggling with his composure, he wiped his tears and took a while to respond. "I don't know. I was too scared to tell anyone in case she found out and didn't feel the same."

Touched by his innocence and struck by the disparity between the two boys, she felt his anguish. "I'm not excusing his behaviour, darling, but I really think if he'd known, he would have left Eliza alone. He loves you, you know that."

"Well, it doesn't matter now; he's fucked it up for me completely...sorry."

Smiling at his apparent inability to censor his discourse, she excused the expletives and, desperate to heal his broken heart, she sought to find a satisfactory solution. "Not necessarily... if you're kind to her and loving, and really supportive, like a boyfriend should be, she might want you instead..."

Looking at his mother, he was suddenly full of hope. "Do you think so? But, I'm not sure I would want to...well...after he has..." He blushed again.

"Oh don't be so silly. Do you honestly think that every girl you meet is going to be a virgin? You're going to be very disappointed, my love! It doesn't matter who she's seen before, just who she's with now."

As he reflected on her theory, he hugged her again. "OK... thanks, Mum – sorry. Should I apologise to Joe?"

"Let him stew for a bit."

After a quick cup of tea, she'd called Joe from his room and confirmed they were happy for her to be present whilst they spoke. Realising his indiscretion, Joe was horrified; Eddie and Abbie were the only people he cared about and causing such distress for them was nothing short of treachery. His apology was profuse in the extreme but genuine and he was determined to remedy his destruction. Eddie, surprised by his sincerity, was happy he'd been forgiven for the beating.

With assurances in place, Joe had approached Eliza again and talked to her frankly, apologising for his behaviour and highlighting his flaws, and she was grateful. "I'm not going to change, Eliza, so please don't waste your time hoping I will. If I gave you that impression, that was wrong, and I am truly sorry. You deserve better; there are decent guys out there..."

Within a week, she and Eddie were together and they enjoyed almost two years, before an amicable split as they both left for university. They'd stayed in touch ever since and still met for lunch every once in a while and Joe was nothing more than an amusing anecdote but, ironically, a catalyst for their deep affection and they were secretly grateful.

10

Abbie wiped her tears and forced herself to shower; whilst there was no escaping her grief, cooped up in a strange room, alone, would only centre the exacerbation and, inevitable as that may be, it was punishing, nonetheless, and a change of scenery, or, in fact, any scenery could possibly ease the pain but, without a shower, she'd be unable to face the continuing life outside. With all efforts concentrated on keeping her mind light, she toyed with her options for the day: shopping – no, not today; a drive through the countryside – too isolated; the beach – that would have to do. She dressed quickly, grabbed her bag and headed out.

Enjoying her stroll in the sun, she watched the world carry on around her: young children fighting to get away as their mothers smothered them in sun cream – she'd been there with Eddie; elderly couples walking hand-in-hand, reminiscing about their youth; cyclists whizzing past, without warning; dogs barking as they ran to chase a thrown ball; young couples sitting on the wall, eating ice-creams, and a large group of half-naked lads playing volleyball on the sand…she headed their way.

Berating herself for being so predictable and obvious – though, to be fair, there was no harm in looking and appreciating their sporting prowess – she settled on a bench a few feet away and sat down before anyone else could steal it, but as she tried to focus on the sea, her mind, and her eyes, wandered back to the volleyballers; maybe this was a bad idea. Turning to look in the opposite direction, she saw a young family building sandcastles. The children were no older than three or four and every time Dad removed the bucket, they smashed his creation with their little hands and their laughter travelled beautifully on the breeze, like petals on the waves, warming her as much as the sun. Absorbed by their delight, Mum noticed her attention and smiled, looking at her boys, then back at Abbie, shrugging her shoulders. With a knowing smile, she left them in peace; this was their fun and she wanted them to enjoy it as a family, without intrusion.

Back to the lads, she was somewhat relieved, if not a little disappointed to see they'd finished their game – perhaps they'd be back later for a rematch – and as they left the beach for refreshments, she spotted an elderly lady slowly making her way along the front with two walking sticks and a determined look that would send a pack of lions on their way. Admiring her strength, she was pleased when she stopped at the bench.

"Would you mind if I sat with you for a bit? I'm getting there, but I don't want to push it too hard."

Abbie smiled. "Of course, be my guest. Where is it you want to get to?"

The elderly lady laughed. "Well, I don't mind really. I used to come here with my daughter when she was a little girl so anywhere will do. Last week, I could only make it to that surfing place down there – do you see? And now I've made it to here, so I'm feeling pretty pleased with myself if I'm totally honest. But if I'd known those lovely young lads were playing volleyball, I would have tried a bit harder; I can see why you chose this seat!"

Abbie blushed a little. "Oh…it was the only one free at the time…" A lame excuse so elaboration was unnecessary. "Anyway, you should be pleased with yourself – that's quite an achievement. Have you had an operation or…?"

"Several, dear, but the last one was just under a year ago."

"Wow! And I complain if I get a headache; you're a brave lady."

She smiled at Abbie. "Oh, I don't think so; it's more sheer bloody-mindedness, really. They told me I wouldn't walk again, but I wasn't having that, so I did everything in my power to prove them wrong...and I did, so they know what they can do with their diagnosis!" She laughed in triumph.

Intrigued by this lady, Abbie felt an instant warmth towards her. "Why did they think you'd never walk again? Sorry if that sounds a little impertinent..."

"Not at all. I was involved in a car accident three years ago. Young lad – out of his mind on drugs – knocked us clean off the road; the car flipped and landed on the roof and they had to cut us both out. I was in a coma for four weeks and when I woke up they gave me the bad news: damage to my spine. 'Like bloody-hell,' I said!" She paused, knowing her companion would likely think her a crazy old fool. "I love to dance, see, and there's no point in living if I can never dance again, and there was no way on this earth some mindless youth was going to steal that from me."

Awed and a little guilty for prying, Abbie apologised. "I'm so sorry, I didn't..."

The old lady smiled and touched her arm. "Oh, don't be sorry, dear; it wasn't your fault...and I'm here, aren't I? And believe me, in the coming months I'm going to dance again. I haven't done so for three years and I'm desperate to. Do you dance, my love?"

"Well, I do around the house...and at parties...weddings, you know..." The memory of her father's demands still weighed heavy, but she could understand her companion's determination.

"It's the best thing for you, did you know that? Dancing is the best thing for you; makes you feel good; makes you feel alive. Do you know, I haven't made a single decision in my life without dancing first – I can't do it!" She laughed at herself. "You feel better about things when you dance; it clears the mind and it's far easier to make the right decision then."

Abbie smiled in agreement. "You know, you could well be right! I'm going to put your theory to the test the next time something crops up; I like it." Whether it would help her currently was a matter for debate, but it was nice idea. "So do you have a decision to make, is that why you need to dance soon?" With thoughts of a little amusing, if not naughty insight into the antics of the older generation, she regretted her teasing when she looked at the sweet face beside her. "I'm sorry, I didn't mean to make fun…"

"Don't worry, my lovely, you weren't to know. Yes, I do; my husband was also in that crash and has been in a coma ever since." Rummaging in her purse, she found a photo of him in happier times, and handed it to Abbie. "They told me there was little chance he'd ever wake up. I've kept him going all this time, but I've been told they want to switch him off." She sighed heavily. "I've been by his side every day for the past three years: talking to him; singing to him, laughing and crying with him, reading to him. I've stroked his face, stroked his hand and hugged him every day; I watch the telly with him and tell him what's going on in the world, though not the nasty stuff – he doesn't need to know that. And I tell him a hundred times a day how much I love him. I know he can hear me and I know he can feel me, yet they tell me he can't…but they were wrong about me not walking again, so…" She shrugged as her eyes filled involuntarily. "They've told me I have to think 'seriously' about turning off the machines." Abbie had long since started crying, but she endeavoured to shield her face from the spirit of this courageous lady. "I know I need to do it really; I need to let him go. I can't keep him for ever, but I just hoped I could have one more day with him. I want to kiss him and have him hug me back, and tell me he loves me and always will. I know he does, but I want to hear his voice again, just the once. I'd be happy with that, but it looks like I'm not going to get the chance, so I have to make this decision and I can only really do that when I can dance again." Her sad laugh acknowledged the absurdity of her words. "I know that sounds ridiculous, but I can't do it any other way." Turning to Abbie, she was horrified to see her distress. "Oh, my dear. I'm so sorry, I didn't mean to upset you with all this. I'm so sorry. Here…" She searched her bag for some tissues and Abbie graciously accepted. "You poor love." She wiped her own tears and gave her confidante a quick hug. "I'm sorry, my dear. I shouldn't have…"

"No, no, please, no apologies. I asked, remember? It's not a problem – really." Abbie smiled.

"Well, you seem like such a nice girl; it was very easy to talk to you, thank you."

Abbie laughed cynically. "Yeah, well you've only known me for a few minutes; give me a little longer and I'll change your mind!"

"I don't think so, dear. I'm a pretty good judge of character." Looking at the generous person beside her, Abbie's tears refused to subside. "What it is my love? You look like you have the weight of the world on your shoulders and I don't think it's my tale of woe. You're too pretty to be so sad – what is it?"

Abbie sniffed repeatedly, trying to stabilise her voice. Several minutes passed before she could speak. "I'm sorry, you seem to have set me off!"

"Well I can see that, dear! Do you want to tell me what's bothering you? Lord knows, I owe you that much after burdening you with my troubles."

With friendly eyes at her side, concerned and compassionate, she attempted an explanation: "My son died at the weekend and…I couldn't save him." The shame was still too raw.

"Oh, my love, you poor thing! Why didn't you stop me? Your poor, poor thing." She hugged Abbie tight and for the first time since she left home, she let herself go. The warmth and kindness of the stranger she'd befriended was comforting and Abbie felt safe, and she sobbed in her arms for what seemed like an eternity. Finally steadying herself, she pulled away from the security. "It will get a little easier, my love; I know that doesn't seem possible right now, but it will."

Feeling exposed, Abbie attempted a little humour. "Maybe you should have pushed a little harder to get to the next bench: it would have been a whole lot more cheerful!" Her forced smile was thwarted by her still quivering bottom lip.

"Yes, I think you're probably right!" Abbie laughed loudly as her friend smiled warmly. "You don't have to say any more, but could I ask what happened?" She may have been wise, but she was very mindful of her companion's misery.

"I'm embarrassed to say after your story..." She took a deep breath. "They think it was drugs...but if I'd got to him sooner, they may have been able to pump his stomach and save him."

"Did they say that?"

"No, but I was in the house when he fell into a coma...I just didn't get to him in time..."

"Oh, my dear, did you know he'd taken drugs?"

"No! God, no. I would killed him myself if I'd known." She smiled weakly.

"So you couldn't have known this would happen, how could you possibly be to blame?"

Were it that simple, Abbie would be at home right now. "Well, we had to put him to bed so I knew he was in a bit of a state, but I just thought he'd had a little too much to drink." That much was true.

"'We'? If you're going to blame yourself, what about this other person – is it their fault too? That's a little harsh, dear, don't you think?" Lecturing this poor woman was possibly inappropriate, but she'd seen enough in her own life to know what was worth worrying about.

"I don't know…I…I've kind of run away for a while…" She was conscious of her childish behaviour.

"Well, I can understand that, but let me tell you, it won't change anything, my dear. And nor will blaming yourself…and this other poor person – is it your husband?"

Finding no escape from the embarrassment she felt, Abbie looked at the ground, avoiding inquisitive eyes. "Er…no…no, it wasn't…"

"Oh, OK. Well, it's none of my business anyway, but it's not fair to blame…him?" She didn't want to assume anything.

Abbie smiled. "Yes, it was a man."

Reluctant to appear rude, the elderly lady paused; her own years living with guilt had been wasted and she was loathed to let this woman suffer too. "So…were you having sex? Is that why you feel you were to blame?"

Abbie nearly choked. "Er…yes…"

"It's OK, dear, I have heard of it! So, if you hadn't been having sex, what would you have been doing?"

"Sleeping, probably…"

"OK…so would you have checked your son if you were sleeping? You didn't know he'd taken drugs…"

"No, not 'til I found him unconscious. I was told by…the man I'd been…with." The complications were proving difficult to voice.

"Forgive me, my love, but how could you have saved him then? I don't wish to be flippant but, surely, you had more chance of saving him by having sex with this chap, because if you hadn't, you would have been asleep. Why are you blaming yourself? Look…" She sighed heavily, uncertain whether she could qualify her own advice and, not usually so open with strangers, she risked sharing too much of her own pain, but she wanted to help, and there was, as yet unknown, common ground; "I lost my daughter fifteen years ago and it took me ten years to stop blaming myself. I should have been there; if I'd seen her more often, I could have saved her, but there was nothing I could have done. And then I had two years grace before we had our accident and Stan has been in a coma ever since. Those ten years could have been spent enjoying my husband, enjoying life, enjoying everything I had left. It didn't mean I had to forget her, but I should have lived my life, not wasted it punishing myself, and it didn't change anything, anyway; it didn't bring my daughter back and she would have wanted me to be happy."

Interrupting her own sorrow, Abbie stared at her adviser, unable to summon the proper words, or, indeed, utter a sound, but the affinity she felt with this remarkable woman was now clear…like it had been with Eddie and Joe so many years before.

"How about this: why don't you go into that restaurant over there, find us a quiet spot and we can sit, drink, eat and pour our hearts out while the other customers look at us with pity? If we're lucky, they might even buy us a drink! It's on me, so if you don't have a better offer…?"

Wiping her tears, Abbie smiled: it was a good plan. "I don't! Come on, let's do it."

Walking slowly to the restaurant, she held the door open, careful not to insult her friend's fierce independence and, requesting a quiet location, they were led the back of the room, where, luckily, as business was quiet at this early time, they secured the seclusion they sought, and ordering quickly, they sat back, drank wine and ruminated on the ways of the world.

"So, my dear, who was this chap…? I'm so sorry, I don't even know your name! Heavens above, where are my manners? Please forgive me."

Abbie laughed. "OK, well, I'll let it go this time, but…! I'm Abbie, and I'm delighted to have met you."

"Well, thank you, Abbie, I shall heed my warning! I'm Joan and I'm delighted too." They chinked glasses and drank to each other before Joan returned to her companion's distress. "Now, this chap that you were lucky enough to be engrossed in – does your husband know...?" Joan felt they'd shared enough to be direct.

"Oh, no, I'm not married...well, widowed; he died years ago..."

"Oh, my dear, I'm sorry..."

"No, don't be! He wasn't a pleasant man and...he died from an overdose..." Her life was sounding increasingly more sordid: why had she never analysed it before?

"How awful for you. Well, you know better than I. So, who was this chap; was he your boyfriend?"

Whilst troubled by the truth she was about to reveal, she hoped she'd earned enough trust to avoid an adverse assessment of her character. "Well...erm..." She sighed. "It's a little complicated: I've known him for a long time, but it was the first time we'd..."

"Had sex? You can say it, dear. I may look old, but up here I'm still twenty-two, and if I ever got the chance..." Joan was interrupted by the waiter bringing their order and she smiled mischievously. "Hello, dear...thank you." Struggling to stifle her giggles, as the waiter left, Abbie collapsed hysterically. "It never goes away, Abbie, but unfortunately I'm slightly impeded."

"Well, that won't last forever, and your time will come..." She smiled in admiration.

"So, what's so complicated? You've obviously taken your time and didn't rush into anything, so why do you feel it was so wrong?" Looking at her friend, Joan could see the continuing torment in her eyes.

"Joan...we didn't wait because we were being sensible... there were always other people in our lives, so that didn't help... but...he was Eddie's – my son...he was his best friend..." She waited for the judgement to begin.

Contemplating Abbie's predicament, Joan thought hard before replying. "Was he the same age as your son?"

No sense in complicating things further by lying. "Yes..."

Placing her cutlery neatly on her plate, Joan looked at her companion with a wicked smile. "You lucky lady!" Abbie laughed, relieved that there was no lecture and no humiliating walk-out. Reluctant to elaborate further, she chose instead to gauge Joan's questions. "Is that so bad? I assume it was consensual… Did your son know?"

"No, he didn't, but it just feels wrong now because Eddie became ill whilst we were…having sex and I didn't know, but it was definitely consensual; in fact, he instigated it."

"Well then, no harm done, my love. As far as this chap is concerned, it would have been a bigger problem if your son were still alive because you'd either have to tell him or carry on secretly, which would have been difficult, given the closeness of their relationship and yours. I can understand your need to blame someone, but it won't help. Believe me, I know. Guilt wastes so much of your life and it ages you. You've clearly embraced life, having sex with a much younger man – something most of us can only dream about – so don't waste it on misplaced guilt. If you don't wish to see him again, let that be because he's not suitable for you, not because he happened to be in the right place at the wrong time."

Listening intently to her elder and recognising the essence of her own experience, Abbie welcomed the unexpected benevolence but wondered how she'd react when the full history was revealed; when Joan knew she'd assumed the role of a mother and unofficially adopted Joe as her son – was that as forgivable? She looked at her companion, cautious to offer further details.

"What is it dear? I can see you're still worried – what haven't you told me? Are you pregnant, is he married, what is it?" Maybe hindsight was a useful tool, but life had shown Joan that few obstacles were insurmountable and she worried that her young confidante would realise a little too late. Observing her reluctance to raise her head, chasing her food around her plate to delay the inevitable, she gently touched Abbie's hand, halting her tactics. "Can it really be that bad, my love? I'm not here to judge; there's very little that shocks me these days, but don't punish yourself – it's the quickest way to an early grave."

With a glass of wine to soften her trepidation, Abbie looked up: did it matter if Joan disapproved? They'd finish lunch and part company, and even if the terms were unsavoury, divulging her shame would alleviate, in part, her anguish and opprobrium, and such a liberating proposition, albeit, a selfish one, was enticing. Breathing deeply, she confessed. "He lived with us from the age of eleven and I brought him up as I did Eddie, like a son…" Awaiting the revulsion, she searched the face of her counsel.

Joan, too, took her time to reply. "And how old is he now?" An obvious question that had escaped her earlier and she silently prayed the answer would at least be legal.

"Twenty-three…"

Smiling broadly, relieved, but keen to show Abbie her lack of judgement, she reiterated for clarification. "Twenty-three? You know for a minute there, I thought you were going to say fifteen and I was trying to figure out what the hell I would say! Twenty-three? I think the term you youngsters use is, 'Get over it', Abbie! It's an unusual situation, I'll give you that, but if you're both happy with it, I don't see you really have a problem, my dear." Whilst aware her sincerity would alleviate Abbie's concern to some degree, her own had been heightened momentarily, and she dismissed her alternative response to more condemning facts, along with the twinge of interest she couldn't completely ignore.

Abbie's ubiquitous gratitude tempered her frown, but why Joan's opinion was so important to her remained unknown; whilst her advice and her insight were comforting, she doubted a change in her own perception and that annoyed her. Her friend was right, however: disclosing her odious self-loathing was liberating.

Sensing her continuing scepticism, Joan sighed. "I know you won't listen to me and I understand why you feel responsible but…I have been in your shoes…well, partly – I've never had sex with a man half my age, but that's not really the point…" Abbie laughed – she was nothing if not direct! "If it hadn't been for my faith, I think I would have given up by now. It may have taken me ten years of prayers and church, but it helped. Do you have faith, Abbie, do you believe in God?"

"No, I'm afraid not." Religion was not generally on her agenda, but now, with recent events still raw and grief unrelenting, the very idea choked her like an invisible noose. Taking Eddie so young – what could possibly justify that? Although she'd conceived the notion that it was a retributive deed to account for her somewhat impure alliances with the younger male generation, it was simply unnecessary to serve punishment to an innocent party for her own carnality, for which she neither sought nor offered forgiveness.

The waiter returned to remove their plates and offer dessert menus. Joan waited for him to leave. "It's what got me through it, my dear…that, and my sister. She had a little grandson a couple of years older than mine and she and my niece would visit as often as they could with him to try to fill the void, but they lived so far away…it was such a lovely thought, but it was never quite enough so I relied heavily on the Church. Stan lost his faith after Eva died. Losing a child was just too much for him and he never got over it, but my faith got stronger."

Abbie laughed ironically. "Well, we're a barrel of laughs!" She smiled sympathetically at Joan. "What happened to Eva, how old was she?"

Her daughter's death, after so many years, was still a difficult subject, but given Abbie's honesty, she felt she owed her. "She was hit by a drunk-driver. I was told she'd stood in front of her son to protect him and it cost her her life; she was twenty-seven. They never found the driver responsible, but I'm convinced it was her husband. He was an alcoholic and he was jealous of the boy, and I'm convinced he was trying to kill him…" Her voice quivered as she recalled her daughter's bravery and she made no attempt to conceal it.

Abbie was horrified. "My God, that's terrible! I'm so sorry, Joan." Her lip trembled too. "Did her son survive?"

"Yes, he did, but his father never let us see him again, so I don't know if he's still alive. We never liked her husband, and told Eva so; he wasn't a nice man, but he was tall and good-looking and charming, and she fell for him, but, like all you girls when you fall in love, she wouldn't listen." She smiled apologetically. "We weren't invited to their wedding and when my grandson was born, he was three months old before we saw him, and that was only because Eva sneaked out with him when her husband was drunk. She was a wonderful mother – you know, you remind me of her a little – and the bond she had with that child was so strong and the bastard – sorry, but there really is no other way to describe him – hated it. When we did get to see them, his little arms and legs were covered in bruises and Eva could always explain them but…I don't know, maybe I'm just an old busybody, but I was sure his father was hurting him." She wiped her tears with the back of her hand. "He was such a beautiful boy, so bright and happy…" As her voice broke, she paused to compose herself. "He'd be…well the same age as your Eddie, now."

As the waiter reappeared, desserts were graciously declined, but more wine was needed.

Smiling, Abbie grasped Joan's hand tight. "He was lucky to have had a grandmother like you and, you never know, he may be looking for you. Have you tried to find him?" With a few hours devouring each other's sadness and tragedy, Abbie was deeply moved and it was clear a reunion with her grandson would heal some of the injustice inflicted upon her, and, determined to keep in touch, she would help her in any way she could, concluding that assisting Joan would facilitate her own recovery as it had Eddie's when he'd comforted her whilst grieving for his father.

"I haven't, really, Abbie, because I just don't know where to start; my husband tried sending letters to the house a few years ago, but we didn't get a response, and we really don't know if they're still living there."

"Could you not go to the house to see? I know it would be difficult, but at least you would know..." The loss of Eddie was unbearable, incessant and torturous, but to lose a child *and* a grandchild...

"We thought about it from time to time, but you just don't know how it's going to affect the child: we wanted to protect him as much as we could."

"Well, let's try again, Joan, what have we got to lose? He's an adult now; he can make up his own mind so it's doesn't matter what his father does or says. Let's go now! Let's pay the bill and call a cab."

As the wine arrived, she looked expectantly at Joan, but she shook her head: she was touched by her companion's kindness and her enthusiasm was extremely infectious, but it was a decision that warranted careful thought...and besides, she wasn't ready to dance just yet. "Abbie, that's so kind, but I can't now, not today. I need time to think about it and I need to talk to Stan...and I need..."

"To dance?" She smiled. "It's OK, I completely understand. I just got a bit carried away, sorry. It would have been nice to end the day on a high...especially as we've both been so bloody miserable!" She sipped her wine and deliberated options. "Well, how about we try social media – are you on Facebook or Twitter?"

Joan laughed. "I wouldn't know how! I'm too old for that stuff. I really can't keep up with it – I do try, but it's for you youngsters."

"Let me do it, then. Where's my phone...does he live far

away?" Abbie rummaged in her bag. *How hard can it be?* She felt an overwhelming compulsion to reunite this estranged family and it was fast becoming as important to her as it was to her new friend.

"Well, he used to live about an hour away, in Halhurst, but I suppose he could be anywhere now. Does that make a difference, will you still be able to find him?" With ill-concealed joy, an hour's wine consumption left Joan ill-prepared for disappointment.

"Halhurst?" *Small world*...and with a growing discomfort, Abbie admonished the alcohol. "No, it shouldn't make a difference, but if I can't find him straight away, I can put a post on Facebook, asking if anyone knows him, add his last known address and ask my friends to share it."

"It all sounds rather complicated to me, but if you're sure..."

Abbie laughed. "It's fine, honestly...here we are. Right, what's your grandson's name, Joan?"

Her face lit up. After fifteen years, she was the closest she'd ever been to finding her grandson. Was it really that simple, was that how Facebook worked? She dared to allow her excitement to surface and smiled broadly. "Joseph Francis."

11

Abbie's smile slowly slipped away, and she knew it but was powerless to stop it. "Joseph…Francis?" Feeling nauseous from the panic shaking her core, she repeated his name, but her voice was barely audible, "Joe Francis?"

Joan, struggling to keep her emotions at bay was rather confused by her saviour's reaction. "Yes, that's it…are you OK, dear?" Maybe the extra bottle had been a bad idea.

But Abbie didn't respond; she felt weak and conspicuous, replaying their conversation in her mind. *Joe? Joe? So, what the…breathe, Abbie…*

"Abbie…are you OK, can I get you something?" Joan signalled to the waiter. "Could you get me some water, please?" Turning her attention back to her friend, she resumed questioning. "Abbie…Abbie, are you alright, dear? Abbie…?"

Finally, she recovered enough to reply. "Yes, sorry, not sure what happened there…sorry…must be the wine…and the emotion…and…" Steadying her nerves, she feigned ignorance to allow her breathing to regulate…but, what now?

As the waiter brought water, she bought herself some time. Sipping slowly, her mind continued to race. OK, Joan didn't need to know; she probably wouldn't be so keen to converse on the intricacies of their connection if she knew…but, then, they'd both been so open and honest…*shit!* "Joan…um…right, well, I…um…"

"Abbie, if you don't want to do it, just say so, my dear…"

Despite the deflation that suddenly engulfed her, Joan reasoned, having met only a few hours ago, she was expecting quite a lot.

"No…it's not that…OK, Joan…I can find your grandson…" *Here we go…*

Joan slowly lowered her glass. When she'd got up this morning, her only plans were to walk a little further than yesterday and to visit Stan in the hospital; now, she had a new friend…and she might, just might, find the grandson she'd not seen in fifteen years – that was a lot to take in. She looked at the relative stranger opposite and then down at the table, not wanting to raise her eyes in case Abbie's revealed a lie. 'I can find your grandson' – that's what she said; she said those exact words.

With the reality of her elder's knowledge of her familiarity with Joe came the risk of her deciphering just how familiar she was, and that thought left her trembling. She drank some more wine – because that would really help – and awaited her trial.

Slowly, Joan raised her eyes, full of tears. "You can find him…?" *Was that what you meant, Abbie?*

She smiled nervously. "Yes, I can…but, Joan…I…" She was unable to offer her defence: Joan had launched herself across the table, knocking over glasses and what remained of the bottle, and hugged her tight.

"Oh, Abbie, thank you; thank you so much!" She released her grip, smiling broadly at her friend and, sitting down, apologised for the mess she'd made, as her tears flowed to compete with the soggy tablecloth.

Their quick-witted waiter averted further chaos and when he left them, Joan looked earnestly at her companion. "Do you know him, Abbie? Do you know where Joe is?" Just saying his name made him feel closer.

"Yes…I do…" *And…?* Exploiting Joan's recovery from the shock of her revelation, she thought carefully about her next move. Discovering your long-lost grandson was closer than you thought was one thing, but learning the person who could get you to him had fantasised about him for almost ten years and realised those fantasies, in part, less than a week ago, in a most base and salacious manner, and continued to think of him only in a similarly debauched way – mmm…that posed a dilemma.

Beaming like a child in a toy shop, Joan had many questions… but where to start? "What's he like, Abbie? Is he is clever? How well do you know him, do you have any photos? Is he married; does he have children? What does he do for a living? I'm sorry, there's so much I want to ask you…"

"I know, and I'll answer as much as I can. I'm not going home for a short while and when I do, it'll be for Eddie's funeral so…"

"My dear, I'm so sorry! I got carried away and forgot about your troubles. Of course – you need to sort out your affairs first; I've waited fifteen years so another few weeks are not going to make a difference – maybe, by then I'll be able to dance! But could I please ask one thing: could you possibly get me a photograph? It can wait until you go home, but I'd just like to see what he looks like, to see if he looks like Eva." Conscious of her demands, she was confident Abbie would understand.

She touched Joan's hand. "I have one on my phone; it's not a good one and he's with Eddie, but you can see what a gorgeous young man he is." With trembling hands, she opened the wedding album and passed her phone to Joan.

Looking at Abbie, as if seeking permission, she slowly dropped her eyes to the phone and seeing Joe's face, she gasped; her hand flew to her face and she sobbed, unabashed, with no apology, clutching the phone like life itself. "He has her smile!" Abbie wiped her tears and smiled as she held on to Joan's hand, feeling this gently lady's pain, relief and sheer euphoria at reconnecting with her family, understanding the emotion she was unable to control. Silently, she thanked the heavens for bringing the two of them together.

When she finally relinquished the phone, Abbie suggested they get some air and whilst Joan's smile was a permanent fixture, the pain of their conversation had originally given more definition to the lines on her face, deepening them almost; now, she appeared to be ten years younger and Abbie couldn't be sure if her imagination was conspiring a little too closely with the alcohol she'd consumed, but she was adamant this recovering patient was quicker on her feet.

Bill paid, the two friends wandered out into the sunshine, very different to the ladies who had walked in. Finding a little shade, they sat down, quieted by their discoveries, both watching the waves, lost in their own thoughts…but both secretly pleased the volleyballers had returned!

Joan was the first to break the silence: "I have prayed for Joe every day for the last fifteen years…" She could feel the tears well again, but this time they were joyous. "Asking that he be safe, and I wondered if that was the reason for our accident. I know that probably sounds silly, but I think God knew that his welfare was more important to me than my own, or, indeed, my husband's. It's not that I don't love Stan, but we've had our lives and Joe's was only just beginning. But now I think the accident was to bring me here, to meet you. If I'd not been in that car, I wouldn't have had to learn to walk again and I wouldn't have been here today, the same day that you decided to come here… and I wouldn't have found my grandson. Do you think that's just a coincidence, Abbie?"

Maybe. Whilst she had no faith in God, Fate was a firm contender, but perhaps it was nothing more than a little luck that, surely, they were both overdue. If there had been a big plan for them to meet, the car accident wasn't necessary; Joan's control over her husband's life – that wasn't necessary; there were easier ways, but offending an optimistic and faithful pensioner was neither beneficial nor necessary, so she played safe. "Maybe not, but we've still got a long way to go, Joan…" Despite the hurdles she had to jump, it was important Abbie demonstrated her commitment.

"I know, dear, and I know there's a chance Joe may not want to see me. God only knows what his father has told him, but knowing he's safe is more than I could have wished for. You've made an old lady very happy...and more at peace." Her face, full of life and hope was warming and contagious, and Abbie was proud to have contributed. "What's he like, Abbie? Is he a good boy...what am I saying? He's a grown man! Is he a nice man, does he still see his father, do you know?" With so many unanswered questions, her interrogation was inevitable, but it was unlikely she'd remember the replies even if it were possible for Abbie to satisfy them all.

"Yes, he is a nice man, Joan. He's a little intense, but that's no surprise, given his history, but he works hard...plays hard, and I think you'll be proud of him." ...*Mostly!* "His father died a couple of years ago, I think, but he hadn't seen him for a few years, although, he tried for so long." She smiled as she recalled Joe's attempts at reconciliation that his father always rebuffed.

"How long have you known him, dear?" Joan envisaged a more recent encounter, but her companion's words suggested otherwise. Having already avoided the detail, Abbie froze momentarily, unprepared for such an obvious and innocent enquiry and her hesitation was evident, but the reason for it, not so. "What's the matter, Abbie?"

Looking at the expectant face beside her, veracity was her only option. "Joan...I've known Joe since he was eleven, when he and Eddie became friends at school."

"So you've watched him grow up? Please tell me he was happy..." Nothing else mattered as much.

Abbie closed her eyes and breathed very slowly. "Yes, I did...and yes, he was happy...well, as happy as he could have been under the circumstances. Joan...Joe is...was...Eddie's best friend...and he came to live with us when he was eleven..."

As her eyes widened, Joan gasped. "He wasn't with that bastard of a father, then?"

"No."

"Oh, thank God! I can't tell you what that means to me; thank you, Abbie, thank you so much." Squeezing her hard, her gratitude erased all previous beliefs as she pictured a more blessed life for a grandson deserving of a happy childhood with this honourable woman who had welcomed him in to her home, shielding him from the excuse that was his father.

Her solace justifiable, but it had distorted her appreciation of the depth of Abbie's disclosure. Uneasy, and with advancing panic, she realised she was compelled to be a little more direct. *Shit!* As Joan released her hold, Abbie looked at her, labouring to devise a suitable explanation, but her efforts were halted. "This is hard for an old lady to take in, Abbie, but knowing Joe is safe is enough for now. I don't know if it's the wine or the sun, or simply knowing I still have a grandson, but I'm feeling a little drained; would you mind if I went home? I have so many questions about him, but they can wait; do you mind?"

Torn between deliverance and despair, Abbie settled for the former. "No, of course not. Let me call you a cab." As she dialled the number the consternation resumed; it would be deceitful to allow Joan to continue her unintentional misinterpretation – wasn't it obvious? – and if she waited for another opportunity, would she not be angry that she'd been misled and discredit the woman she'd trusted and praised? She reserved the taxi and put her phone away. "He'll be about fifteen minutes – shall we walk to the car-park?"

"Yes, dear, thank you. Well, what a difference a day makes! I've got so much to tell Stan later; I don't know where to start! Thank you, Abbie, for everything: if Joe had played no part in this, I'd still be grateful; you've given me the best part of your day and listened to my woes, and you've given me understanding and love. You haven't treated me like an old fart; you've treated me as a friend and I'm grateful for all those things…but, knowing my grandson has been safe with you for all these years…" Unable to censor her tears, she permitted their emergence – she knew they'd come anyway. "I can never thank you enough for that." She held onto her saviour, savouring the link to her family, but she had to leave…and she had to tell Stan. "Here's my number." She scribbled on the restaurant receipt and closed Abbie's hand around it. "Please don't lose it, Abbie, but please call me when you feel you can. I'll be thinking of you and praying for you, and I hope that after Eddie's funeral you can start to rebuild your life. I will be there if you need me, I promise, but when you feel able to move on, I would love to meet Joe." She kissed Abbie's cheek as the taxi pulled into the car-park.

Opening the door, she watched her friend struggle to get in and her decision was made. "Joan, I need to tell you something…I need to tell you about Joe…" Leaning forward, she gave the driver her address. "Joe was the one…"

"I know, dear, I know…look after yourself, Abbie…and my grandson." She smiled as she closed the door and Abbie stood motionless, watching the car drive away and when it finally disappeared from view, she sat down on the nearest bench. She knew; Joan knew about Joe.

***

Making her way slowly back to the hotel, Abbie felt tired, very tired indeed, and although she'd consumed enough wine to secure the industry for the foreseeable future, she knew it wasn't the only culprit; the emotions of the day had certainly taken their toll, and, of course, there was always the sea air. As she closed the door behind her, she was reassured that at the very least, her fatigue would put a stop to her constant analysis and guilt, and that alone was reward enough for the turmoil of the day. A quick glass of water…and sleep. Oblivious to the time, she made no attempt to check – what did it matter, anyway? She had no plans and, later, when she woke crying, unable to regain that blissful state of lethargy, the brief cessation of misery would have enabled more rest than of late and that was a blessing.

Buried under the duvet, she was asleep within minutes and remained so, without interruption, all night and for most of the following morning, until, slowly, she became aware of her phone ringing but, choosing to ignore it, she rolled over and drifted back into a deep slumber, feeling safe and warm. When she finally stirred, it was past two o'clock and although aware of the gurgling in her stomach, at this time, waking up was the priority. Forcing her eyes open, she wandered into the bathroom and stood motionless in the shower, allowing the cool water to shock her body into life, and when finally close enough, she upped the temperature as she thought about the events of the previous day…assuming it had been the previous day, but before she checked her phone, she couldn't be completely sure. To dismiss it as a dream would be a little too dramatic, yet it was all a little coincidental. Maybe Joan's assertion that an act of God was at play had more credence than she'd allowed for, although her current state of mind dictated it was, however, implausible. Retracing her steps would be erring on paranoia, but it was a serious consideration, and if, indeed, the facts edged towards an accurate perception, what then? It would be easier to believe that Joan had been a manifestation of all the things wrong and missing in her life than to deal with the repercussions that their meeting would impose. Joan, understandably, wanted to see Joe and so did she, yet she'd run away like a child to avoid confronting her contrition, presenting her with further complications to consider. The pain of losing Eddie was crippling and unwilling to release its hold, but had that changed because she was here? Any contact with Joe took her back instantly to a night of sensuality and intense gratification, but it wouldn't end there. It had to pursue a dark path to panic and hysteria, the simultaneous numbness and pain, confusion and denial, and the morose after effects of the death of her precious son, and it persisted until it forced her to punish herself for her one vice, her one flaw: young men...and their touch, their bodies, and, oh God, their sex. Without blocking that path – separating the two events – she couldn't face Joe and that would make things a little difficult for Joan.

Stepping out of the shower, she headed back to the bedroom, checked her phone to confirm the day and found Joan's number on a scrappy bit of paper, authenticating the reality of the previous day. There were several missed calls from Rose, naturally, and one from Joe – surprising. With only one voicemail, the odds suggested it was from her friend, but maybe, just maybe...Listening carefully to the number, she lurched from elation to despair: Joe. She ended the call quickly but, regretting it, dialled again and held her breath as she heard his voice: "Abbie...hi. I won't trouble you again, but I just wanted to say thank you. If it weren't for you and Eddie, I wouldn't be here now; I would probably have taken my own life, or my excuse for a father would have taken it for me. I never thanked Eddie, but I think...I hope, he knew, but I can thank you. You have given so much to me, which I have mostly taken for granted and I took for granted that you would always be here. I hope you'll be happy, Abbie, and I hope that eventually you'll be able to forgive me." Instinctively, she saved the message and ended the call. Motionless, she stared at her phone, unaware of the tears trickling down her face as she replayed Joe's call in her head. Dialling her voicemail again, she listened closer, pushing the phone hard against her ear, in a futile attempt to feel him. She could smell him, could feel the warmth of his hands on her skin and his breath on her face; she could see the intensity in his gaze and the smile loaded with promise. Again, she ended the call and her body shook as the sobs emanated from her like the cries of a young child – searching for its mother, desperate and frightened

– but no matter how much she ached for him, her heart yearned for Eddie. The love she felt for her son and the love she received from him were unlike anything she had ever experienced. With no memory of her mother, those of her father were tainted with the vulgarity he'd craved. He'd loved no one but himself and his dick, so long as it was buried in some poor innocent teenager, or in his hand, dancing in unison with her; Pete, with his love of all things chemical, and illegal, and the power he felt when his fists connected with her stomach, or her back, was no better. Consequently, the feelings she'd experienced for her son were completely alien and she'd told nobody for years, fearing they were the replication of her father's behaviour, but Pete died and people saw how she guided and supported Eddie, nurtured him and encouraged him, and marvelled at their 'bond'. Slowly, she began to understand that this was 'love' she felt for her son – nothing sordid, nothing sleazy; it was natural and it was what had been missing from her life and now it was missing again. Now, she had no one to love and no one to love her, but…that would have to do. Few would understand what she'd shared with him, and fewer still would ever know; it was hers and nobody else's, and she wanted to keep it that way, unwilling to betray its supremacy. It may have been her one and only love, but it was pure, sincere and had changed her world, and, whilst no one could ever replace it, she wouldn't consent to it anyway: she wanted no more. And she wouldn't allow it to fade; she would, instead, sustain it, indulge in it and harness its power to facilitate her recovery rather than succumb to the hopelessness that had dictated the days since Eddie died. With a sudden sense of disappearing pusillanimity, she felt stronger. No more weakness, no more desolation; she would bury her grief before she buried her son and move on with her life in his honour. Her father and her husband had punished her for their sins, compelling her to punish herself, but she'd served her sentence; whatever they'd taken from her, Eddie had given back to her and she would never lose sight of it, but she would have to face the fact that before she could expect Joe to forgive her, she would have to forgive herself, and that would be a priority.

Her phone rang again as she quietly congratulated herself. "Abbie? For fuck's sake: where have you been? I've called, like, a hundred times; why don't you call back?" Despite her tone, Rose's relief was unmistakable.

"Hey, Rose. I'm sorry, I've been a little distracted. How are you?" The sound of a familiar voice was comforting and Abbie now realised how much she'd missed it.

"Don't worry about me, how the fuck are you? *Where* the fuck are you? You've had me worried sick, Abbie!" There was truth in her words though she knew her friend needed space.

Apologising, Abbie knew it couldn't have been easy for Rose; with her disappearance and the inevitable fall-out from Joe, she was battling her own grief from the loss of Eddie, coinciding with the wedding of her daughter and that was a difficult blend. "I'm fine, Rose. I've been very up and down, but I think I've levelled now. I managed to speak to my doctor and he gave me some sleeping pills, but given the amount of wine I've had lately, I didn't think it was wise to take them. Anyway, how about you? It does matter; I know you've had a lot to contend with." With a little clarity, she felt sure she'd hurt Rose, however indirectly, and being so fond of Joe, the inability to help him would have distressed her enormously: a simple 'sorry' seemed a little inept.

Rose sighed heavily and the quiver in her voice was distinct. "I'm OK. I'm happy I finally got hold of you. I know you needed to escape but, boy, you could have at least let me know where you were."

"I know, I'm sorry, my darling. I'm staying at the Seaview Hotel, in Tilden Bay. I've booked in for the week, but I'm going to see how it goes; it gets a little lonely in the evenings."

"Yeah, well, I can understand that." She paused; the inevitable question burned her lips but she was loathed to upset Abbie, especially as she sounded settled. "Have you...spoken to Joe... at all...?" *Done – phew!*

Recognising her dilemma, Abbie smiled. "No, I haven't; I'm not sure what I'd say to him. He called me...yesterday, I think... it could have been today...anyway, he left a message...quite a sweet one, actually; not what I expected at all. Have you seen him, is he OK?" It felt good to hear his name without wincing.

"Er...yes, a couple of days ago. I called him Sunday night, to tell him you'd left, but he was in The Well and I think he'd had a little too much..."

"Joe, really? That's not like him..." Like Eddie, Joe was never short of a drink but, unlike Eddie, he knew when to stop.

"I know, but I suppose it's understandable. Anyway, it got a bit heated, and not in a good way, so I called him Monday morning...and then the shit *really* hit the fan..."

Abbie closed her eyes. "I'm sorry, Rose. I didn't think about that when I left...I didn't think about anything, really."

"Oh, for Christ's sake, stop apologising! If that's what you thought would help, then you had to do it. Convincing Joe of that...well, that was a wee bit difficult!" She paused; it was unfair to burden Abbie with any more guilt, but equally unfair to ignore Joe's distress. "He...well, he didn't take it well – no great surprise there – but, I need to be honest, Abbie...he was really hurt. He hid it well...behind his temper...and, well, his... advances, but..."

Abbie gasped. "He made a pass at you?" *Shit*...but she thought...

"Oh, you know what he's like; he's always messing around; don't take it too seriously – it was his way of lashing out at you. You know it's always you..." Feigning jealousy, she had to concede it wasn't entirely false..."But he was so shocked, my love, and, I just don't think he knew what to do. He couldn't deal with it; he couldn't understand why you left...but he will; he just needs a little time. I haven't spoken to him since; I thought I'd give him a little space. Are you going to call him, or do you want me to…?"

Images of him with Rose flooded her mind and though scared to ask, she wanted to know more but was convinced her friend would brush it off and she'd be no wiser…maybe it was better to remain ignorant. "I don't know, Rose, I don't know. I don't think it's a good idea to speak to him just yet, especially as he's so angry…but he left me such a sweet message…I need to think about it. By all means, call him if you want to – I don't want him to feel totally neglected – but, Rose: touch him, and I'll kill you!"

Whilst Abbie's laugh may have disguised the solemnity of her statement, Rose knew no humour was intended. "Yes, Mum! Abbie, you know I wouldn't…"

"I know." Ignoring the questions screaming at her, she found a more congenial subject. "How's Michael, by the way…and Frankie – is she on her honeymoon yet?"

"Michael's fine – worried about you, but fine otherwise. Yes: they flew out Monday. They were going to postpone, but I assured them they wouldn't miss Ed's funeral. They send their love."

"That's sweet. Please thank them when you speak to them."

"Yeah, of course. Oh, and expect a call from Jesse. I only managed to speak to him yesterday, but he was in and out of meetings all day. He was rather upset, bless him."

Abbie smiled. "OK, I'll call him tomorrow if I haven't heard from him."

With her agenda satisfied, Rose felt a little lighter. "So, do you have plans tonight?"

"No, I was out for most of yesterday and I met a wonderful lady. You won't believe what happened, but I'll tell you more when I see you. We chatted and had lunch, and…well, she was amazing and…she helped me make sense of this awful mess I've caused, and I managed to sleep last night and for most of the day, so I feel a lot better. I thought I might go for a swim later and get an early night."

"OK, well, take care, my darling, and please let me know when you decide what you're doing; if you're going to stay there for a while, I'll drive over and see you – I'm missing you so much."

"Thanks, Rose. I miss you too, but I needed to get away. I hope you can understand that."

"Yeah, of course, but not for too long, OK?"

"Yes, Mum!"

"Take care, you – love ya!" Rose fought her tears.

"Love ya more!" Smiling as she ended the call, Abbie grabbed a bag and headed for the pool. A gentle swim should hopefully eradicate any thoughts of Joe with Rose and help her sleep again.

As she entered the water, she noticed a group of young lads to her left paying her a lot of attention, exhibiting their aquatic prowess, and smiling, tempted to swim to them, she was alarmed by her indiscernible decision to exercise discretion and remain in her half of the pool. As the tumultuous psychological debate ensued in her mind she resolved to call Jesse first thing in the morning.

12

Abbie was jolted awake by her phone ringing and bleary eyed, she fumbled to answer. "Hello?"

"Abbie, hi. Rose told me about, Eddie but I couldn't call you until now. I'm so sorry..."

"Hey, Jesse. Don't worry, it's been a difficult few days and I know how busy you are; are you OK?" It was a pleasure to hear his voice.

"Yeah, yeah, I'm fine, but how the hell are you? Rose said you'd left – where are you?"

"Yeah, I needed to get away from the house, and...everything, really..."

"Yeah, of course. How are you?" His concern emanated through the phone and Abbie was touched.

"OK, really. I know it's going to take a while, but I'll get there." She rubbed her eyes: the softness of his voice could easily lull her back into a deep slumber.

"I really don't know what to say; he was a good kid, Abbie, everyone loved him."

With a quivering lip, she smiled into the phone. "I know. Thank you, Jesse."

"Where are you? I'm free for the rest of the week if you wanted to meet and chat..."

That would certainly be a start... "Yeah, that'd be nice. Where are you?"

"I'm still at Hayward's."

"OK, well, what's today – Wednesday? I'm free today…or tomorrow…"

Another day would give her the chance to change her plans so Jesse jumped in quick. "Let's do today. Do you fancy lunch at Stanley's?" He was a little concerned she'd find Hayward Manor a little too traumatic.

"Yeah, lovely; one for one-thirty?"

"Yep, sounds good. I'll book it now. Do you want me to pick you up or send a cab?"

"No, don't worry, I'll drive; I can always stay over if the wine's too good!"

"The wine…?"

Abbie laughed. "You're always too good. Thanks, Jesse, it'll be good to see you."

"No worries. But drive carefully, yeah? See you later."

With a focus to the day, she felt brighter, and if it happened to be Jesse, that could only be good. Having left so quickly, with few belongings and clothes, she had little to choose from, but there was always something for Jesse, and smiling, she lost herself in reverie, anticipating a satisfying antidote to the week's despondency. Disregarding the polemic nagging suggesting she reconsider her intentions – for it was the same voice that steered her into the abyss that castigated her for her role in the death of her son whilst exploiting the delectation of nature's evolutionary processes – this was a chance for her to instigate the delicate operation of self-forgiveness, consenting to the very activity that initiated the agony that had subsequently governed her life, and whilst it was Joe that would potentially challenge her resolution, aside from the obvious benefits, time with Jesse would certainly demonstrate that her self-condemnation was irrational, and right now, she needed that exposure.

Showering quickly, she tried to subdue her wandering mind; the demons persisted, but so did the expectation of a fulfilling afternoon and, thankfully, that notion prevailed: lunch would be more than just sustenance and no matter how considerate he may be in light of recent events, Jesse would be unable to resist even the subtlest of suggestions that they conform to their traditional practices and defer to his suite, and she knew, as well as he, that despite recent events, she would agree. Lunch would be fun, but the sex, more so, and God, did she need a little fun…but, with her enforced, albeit short-lived celibacy refuted by her new-found perspective, her refusal to participate in any cordiality with Joe made for a very delicate position, and should he find out…fuck! A concern for another day and, with only half an hour before she had to leave, focussing on the negative repercussions was counter-productive, time-consuming and hardly conducive to the prospective pleasure of Jesse, so, dry and dressed, she looked long and hard in the mirror: today was a better day. Carefully applied make-up and casually styled hair increased her optimism and she texted Jesse, warning him she may be a little late.

Ten minutes over schedule and she was on her way and, driving a little too fast, she was careful enough to not get caught, arriving just five minutes later than planned. As she left her car, she dismissed her nerves as excitement, refusing to let anything distract her from the promise that awaited her.

Opening the door to the restaurant, Jesse stood out a mile – he looked more appetising than anything on the menu. Diverting from his usual casual, yet equally delectable attire, he'd opted for a beautiful black, pin-striped suit and crisp white shirt, with an absent tie and, no doubt, his trademark boots. With his own marvellous way of interpreting the rules, some changes were completely unnecessary. Abbie could see other diners looking at him slyly, asking questions, but he kept himself to himself, waiting patiently. Standing up to greet her, his smile alone was worth the drive over and as he hugged her tight she relaxed. Once they were seated, he took her hands. "You look beautiful, Abbie."

She laughed. "You lie very well, Mr McKenzie!" Her gin and tonic arrived instantly.

He smiled. "Do you want to order now or wait a bit?"

"Let's order now; get it out the of the way."

When she worked at Hayward Manor, she would bring clients here; the service was impeccable and the food exceptional, and she'd brought Jesse here when he'd asked to perform at her festival and, full of self-imposed obligation, he'd insisted on paying the bill…before he'd seen the prices! She'd managed to avert any embarrassment by suggesting she used her expense account, but ever since, he repaid her generosity.

The extensive menu was lavish, as always, but Abbie kept it simple with a salad, whilst Jesse, anticipating the need for a little more nourishment, preferred something more substantial and settled on a steak, and with wine necessary from the outset, they were free to review the days since they last met.

Jesse, with bewildered eyes and conscious of their surroundings, was keen to satisfy his curiosity without causing too much distress. "I'm so sorry, Abbie. I can't imagine what shit you're going through."

Smiling, she could see the sadness in his face. "Thank you – it's been tough for a lot of people…and I haven't helped by running away, but it seemed right at the time." She sighed deeply. "I spent a little time yesterday thinking and talking about everything that had happened…and I think I've come to terms with it a little better. I think it'll be a while before I fully appreciate Ed won't be coming back, but…that's just the way it goes, I suppose."

"Why did you run away?" It was a strange reaction from a woman he knew to be strong and resilient.

With a sardonic laugh, the inevitability of the requisite explanation weighed heavier than she'd calculated and she struggled to compose a sensitive mitigation. "Well, aside from the memories of Eddie everywhere I looked and knowing they were all I had left of him…I had more recent memories that I couldn't…face up to." She sipped her drink, hoping, unrealistically, to deflect any further questioning.

But her lack of specifics revealed more than her words and Jesse wouldn't concede. "Memories of…?"

Replacing her glass, she smiled in defeat. "Memories of Saturday night…"

"And what do those memories consist of?" Whilst, deep down, he'd prefer to remain ignorant, her reluctance to elaborate had already planted an unsavoury seed.

"Joe."

Reaching for his drink, Jesse sought to disguise his derisive smile. There was no surprise, but there was always hope, although, this time, unsatisfied, but as he sipped slowly, he concurred that whilst he was unwilling to enter into a relationship currently, he was by no means faithful to whatever arrangement he and Abbie had, and that, if he were Joe, he would have exploited his position way before now so any judgements would be wholly hypocritical. Having known her for a few years, their time together consisted of dinner or drinks and sex, and the conversation usually revolved around his career and what delights lay in store; they'd never discussed Joe, and until Saturday night, Jesse had had no reason to suppose he was, in any way, significant, such was the nugatory status he seemingly held in Abbie's intimate affections. Sure, he'd always appeared apathetic to Jesse's presence, but with his own reputation at stake, Jesse assumed he was a potential threat to Joe's conquests. He steeled himself for an unpalatable response before enquiring further. "So, what happened with you and Joe?"

Laughing nervously, she knew clarification was superfluous and that his inquisition was designed to confound her but, in fairness, he was justified. "Well…he helped me get Eddie to bed as there was no way I'd manage alone…and I suggested a glass of wine as a thank you…"

Jesse smiled. "A 'thank you', yeah?" Feeling the involuntary blush, Abbie averted her eyes, but her discomfort was eased somewhat by the arrival of lunch. Finishing her drink, she reached for the wine bottle and filled their glasses; detecting her procrastination, Jesse allowed the waiter to leave before prompting resumption. "Go on…"

"Jesse, do you really want to do this?"

"Yes, I need to know what I'm competing against."

"It's not a competition!"

"You know what I mean; cut the crap, Abbie, and tell me what happened."

She sighed deeply. "OK. Well, there's always been something between us, I think, but I brought him up for about six years, so it's a little awkward and he's never really given me any indication that he wanted anything more… There's been the occasional innuendo, but that's it…and then Saturday night… I don't know if he'd planned it or whether it just happened…but it definitely happened…and, boy, did it!"

Dismissing the envy clawing at him like a feral cat, Jesse laughed. "Thanks, Abbie!"

"Sorry…but you asked."

"Well, judging from his behaviour on Saturday, I'd say it was planned – he couldn't have been any happier when you had to leave early."

"I don't know about that – I was just focussing on Ed."

"Trust me…but it doesn't make any difference…and I'm guessing, despite his arrogance, he didn't force you…"

Abbie played with her food. "No, of course not." She looked at him with complete sincerity. "You know I love what we have, Jesse. Christ, the very thought of you turns me on, but Joe…was different; no better, no worse, just different…*very different!*" She smiled sheepishly.

"Yeah, let's leave it there…" As every mouthful stuck in his throat, he drank quicker. He'd heard enough, but the ambiguous impact on his own standing needed to be addressed. "So where does that leave us, Abbie? I never expected you to wait dutifully for my return, but I've never had any direct competition before…"

Laying her cutlery down, she frowned. "Come on, you're Jesse! Everyone knows who you are; how long do you suppose this is going to last? It's only a matter of time before you find some sexy young thing – Christ, you could have anyone you wanted – and do you think she's going to put up with you screwing me when you're in town? What do you do, Jesse, when you're out on the road? Do you wait for me or do you help yourself to whoever's on offer?"

"OK, OK…but…Joe? Isn't he a little intense…and controlling?"

She smiled mischievously and leaned in closer. "Most definitely!"

He laughed as he shook his head. "You're bad, Abbie!" With his lunch now slightly less appealing, he pushed his plate aside. "So, does he know you're here? Fuck, he'll kill me!"

Her smile dropped. "No, I haven't seen him since Sunday. I left rather quickly and didn't tell him so he's not taken it too well. I felt we were responsible and that if he hadn't been there, Eddie might still be alive."

Jesse chose his words carefully; despite their mutual loathing, it was unfair to condemn Joe for something beyond his control. "But if he hadn't been there, what would you have done, gone straight to bed?" Abbie shrugged. "Well, then, you would have found Eddie the following morning, alone – fuck, Abbie, that would have been harder… Look, I'm happy if you never see Joe again, but if Eddie didn't die Saturday night, he might have died today, while we're having lunch…or later…when maybe we're not…" He smiled sweetly. "It's not his fault, or yours…and I understand you're looking for someone to blame, but you can't punish him, not for this." He took her hand, his voice tender.

"Eddie knew about us and I'm pretty sure he knew we didn't just meet to chat, but he didn't care. So long as you were happy, he was happy. Don't you think he'd prefer you were…enjoying yourself rather than alone, when you found him? Have a break, go and see someone – a counsellor or a shrink, whatever – but don't do this to yourself, Abbie, or Joe, especially now…fuck, what am I saying? Forget that; blame Joe!"

With eyes full of tears, she laughed and gently touched his face. "Thank you, my darling. I know you're right but…he's…he *was* my child and I let him down."

"Yeah, he was *your* child but he wasn't a child and you can't be responsible for him all the time, any more than my mother can for me. Christ, she wouldn't let me out of her sight if she knew what I got up to…but, I'm responsible for myself as Eddie was, so it's out of your control."

Abbie eyed him suspiciously. "So what do you get up to?"

Jesse laughed. "You know that better than most…" Filling their glasses as their plates were removed, he felt a little melancholy, but they were never exclusive and he couldn't lay claim to a woman he met, at best, twice a year. Changing course, he hoped to prevent negativity pervading his afternoon. "So when will you know what happened?"

"In a week or two, I think, but I'm pretty sure they'll tell me what I already suspect. You know, I was so convinced that losing his father like that was enough of a deterrent, but maybe I was a little too complacent. He wasn't like his father – he used everything he could get his hands on – but, clearly whatever Eddie used was enough to kill him. Joe tried to stop him, but Ed wouldn't listen and I know he feels guilty about not telling me, but as you say, Ed wasn't a child and Joe wasn't his keeper. I don't suppose it would have made any difference if I had known, but I would have liked to have had the chance to help him, you know?" Losing her resolve to maintain her composure, she stopped to avoid her emotional disintegration.

Jesse smiled. "I know. But he was happy, Abbie; he was a very lucky boy and he knew that, and he wasn't shy about showing how much he adored you. The first time I met him, I thought he was going to punch me! I don't think he knew about us then, but I thought everyone knew. I never mentioned it, but he wasn't stupid, and I'm pretty sure he would have made it clear if he had a problem with me…rather like Joe does!"

Abbie laughed. "Mmm…I'm afraid that's unlikely to change."

***

Having resisted desserts, they ordered coffee and more wine and veered towards more light-hearted conversations, both palliated by the absence of Eddie and Joe and appreciating the subtle flirting that was always part of their time together, but Abbie struggled to silence her underlying fear that, given her revelations about Joe, and his own tremendous success, this was quite possibly the last time she would share herself with Jesse.

Bill settled, they headed for the door and, reluctant to appear insolent, Jesse tried a subtle approach. "So, do you want me to call you a cab…or…?" Eyes wide with expectation but wary of temerity, and biting his lip in that irresistible, boyish way that made Abbie melt, she wondered if he knew the effects of his innocent manner or whether it was natural appeal.

Taking his arm, she smiled. "You don't give me a choice!"

With a knowing laugh, he silently congratulated himself.

The suite was stunning; beautifully decorated with sumptuous furnishings, in a mix of traditional and contemporary styles, with black and white photographs of the Manor, its occupants and staff performing their various tasks, both inside and out, framing a large monochrome image of the entire estate, taken in 1885. To the right were what appeared to be the original plans for the building, with quotes and invoices from the architect, Samuel Ferris, and to the left were various letters written by the male residents to their loved ones during the Crimean War, but in particular, from John Hayward-Smythe, during the First World War. Touching them softly, Abbie was reluctant to read their contents for fear of intruding or identifying a little too closely with their sentiments and reliving the pain of the weekend. She wondered who would have used these rooms and if they would have been employed for the kind of entertainment they would see today.

The breath-taking view of the grounds was more vivid at this time of year, with a sea of lush green interspersed with ancient trees – proud and undeterred by the swarm of schoolchildren clambering indiscriminately over low-slung branches, reaching ever-higher, impervious to their legacy – bordered by clumps of delicate yet robust wild flowers in soft pinks, vibrant yellows and pure whites, dancing elegantly to the will of the breeze, and with the windows closed, it was almost possible to smell the honeysuckles and lavenders in the carefully designed courtyard, gently bowing their heads as the bees left their evolutionary mark. Abbie wanted to stay here, right here, in this particular moment, forever, filled with anticipation for what would unfold and hold on to it, surrounded by the splendour both inside and out.

Jesse handed her a glass of wine, having selected some appropriate music. He lived and breathed music, couldn't be without it, and she knew he chose his restaurants by what they played, and if he recognised the beat of one of his own intros, he would beam, though ever so slightly self-conscious. He would interrupt conversations to write notes that he would later convert to lyrics and if she commented on a particular favourite song he would question her to determine why it was so important. When he wasn't touring or writing, he would frequent many bars and clubs seeking new talent that he could promote as opening acts for his own shows and often performed at charity functions to raise much-needed awareness and funds, which only added to his charm.

She looked at him as she sipped her wine. He remained unspoiled by fame: unpretentious, subtly coy and overtly courteous, yet he exuded an inherent sexuality that contradicted his innocent manner and enhanced the beauty of his face. She could keep him here, lock him up and use him at her leisure, feel his hands on and in her body and feel his breath on her face as he came inside her, submit to his tongue as it gently explored her pussy and encourage the twitching of his cock as she sucked it hard...

Abandoning her glass, she pulled him towards her. He finished his wine and smiled wickedly, perspicaciously intent on fostering her discomposure, for he knew that one simple act could make her come if she thought about it long enough, and as she kissed him passionately he responded intensely, fuelled by the deprivation of their last encounter, engendered by the presence and intentions of Joe. As she walked him carefully towards the sofa, her hand wandered tentatively down his body to his belt, tracing its edge before eagerly reconnoitring his crotch. She pulled away and smiled seductively, examining the source of her proposed profligacy and the results of her propinquity, and as her eyes devoured the vision before her, they rested on Jesse's groin, meeting his approval. She sighed deeply. "There's something about a hard-on in a suit..." Moving close, she unbuttoned his shirt and kissed his chest, licking each nipple tenderly before biting a little too hard, whilst her hand gently groped the tumescence she craved, but her impetuous beneficiary removed her hand and placed it on his belt, keen to precipitate momentum. Willingly obedient, she dropped to her knees, but intensified his frustration by undressing him slowly, watching his face as her tongue lightly caressed his cock. Closing his eyes, he breathed deeply, savouring the munificence of her mouth, excruciatingly superlative though long overdue, and whilst he'd happily come in her mouth later, now he wanted to fuck her and he gently pulled her up to face him, kissing her hard and tugging at her dress. Pushing him down to the sofa, she straddled him, rolling her hips and grinding hard on his dick, holding his gaze as she kept his hands at bay. His smile reflected his aspirations and she enjoyed his appreciation as she slowly removed her dress and dropped it to the floor, writhing around, denying his urgency but, struggling with her restraints, Jesse's smile wavered and he repudiated her command, pulling her down and forcing himself inside her. Gasping as he pushed harder, her body ached for the atavistic, almost brutal side to him that emerged only when he fucked her, and acceding to his visceral volition, she held him tight, searching for his mouth to taste the sweetness of his exigency, but he refused her, watching her face instead, as his jaw tightened. Piercing the skin of his lower back with her nails, endeavouring to provoke a fierce corollary, she studied his face, her breathing controlled by his movements and ferocity, her body alive with the sensations generated by the force of his, and when his climax took hold and he held his breath, she filled his mouth with her tongue, welcoming the aggression he returned. Closing her eyes as Jesse collapsed on top of her, she stroked his exquisite body, enjoying his weight and the delicate sweat on his skin.

Finally raising his head, he smiled at her. "That's my kind of lunch!" He kissed her tenderly and stroked her hair but became uncharacteristically serious. "If it weren't for you, I wouldn't have the life I have now, but because of that, I'll never be around long enough to have you to myself. I know I've dreamed of it since I was five, but it takes me away from you and if I thought for one minute that I stood a chance, I would stay and give it all up...but something tells me there's no point."

Taken aback, Abbie was confused by his revelation; for her, it had never been anything more than indulgence in mutual hedonistic pleasure and he'd never given her any controvertible indications. "But we never took it seriously, Jesse. It was only ever a bit of fun – just as much sex as we could cram in while you were back and I'm always waiting for you to call to say you've met someone…and I thought you felt the same…" She'd always known it was a gamble, but one worth taking.

Feeling foolish, he looked down. "Yeah…I know…" A change of subject was necessary. "We best get on with it then…"

She smiled and kissed him softly as he pulled her to him and held her tight, kissing her face and neck. Picking her up, he carried her to the bed, laid her down and lay on top of her, kissing her body as she sighed and ran her fingers through his hair, watching him devour her, searching her body for uncharted territory. Abbie's curves pleased him, impelling him to examine every inch of her with every inch of himself, methodically and unhurried, for fear of missing something that might assist the onset of his next erection and when his hands were satisfied, his tongue superseded to ensure accuracy of his mission and increased stimulus for Abbie. Licking her stomach, he slowly dragged his tongue to her breasts, whilst moving his hand further down until his fingers found their way inside her, deep inside her. She pulled him up to kiss him, wrapping her legs around his waist and he studied her face as he removed his fingers and placed them in her mouth, smiling contentedly as she dutifully sucked, provoking that familiar sensation in his crotch.

"Sing to me, Jesse."

A predictable precedent given his talent, but one that, until now, he'd avoided. Abbie, however, merited compliance and he sang softly in her ear, feeling his cock harden with her appreciation. Thrusting aberrantly gently, he watched her closely before withdrawing, continuing to sing, but toying with her patience, knowing if he teased her long enough she'd beg. Barely touching her, his voice served him well, eliciting breathlessness from his audience that signalled her desperation and, prolonging her agony, he brushed her pussy with his dick as she wriggled beneath him, seeking a more satisfactory progression, but he resisted her, battling with his own self-control, awaiting her imminent supplication, and, predictably, her intolerance escalated and she secured his victory.

"Please, Jesse, *please.*"

Ambivalence was rare for Jesse, but feeling disquietly ominous, a determination to transcend Joe prevailed and with his voice seemingly a trigger for Abbie's pleasure, and, an advantage over his adversary, he allowed it to tease her as his body did, accelerating her frustration and, ultimately, her consummation. As she edged closer to orgasm, she tugged at him, frantic for intense penetration but, remaining ascetic, Jesse relished the ease with which he could affect her and delayed the pervasion of his cock until she succumbed to her own body's ultimate inevitability. Finally, as she moaned softly, he fucked her as hard as he could, his tongue seeking hers, exploiting the fragility of her senses. Still breathless, she allowed him to control her, cosseting his own climax until he crumpled in a mass of groans and sweat and she held him tight, luxuriating in the feel of his body and the smell of his skin and the gentle throb of his cock, still inside her, happy if he never moved, but once recovered, he rolled to her side and stroked her skin, running a finger just below her breast and down to her stomach, watching her flinch as his hands tormented her.

"What time do you have to go?" He gently traced her navel.

Raising herself onto an elbow, she looked at him, stroking his cock with one finger. "I don't…"

Leaning forward, he kissed her through his smile. "Would madam care for room service?"

"Well, I feel I've been serviced already but, if you're hungry go for it. What's available?" Food wasn't on her mind – she was hopeful for much more of what she'd already had and she wandered into the bathroom to freshen up.

"There's a menu somewhere…" Jesse got up to search and as she reappeared she studied his body. Jesus, he was beautiful naked! He was beautiful clothed, but naked...that took some beating, and when he returned to the bed, she was lost in reverie, picturing more deviant ways to entertain themselves.

"You OK?"

She smiled wickedly. "Absolutely!"

Mirroring her smile, and with interest piqued, he enquired further. "What were you thinking?" Assured of an appropriate reply, he could feel the sensual tension rise.

"You didn't give me much time, but I can tell you it involved a certain part of you...my mouth and some sucking."

He groaned. "Do we need to eat?"

"Well, my mouth's going to be full, so..." She shrugged and laughed as he pounced and kissed her passionately.

"Shit! You make me so fucking horny, Abbie."

Her hand wandered down to his crotch to encourage truth in his statement as she watched his face. "Well, let's order and find a way to fill our time whilst we wait."

With flagging interest, Jesse's priorities changed. "Just order everything; I can't wait for you to decide. See if they've got some fruit..." His eyes travelled down her body. "We need our five a day...and some more wine."

Abbie released herself from his grip and headed for the phone. "Do they know you have a 'guest'?" Thoughts of the inevitable gossip amused her.

"I'm a good customer..."

Whilst she waited for her call to be answered, Jesse kissed her back and as she placed her order she could feel his exploratory hands inside her bra, delicately pinching as he whispered in her ear. "I want to come over your tits, Abbie. Hurry up, I need to come!" He breathed heavily. "I'm coming, Abbie...Abbie, feel my cock...*please!*"

Having spluttered over her order, she hung up and slapped him on the chest as he giggled like a child. "I wasn't lying."

"That was unfair – she asked me if I was OK! Maybe I should

have told her you're not as sweet and well-mannered as you would have people believe; perhaps I should dispel the myth that surrounds you…"

He grabbed her roughly. "Maybe you should have, she might have asked if she could join us." If confirmation of his sincerity were needed, his smile provided it.

Abbie feigned offence. "I'm not enough for you?"

Biting his bottom lip, innocence glowed convincingly. "I can never get enough Abbie, but I wouldn't mind sharing you; in fact, I think we should try it."

Grabbing a pillow, she struck him, but before she had another chance, he pushed her down, restraining her as she wriggled to free herself. He allowed her a little respite to enjoy the sight of her body as she escaped and attempted to punish him further, pinning him to the bed and resuming control, surprisingly tough and determined, whilst her diminutive frame undulated provocatively, in unknowing deference to his hunger, forging a pleasing alliance with his impatient wait, and when he'd witnessed enough to ignite sufficient intemperance, he seized her hand and dragged her playfully into the bathroom as she tried to resist to appreciate the tension in his body. Turning on the shower, he slowly removed her underwear whilst it heated up, stepped back into it, pulling her close and kissing her softly. He smoothed her hair from her face before lifting her and pressing her against the tiles, pushing his cock deep inside her, thrusting gently, knowing her need for a little more force would surface with an urgency that would compel him to comply but, instead, she stopped him and slowly slid down his body, licking the water from his skin as it trickled down his stomach, creeping ever closer to her target. Observing the pleasant change of direction, Jesse gasped as her tongue caressed his dick, gracefully circling its prey before her mouth engulfed it, hungry for his submission. Closing his eyes, he held her head, swaying instinctively as she sucked hard, barely resisting the urge to bite down. The sound of running water was silenced by his breathing, consumed, as he was, by her presence and her expertise and, with her hands gently squeezing his balls, attempts to defer his climax were futile, and in recognition of his defeat, he pushed hard into her throat, coming suddenly, charged with a potent force beyond his control that gradually dispersed, leaving him trembling and alive. Abbie remained still, swallowing his cum and enjoying the throb of his cock as it started to soften.

Allowing a few minutes recovery, he pulled her up and kissed her neck, but she found his mouth with her tongue, eager for him to taste what she could, scrutinising his face as she kissed him, although, less enthused by the prospect, he pulled away, pulling down the shower hose as he pushed her against the tiles. Assuming an authoritarian attitude, he parted her legs and aimed the head at her crotch, far enough away for the water to gently massage her pussy whilst he held her in place, focussed intently on the impromptu performance he'd devised. Grabbing his wrist, she guided his hand, breathing deeply with the swirling of the shower head, committed to satisfying both herself and her advocate, aroused further by his unbroken concentration which ultimately effected her orgasm and, closing her eyes, it washed over her as the water did, warming her very core and soothing the exhilaration that had led her to this point. Looking into his eyes she smiled contentedly as she attempted to steer the hose away, but he held firm, refusing to acknowledge her fulfilment as motivation to conclude his show, choosing, instead, to witness her sensitivity turn to discomfort.

"That's enough, Jesse."

Compromising reluctantly, he turned the water off and dropped the hose, pulling her to him and kissing her aggressively and, whilst usually content with his primeval approach, she was somewhat disturbed by its intemperance and, hearing a knock at the door, she gently pushed him away, but he refused to be impeded until he heard the second knock.

Regaining composure, he grabbed a towel and headed towards the door and, alone, Abbie closed her eyes, presuming she'd misconstrued his intentions and concluding that, for the most part, his manipulation was acutely erotic, lusciously savage, but rare, and that added to its appeal. She shivered as she wondered how many others had witnessed and succumbed to it.

Wrapped in a towel, she went to find him. Watching closely as the waitress wheeled the food trolley through, his smile had returned, but whilst the demon in his eyes was clear, his aims were less so and the poor girl tried hard to avert her eyes as her stood before her, half-naked, dripping with water. "Thank you…?"

"Er…Kate."

"Thank you, Kate. We've got far too much food here, would you like to join us?"

Kate blushed. "I-I'm sorry, but I'm working all evening, sorry…" She smiled awkwardly and headed for the door.

"OK…but if you change your mind…" He touched her arm and smiled angelically, reminiscent of Joe as he opened the door for her.

As he closed it, he looked at Abbie and shrugged his shoulders. "What?"

"You asked her to join us? Jesse!"

"I thought it might be fun…"

She tugged at his towel. "Have you not had enough 'fun' already?"

He grabbed her. "Not yet."

Laughing, she pushed him away. "Well, I need to eat."

He removed his towel. "Go ahead…" If his smile was playful, his eyes were serious.

Grasping his offering, she pulled him slowly towards her, before pushing him onto the bed and turning her attention to the food trolley, perusing its contents for an irresistible treat, but an impatient Jesse sat up and dragged her across the bed, intent on generating his own. The smile had gone; he'd done playing games. With the progression of the afternoon came the realisation that once she returned home, Joe would stake his claim, unopposed by Abbie; a decision he neither venerated not accepted...but to what end? Unwilling to renege on her unspoken but clearly evident attachment to Joe, she'd already dismissed his own delusionary declaration and with that came the subtle suggestion that he would no longer feature in her life... at least not as he had previously, and that wouldn't be enough. As a constant in his mind and his life for the last six years, she'd been a comfort during the long months away from home and a worthy reward for the pressures synonymous with his career, but the crude discovery that he was no more than a stop-gap whilst she waited for a slot in Joe's schedule, and of his own part in their little sexual theatre, choked him like an invisible hand around his throat. Abbie's sated smile appeared to mock him and he yielded to the compellable desire to raise a hand to her neck and press hard, and as he did so, her expression changed dramatically, struggling with comprehension, frightened by his force and involuntary grimace. In an attempt to release his grip, she secured it, procuring adequate rigidity in his cock to succour penetration, and he fucked her hard, though in her fragile position it was less appealing but, mercifully, the arousal of her vulnerability hastened his orgasm and coming violently, he removed his hand to grasp her hips, pushing deeper inside her, heightening the thrill. Exhausted and finally cognisant, he covered his face in shame as Abbie recoiled, scared and shaken by his anomalous behaviour. With vicarious alarm, he sat up, mindful that a tenable explanation was doubtful.

"I'm sorry, Abbie...I'm so sorry. I just...lost it..." He stroked her hair in a vain attempt to prove his words.

She carefully removed his hand and herself from his reach, and looked in his eyes. The danger had gone, thankfully, and they were, indeed, full of regret, but there was something else:

he looked despondent – the sparkle had gone and he appeared very young. "You scared the shit out of me, Jesse. What the fuck was that all about? I'll take a certain amount of pain, but I prefer to be able to breathe." Deeply burdened by his own conduct, he wasn't sure how to proceed and pacified, somewhat, by his remorse, she tried to reassure him. "What happened? That's not you…" Discomfort was, for her, a welcome consequence of their pursuits, but this was different; this wasn't Jesse.

Smiling apologetically, he took her hand and kissed it gently. "I know…and I'm so sorry…but I know that when you leave here today, I won't see you again…and that scares me…"

His sincerity touched her. "We both knew this would happen…"

"No, Abbie. I told you; I didn't think it would, but then I didn't know about Joe. Why didn't you tell me before?" He felt a little cheated.

"Because there was nothing to tell; nothing happened until last weekend and I don't know if anything else will – he's not particularly amused that I left. But you haven't told me about everyone you've slept with over the past six years…" Neither had promised exclusivity so she couldn't quite see his point.

"No…but that's different…"

"Why, because it's you? Don't do this, Jesse…" Getting up, she searched for her clothes but he grabbed her arm.

"I'm sorry, please don't go. C'mon, please…" He pulled her towards him, his face a picture of innocence and she relaxed. "Just promise me you'll keep in touch; there's no reason why we can't still meet for lunch. I know we won't have any more afternoons like this, but I don't want to lose you completely."

Touching his face, she smiled. "Jesse, right now, I'm the last person Joe wants to see but, even if that weren't so, relationships aren't his thing and I'm not vain enough to suppose that's going to change for me, and I'm not sure I would want it to anyway. Of course I'll keep in touch, why wouldn't I? But you need to find yourself someone that can give you what you want…and that's not me. Until then, I have no plans to change anything." She kissed him tenderly. "Now let's eat something before it spoils."

As they enjoyed the feast before them, the atmosphere lifted and they joked whilst feeding one another, both anticipating what their games would lead to and, fuelled by more wine, they reminisced about their history, delighting in forgotten times and musings from a perspective other than their own, leading to the desire to relive their mutually favoured recreation, but this time, the pace was slower and, accustomed to a more sordid, albeit, passionate experience, the solemnity in Jesse was unfamiliar; whilst not unpleasant, it was laden with nuances that made Abbie a little uncomfortable. His take on life; his permanent smile and ability to surmount every obstacle with humour, along with the promise of the most decadent and rewarding sex, was the attraction and aroused her when he crept into her mind late some evenings when he was due home. The intensity, that was for Joe.

With fervent kisses, she hoped to effect a change and entice the animal he happily exhibited when usually inside her. As he pulled away, he looked in her eyes and recognised the wildness he'd temporarily lost, remembering all they'd ever been about and how their relationship had begun…and the smile returned, the animal returned: Jesse returned. He rolled over, sat up and forced her down hard on his cock, acknowledging her triumphant smile before she kissed him again, longing to taste his breath as his orgasm exploded through his body. Holding him still she could feel the beating of his heart and the sweat from his face on her breasts, whilst his dick pulsed inside her, and she closed her eyes, clinging to the last moments of the day, wishing they would remain forever, but knowing, as Jesse did, that they couldn't.

***

It was almost seven before Abbie stirred, and it was a while before she realised where she was. Hearing Jesse in the shower, she awaited his return – wet, warm and smelling divine. With a grumbling stomach, she pulled the food trolley towards the bed, but nothing looked appetising...certainly not as appetising as Jesse would in a few minutes, but when he appeared, he dressed immediately, unaware she was awake. She tugged at his shirt. "Hey, what's this all about? I've not had breakfast yet." She sat up to kiss him, but he pulled away. "Are you OK?"

With the smile of an angel, he reassured her. "Yes, I'm fine, but I need to go; I forgot I have a meeting this morning, but I won't be long. Stay here and I'll come back and find you later." He kissed her quickly, grabbed his jacket and left.

Shit. Damn you, important music people! She revisited the food trolley and settled for some slightly stale brioche and cheese, hesitated at the wine but thought better of it. She ambled into the shower and stood for an age, allowing the water to gently cleanse every inch of her body without any effort on her part, and her mind wandered back to the previous day with Jesse in the shower, but her thoughts quickly turned to Joe and her body ached for him. Washing absent-mindedly, she imagined his hands on her body, caressing every curve, seeking every crease and crevice, pushing inside wherever they could, but feeling decidedly disloyal, she turned down the heat and gasped as the cold water hit her, although the shock diverted her attention from Joe. Stepping out, she dried herself and dressed quickly, still feeling the chill of the shower.

As she warmed herself by the window, she studied the visitors, like she did frequently when she worked at Hayward Manor. She'd spotted Jesse amongst the crowds – easily – before he'd approached her, and had watched him wander around, presumably asking staff who he needed to charm. Luckily, her name had been offered and as he sheepishly knocked at her office door, she was irritated at the interruption when she was so busy organising the festival, but when he walked in, her mood improved instantly. He'd been polite, he'd been endearing but, mostly, he was convincing, yet she was still a little anxious about letting a complete unknown open her third, and by far, biggest event; thankfully, her worries proved unfounded and he'd delivered on all his promises. The boys had joined her to watch, and although Joe had openly enjoyed Jesse's music, once Abbie began to marvel at his talent...and quite possibly his beauty, his opinion changed, and although his reasons were obvious now, she hadn't registered then.

Those were her happiest days: busy with the Manor, busy with the boys, seeing the beginning of Jesse's illustrious career and relishing the attention she was getting from pretty much every male she knew...or, at least, every male the boys knew. No regrets, no parameters, just freedom...and sex – lots of sex.

As she reminisced and lost herself in the sounds and senses of that particular time, she felt a tear on her cheek and chastised herself for being so melancholy, but as she wiped it away, she knew that Jesse's words were true; as much as she adored him and everything about him, Joe had a hold over her that she couldn't escape and was beyond her own understanding, but if it meant giving Jesse up, she would. She knew Joe was a risk, and his history dictated that she'd had her share of him and that he would never settle, but she wasn't entirely convinced she wanted any more than that herself, and perhaps that was the attraction: all the fun without the commitment, all the intensity without the baggage, all the sex without the responsibility. When Jesse returned, she'd say goodbye and return to her hotel...but he would probably be expecting that.

Within half an hour, the door opened and in walked the devastating smile that always took her breath away, and, removing his jacket and throwing it on the chair, Jesse picked her up and spun her around. How could she resist him? "Do you know how sexy you are, Jesse? Do you know what you do to us poor, defenceless women?" He laughed provocatively… or maybe he just laughed but, intentionally or not, it was irresistible. Abbie wrapped her legs round him as he tasted the lips he'd been pining for all morning and, feeling that delightful bulge in his trousers, her resolve weakened and her earlier determination flew out of the very window that had warmed her and led to such a rash decision, but as he pushed her against the wall, unfastened his belt and trousers, and gently manoeuvred himself inside her, she realised she'd be mistaken – her departure was not what he was expecting. Teasing her with his mouth, he watched for her reaction, waiting for her demands, aware of her immediate desperation as she wriggled her hips to feel the most from his cock.

"C'mon, Jesse, don't play with me." She bit his lip, holding his gaze and imploring a more congenial rhythm. Amused by her inexorability, he obeyed her silent intimation, delivering her preferred approach as his mouth devoured hers, his tongue searching, needing to connect with hers. She smiled. He knew her well, knew what she wanted, what she *needed* and always gave it to her, never failing her and never leaving her wanting; she was always excited and always fulfilled. There had been no shortage of men over the years, but none had made her feel quite like Jesse; his dick was like a magnet for her pussy, for her mouth, too, and she was incapable of abstention…until Joe's sudden and unexpected interest had educed a new yearning, and although his reputation dictated he'd satisfied his curiosity, hers raged…but she would miss Jesse – his body, his touch, his exploratory tongue, and that luscious cock, and as it concluded its final assault, she held her breath focussing on the contiguity of every part of his body. Slowly and carefully, he put her down and redressed himself, and although the smile was there, there was sadness and resignation in his eyes.

As she straightened her clothing, he found the remaining provisions and routed through to counter the nausea that he hoped was a lack of sustenance, coupled with the exertion of his welcome back and, with less resolve than Abbie, he washed it down with the remnants of the previous night's alcohol.

With one hunger slaked, he wandered back to her and took her hand. "I know you have to go, Abbie, and I know, no matter what you say, things will change, but don't lose touch…" Before he could finish, she kissed him passionately, running her hand down his stomach. He smiled as he ran his hands down her back. "Christ, Abbie, I'm going to need a little more time!"

Laughing, she had other ideas. "You know, you could always join us…"

His eyes narrowed as he struggled with comprehension. "Join you for what?"

She smiled provocatively, hoping to elicit a full understanding; as he studied her face he laughed loudly at the absurdity of her thoughts. Unperturbed by his unexpected reaction, she kissed him teasingly, as her fingers crept under his belt trying to persuade him to think a little more. "What's so funny?"

With a genuine belief that she was joking, he was surprised to find he was mistaken. "Are you serious? What, you want me to take part in a threesome with you and Joe? No way, *no* way! Sorry, Abbie, really not my thing!"

"How do you know – have you tried it?"

"No. But you know what, I haven't tried jumping out of a plane without a parachute, and I'm not about to give that a go either!"

With such an unreasonable comparison, she was unwilling to give up and tried her sexiest voice. "But I'd do it for you…" She kissed him again as her hand caressed his crotch. "You asked the waitress to stay last night and I didn't complain…"

"Yeah, well, that was different." Very different.

"Why's that, Jesse, because it's what you wanted?"

"No, because I don't do blokes!"

"Well, I don't do women, but you didn't stop to ask me last night when you invited that girl to join us! Don't be so bloody pig-headed, Jesse!" She unbuttoned his shirt, stroked his chest and gently pulled at his nipple. "You know I would have happily played with that girl last night, while you watched; I would have kissed her and touched her...anything you wanted...so why can't you think about it for me..." Licking his tongue, she could feel his erection, aroused by the images she'd just described, images she would have liked to convert if she'd had the chance, but only if he was prepared to repay her kindness...

He pushed her down on the sofa, tore open her dress and quickly unfastened his trousers before thrusting his cock inside her, imagining the waitress in her place whilst Abbie watched. With a conceited smile, Abbie allowed his fantasy to play out in his mind for a while before playing on his aroused senses to persuade him to reconsider. "Are you fucking me, Jesse, or the waitress?" She kissed him aggressively. "She tastes good doesn't she? Fuck her hard...that's what she wants...that's what I want. Make her come...I want to watch you..." Aroused by her own commentary, she regretted Kate's departure..."But Joe could watch as you make me come; he could see how hard you fuck me, and when you come, he could take over while you watch. Wouldn't you like that...Jesse?" Hearing his name again, he exploded violently inside her, fuelled by her words and the images she'd initially engendered. Trembling, he collapsed on top of her, his mind littered with some very disturbing pictures.

She kissed his hair and stroked his back as he slowly gathered enough strength to remove himself from her body.

"You OK?" With an innocent smile, she looked at him, but didn't really need an answer.

Impressed by her strategy, he smiled, tracing her ribs, moving ever-closer to her breasts. "Was that your plan, Abbie; get me so horny, I'd agree to your suggestion? I have to hand it to you, you did a bloody good job!" His finger moved up between her breasts to her face, and rested on her lips, gently prising them apart, forcing its way inside.

She licked it before gently biting the tip, and as he removed it and gently ran it along her bottom lip, she tried again. "Well, it would be fun; you wouldn't have to touch Joe, if you didn't want to…I wouldn't mind if you did, but…" She smiled devilishly. "You can leave all the touching to me if you want…and all the stroking…all the sucking…"

He returned her smile but refused to commit, despite her perseverance. "That's enough! Get up – you're leaving!" He man-handled her off the sofa, buttoned her dress and grabbed her bag, as she protested like a prisoner on death-row.

Kissing him softly, she stopped his game and hoped she would leave a lasting impression that would encourage him to rethink his stance. "Thank you for a wonderful time, Jesse. You've worn me out…but it was worth it. I'll probably sleep for the rest of the week, and hopefully have some very sweet dreams…of you…and me…and Joe…" She kissed him again, reluctant to let him go.

"I want to be in every one of them, Abbie and you can tell me all about them when I see you next, but you can spare me the ones about Joe." Kissing her neck, he pulled her close, conscious that if she stayed much longer, he wouldn't let her go and that when she was gone and his memories created another stirring in his groin, he was on his own. He sought a safer path. "Let me know what the coroner says, please, and when you finalise the funeral details. If there's anything I can do, make sure you phone me, OK? Good luck with Joe…but be careful, yeah?" He hugged her tight, breathing in her scent, feeling the curve of her breasts against his chest and, for a moment, felt tempted to pick her up and carry her to the bed, but the inevitable conclusion would have to arise and that would only prolong the agony.

Sensing his indecision, she pulled away, stroked his face and picked up her bag before reaching for the door. As she opened it, she turned and kissed him for the last time and couldn't resist a final grope of his crotch. Jesse, caught completely unawares, groaned deeply and smiled before closing the door behind her and, heading straight for the shower, his smile disappeared.

13

After lying low for a few days, catching up on some sleep, and easing up on the drinking, Joe thought about how to fill his day. Knowing he'd over-stepped the mark with Rose, he felt an apology was probably in order; besides, she was his only link to Abbie currently, so prudence was necessary. As he dialled her number, he smiled, recalling how close he'd come to fucking her and he knew had he persevered, she would have caved, but no matter how pissed off he was with Abbie, fucking Rose? He probably wouldn't come back from that. "Hey, Rosie, how are you?"

"Morning, Joe."

"I've missed you, missed your voice…and your touch…and feeling you so close…we were so close Rosie, so close, but you rejected me. You know it'll only make me want you more…"

"I can see you had a good night…" Although still somewhat concerned about their encounter, Rose knew his motives were superficial and driven by his unacknowledged fear, and she held no grievance.

"Do you want to hear about it, Rosie? I can tell you over the phone, but it would arouse you too much and I wouldn't want to leave you in that state, alone…so why don't you come over and I'll show you…" Jesting or not, it was a nice idea.

"Thank you, Joe, but I'll pass…this time…" His games she was happy to indulge in…anything else was a little too perilous.

"Ooh, Rosie, you tease: I like that; I can't wait 'til the next time."

"OK, Joe, aside from propositioning me, what do you want, my darling? As lovely as this conversation has been, I do have other things to do."

He laughed. "I thought I should apologise for my behaviour the other day – I was out of order. Abbie had really pissed me off…and Ed… It was all a little too much, I'm sorry."

Impressed by his sincerity, she had to admit that, even in apologising, this man was damn sexy. *Wake up, Abbie…* "That's OK, I know it's been tough."

"You do know that if you'd let me, I would have fucked you and if I ever get the chance again…"

Laughing, and ignoring the temptation, she felt now was a good time to terminate his flirtation. "Joe, you've just completely wiped out your apology."

"I can't lie…"

"Well, thank you. I appreciate your honesty."

Changing tack, he needed some honesty from her. "Have you spoken to her, Rose? Do you know where she is?"

She sighed. "Yes, my love, I have spoken to her and I know where she is. She's fine…she was quite upbeat, actually, which surprised me rather…"

"Is she coming back? I know she's got to come back for the funeral, but after that?"

"I think so; I don't know for sure, but judging by her mood, she'll be home soon. She got your message…"

"Good…that's good." Finally, a smattering of relief from the uncertainty of late. "So, my darling Rosie, what are your plans for the day? I'm free if you fancy something dirty; just say where and when…"

"Tell me, Joe, why did you apologise?"

"For failing to fuck you when you quite clearly wanted me to…"

"Ah, that was it…now get off the phone before I call the police!"

Ending the call, he smiled; if she was wrong, and Abbie didn't come home, he would make good his promise, whether she wanted him to or not.

***

Whilst Abbie had never questioned Joe about his mother, or what his father had done, unbeknown to her, Rose had approached him when he was fifteen and had just seen his father for the last time. She'd noticed that Christmas that he was different: happier, less troubled, more carefree and, fearing the worst – drugs, alcoholism – she'd enquired – away from Abbie and delicately, she'd hoped – what had prompted the change. Joe, still revelling in his conquest of Carl and, indeed, his father, and fuelled slightly by a couple of glasses of champagne, told her he'd beaten the bastard! Unwilling to dampen his spirit, she'd asked him to pop round when he was free to explain what he'd meant and, surprisingly, he'd agreed. A week later, he'd dropped by and spent three hours revealing the truth of his early life, the sadness of losing his mother and the torture of living with his abusive excuse for a father, without expression, without emotion, and, astonishingly, without malice. She'd cried openly, yet hidden her anger well, but his sexual confessions had shocked her tremendously! His reputation, at fifteen, was well established, but she hadn't realised how many of the rumours were, in fact, true and, concealing her surprise, she'd listened without judgement but with genuine concern, and he was extremely grateful. When he'd finished his tale, she'd hugged him tight, hoping to love away some of his pain and promised she would always be available if he needed a shoulder, but he swore her to secrecy and no amount of coaxing could persuade him to confide in Abbie; she was the only person to love him since his mother died and he would do nothing to jeopardise that, convinced, as he was, that revealing his father's true nature would impact on their relationship.

Rose had tried again. "She won't condemn you, Joe. She loves you – you know that – and she knows what a bastard your father was. Christ, she was the one that took you away from it all." But he'd threatened to leave if she was ever told and Rose had calmed him with sincere reassurances that she would keep her mouth shut. Watching him leave shortly afterwards, she'd cried again for most of the night and when Michael returned, she'd sobbed uncontrollably, unable to communicate with him for the first half-hour. Keeping her promise, she'd never told Abbie and Joe never discussed it again, though he felt safe knowing she was there.

Recalling that evening, Joe thought about his home, the home that had only ever been a home when his mother was alive; the same home that had become hell the moment she died. Always aware of his father's contempt, when his mother was around it was immaterial for her love was all-consuming and unconditional; the kicks and occasional punches were bearable because he had her, but without her comfort, without her love – enough love to heal his broken world – it was tough, really tough, and without her there, life just wasn't worth the effort. Inventing ways to end his own life had become a way of passing the endless hours, locked in his room, and in the three weeks before he'd met Eddie, he'd planned two methods in the hope that one would succeed and was waiting for half-term, when his father would kick him out of the house every day, to try them out. But then Eddie arrived and everything changed.

Smiling at the memories of his friend and the fear Eddie had felt on the one occasion he'd met his father, he felt a strong urge to visit the house, to see how it differed as an adult. Was it still as menacing or was it just the perception of the fragile mind of a disturbed seven-year-old, grieving the loss of the mother he would gladly have died for himself? Without time to reconsider, he grabbed his keys, jumped in the car and drove slowly, trying vainly to calm the nervousness that filled his stomach as it had daily in the four years before Eddie had found him, and had remained a constant for the first six months at Abbie's, convinced as he was that she would change her mind, or that his father would demand his slave be returned. As he drew closer, he could hear his mother's voice, her laugh, and he could smell her, as he had when she'd hugged him tight, squeezing love into him, and as his father tried to force his way back into those memories, Joe blocked him, refused him any time, any space, as the man had refused him for his entire childhood. Pulling up a few doors away, he faltered – was this really a good idea? Whilst sensitivity was not a trait he usually associated with, the past few days had been an emotional whirlwind that he had constantly fought, but this could very easily see him defeated, forcing him to face his younger self and see the damage that his mother's death had caused, that could have been minimised, and quite possibly repaired, had the father he'd been given had any idea what the appellation bestowed upon him really meant; see the fear that was a part of his being and the guilt that was ever-present but had no foundation and no right to control the child that it did. Despite his mother's love, it was his father who had dictated his preference to remain single, to never settle, to never have a family. He had killed Joe's ability to feel, to love and to allow himself to be loved. Yes, Eddie and Abbie had been exceptions, but there was still a distance, a detachment, a buffer that he'd instinctively, yet unintentionally, put in place to protect him from ever enduring such emotional mutilation again. He needed Abbie, but he needed to fuck her, needed to control her…needed to own her. Love? Well that just didn't feature.

Getting out of the car, finally, he walked to the gate and saw, like ghosts, himself with Eddie, running out of the house as if being chased and Abbie closing the door behind them, on the life that had shaped him and the memories, both good and bad, that he'd buried that day. Lost, again, in a world full of dread, anxiety and blame, he could feel his heart beat faster as the front door opened, and he gasped – regardless of his knowledge – as a stranger appeared, instead of a foul-mouthed, alcohol-sodden, skeletal sneer. "Can I help you?" He took a while to recover. "Hello?"

"Yes, sorry, hi. I was just…I used to live here, a long time ago, and as I was passing, I thought I'd just drop by and relive some old memories. Sorry if I startled you." His smile was enough to halt any rumblings of hostility.

"Oh…hi! No, that's fine. I thought you looked a little familiar…" He felt slightly nervous: he didn't recognise the face smiling at him, why was he known to her? "When we moved in we found loads of stuff in the loft: old photos, school reports and baby clothes – do you want to come in? We kept them just in case."

He froze. Not only was he being invited into his prison, he was being offered physical memories; possessions that he was completely unaware of, that could bring him closer to his mother, to the only thing he had ever truly loved, the only thing that had ever truly hurt him, and he wasn't sure he could deal with it.

Sensing his indecision, the kind stranger smiled and tried to encourage him. "I don't bite…"

Now, detecting a note of flirtatiousness, he agreed.

He was immediately struck by the different smell. Having barely bathed in the four years he was under his father's control, he was fastidious about cleanliness, both personal and in his apartment, and now, this house was fragrant, flowery and finally pleasant.

"Come through. I'm Eva, by the way."

Registering what she'd said, Joe stopped and stared intently at his host but managed to bounce back rather swiftly. "Sorry – Eva, did you say? That was my mother's name…and she was pretty, like you; I'm Joe." Shaking her hand gently, he held on a little longer than necessary.

She smiled and led him through to the lounge, offering him a seat as she filled the kettle. "Tea or coffee?"

"Coffee, please. Are you sure this is no trouble?"

"Of course! My husband moans constantly about keeping somebody else's stuff, but I've got kids so I know how important these things are to mums. Milk, sugar?"

"No thanks – black." Relieved the house was unrecognisable, he surveyed the room, picturing various altercations with his father and the television that he wasn't allowed to touch, and the night he told his father about Carl. He smiled, still able to feel the victory he'd secured that night, enjoying the disgust and fear in the old man's face…the last time he'd ever had to suffer it.

Eva returned with drinks. "There you go; I'll just nip upstairs and get your stuff."

"Do you need a hand?" His smile divulged his intentions and she accepted his offer.

The stairs were narrower but firmer than he recalled, and full of light – he couldn't remember any light. His life with Abbie and Eddie was full of colour, all summer days and barbeques and parties; here, it had been winter for four whole years, but winter without Christmas. Walking into the master bedroom was a completely new experience. He'd been forbidden to enter by his captor and, although his mother had always allowed him to sneak in and cuddle up in bed, he couldn't remember the room, only the feeling of being so close to her.

Eva removed two boxes from her wardrobe, placed them on the bed and sat down, expecting Joe to start rummaging, but he was wary of the consequences. "Would you mind if I took them home? I fear I may get a little emotional and that's not something you'd want to see." She smiled, slightly disappointed.

Moving the boxes to the floor, he sat down beside her, perceiving her anticipation. "How long have you lived here,

Eva?" He studied her face closely, enjoying her discomfort and excitement at his presence.

"About three years now. We love it; it has a nice feel about it." She avoided his gaze, alarmed at the ease with which he'd charmed her, and regretted her actions, though not enough to prompt a renunciation.

"And where's your husband?" Turning slightly, he moved closer and gently stroked her hair.

"Um…he's at work…" She could feel her heart thumping. "Should be home around six…"

"That's lucky." He kissed her softly, listening to her unconscious sighs.

"Joe…I'm not sure…"

"Shh. I am, Eva. Very sure." As he kissed her again, he took her hand, placed it on his crotch and rubbed gently. "See…"

She gasped and surrendered, mesmerised by his scent, and his touch…and his cock; she didn't care where he put it, so long as it was inside her. Laying her down, he slowly removed her clothes and studied her underwear, electing, as always, to leave it in place; Eva, less patient, longed to feel his skin against hers and undressed him fully – amusing him with her desperation – and rubbed his dick against her pussy, eager yet reticent, closing her mind to the betrayal she was powerless to preclude. Sitting up, Joe pushed her underwear to one side and pulled her onto his cock, studying her face. "What's your husband's name, Eva?"

She opened her eyes, surprised at the question. "Gary."

He smiled. "Does Gary know what you do when he's at work? Does he know you invite strangers into your home and fuck them?" Ashamed of her behaviour, she couldn't deny the parallel excitement. "Do you think he'd like it? Would he like what I'm doing to you, would he want to watch us?" With a mordant laugh, he whispered, "Would you like him to…?"

Smiling in agreement, she visualised the scene he was creating for her but suppressed her response; she was content to listen and continue with the performance in her mind but conversation was unnecessary.

He attacked her mouth whilst pulling her down hard, deeply imbedding himself inside her. Tightening his jaw, he adopted a more violent motion and she winced slightly, serving only to encourage him. "Joe, you're hurting me."

With an accomplished objective, he sneered; he had no intention of pacification. "That's the risk you take when you fuck a stranger, Eva." Pushing harder still, he looked for her distress. "Does that hurt, is that good?"

Panic pervaded her and she seriously considered whether she would survive this encounter. "No, it's not. I don't like it."

He laughed. "I do." He held her hips tight, restricting her escape, revelling in the pain he was inflicting in his attempt to eradicate the pain he had felt in this god-forsaken house. It may have had a make-over, it may have had new life breathed into it, but underneath all that superficial embellishment, it was still the hell-hole that had shaped him and this was his chance to avenge that injustice, in his own perverse way.

Eva whimpered with her discomfort, but rather than impede him, it aroused him, and as he came, he pushed harder still, until he could go no further, and groaned triumphantly as his cock throbbed. Slowly, he became aware of the change in her manner. Continuing to hold her, he waited for her to move but she remained and, enjoying her distress for a little longer, he finally released her and watched as she removed herself and self-consciously covered her body. He grabbed his clothes and dressed slowly, all the while looking at her, satisfied with his work.

He picked up the boxes as she sat nervously on the bed and, leaning towards her, he kissed her cheek. "Thank you for making me very welcome." His mocking tone faded as he became more serious. "And thank you for keeping these boxes; they mean more to me than you could possibly imagine. But please do me one more favour: leave this house; sell up and move as far away as possible because it will destroy you. The evil here cannot be covered up with pretty pictures and cushions; if you value your marriage – and think you do – forget about today and go and be happy with your family somewhere else. You don't deserve the malevolence concealed within these walls." He walked back down the stairs, picturing the eleven-year-old boy bounding down before his father could change his mind, and lingered at the door, closed his eyes and sealed those memories for the last time. Leaving the house, he didn't look back; he placed the boxes on the backseat and drove away without a second glance.

Stopping at the supermarket on the way home, he grabbed some lunch and a couple of bottles of wine, feeling the need should he spend the afternoon engrossed in the boxes he'd just retrieved. Eva had, thankfully, lightened his mood enough to enable him to at least open them and he hoped the wine would facilitate the rest, and back at his apartment, he sat down with a bottle and a glass and lifted a lid, scared that uncovering these memories would evaporate them before he'd had the chance to experience them, but as he stared at the undisturbed contents, he could feel his mother again, feel her arms surrounding him, holding him tight, helping him through this moment. As he peered in, he was hit by the sudden rush of nostalgia, remembering a time before she died; a time he'd not visualised since that harrowing day, and he smiled and cried and laughed as he picked through the collection of odd items that she'd kept: his favourite story about a dog called 'Bonkers'; his school reports; his first socks; his beloved cuddly kitten, Jasper, who his father had insisted on removing when he was six – "He's too old to have a cuddly toy now, for Christ's sake." – but who Joe had longed for the night his mother died, needing the comfort he'd always provided; his nursery Sports Day rosettes; all the cards he'd ever made: Mother's Day, Christmas, birthday; and photos – so many photos – of him, some with his mother, a few of her alone and two with his father. He studied them and very carefully tore off the intruder, found his lighter and watched both of them burn, before carefully replacing the remnants back in the box. There were photos of his grandparents too – *grandparents* – he had no idea he had any. And, finally, he discovered a small baby diary. Pausing before opening it, he opted for more wine and a cigarette first, in the hope they would calm, if not numb, his senses. Slowly turning the pages, the tears fell freely, threatening to smudge the affectionate leaves, filled with observations, comments and footnotes, all of which were filled with more love than he would ever have expected, such was the time without. His mother's love was once unmistakable and he knew he was her world, but the devotion and the emotion contained in her words was overwhelming; the passion, the generosity and the sheer joy of having a child emanated in a way he was totally unaccustomed to and it moved him immeasurably, piercing his defences simultaneously. Battling the uncontrollably sentimentality, he whispered, desperate to connect with her just one more time, "I love you too, Mum." He replaced the diary, closed the lid and downed his glass. The second box would have to wait for another time.

Calming himself with more wine, he reached for his phone, ready for a night out. "Hey, Mark, how's it going?"

"Hey, man. Christ, I was just going to call you! How ya been?"

"Yeah, good. Need a night out though, you free tomorrow?"

"Yeah, yeah, sounds good; I'll speak to the lads and we'll make it about eight, yeah? Do you want to eat there…is Mike doing food?"

"I'll check with him but should be OK. Let me know numbers, yeah? See you tomorrow. Cheers, mate."

"Yep, will do. Speak to you later."

Before calling to check food availability, Joe showered;

he hadn't spoken to Mike since they'd fucked and he was interested to see how he'd respond. "Hey, Mike, how you doing?"

"Joe, hi! Yeah, good, you?"

"Yeah, good, thanks."

"It's been a busy week here; you've missed a lot of opportunities…"

Joe laughed. "Well, why the hell didn't you call me?"

"Never know what you're up to…or who!" No animosity; not his style.

"Fair point! We're coming over tomorrow night, around eight. Are you cooking? Probably a good idea to soak up some of that alcohol you insist we buy."

"Yeah…I've got to sustain this lifestyle somehow. No worries, how many of you, Joe?"

"Don't know for sure yet, but probably the seven of us, unless James wants to bring his girlfriend: let's hope he's not that foolish."

"Yeah, that's fine. Just let me know as soon as, yeah?"

"Will do, see you later."

"See ya, Joe."

Putting down his phone, Joe stared at the unopened box, inevitably torn between further investigations into his past and ignoring it. Another glass of wine and another smoke aided the decision-making process, and sure enough, cigarette extinguished, glass half-drained, the lid was removed. Beneath the carefully placed tissue paper was a pile of neatly folded clothes, each in its own tissue envelope, with its own photo, details of his age, weight and height, and the date it was first worn. There was the tiny sleep-suit he'd left the hospital in; his first Christmas outfit, with a tiny little hat; a set of clothes for every birthday; his first, second, third – in fact, every pair of shoes he'd owned before his mother died; his first school uniform, including PE kit and school shoes; his Beavers uniform – only worn for a year – with all badges neatly sewn on to the sweatshirt, and two pairs of swimming shorts with their associated badges. At the bottom of the box were certificates, Head Teacher awards, trophies and rosettes that he'd long forgotten, and another diary only partially filled. His mother's words, again, were full of pride, love, understanding and praise, and he could hear her voice as he read and reread her comments and observations, closing his eyes to visualise her just once more and feel the force behind every hug as she endeavoured to confirm, if she ever needed to, how much she cherished her only child.

Folding each little piece of clothing and placing it carefully back in its envelope, he smiled, commending the decision to make the journey to the disregarded happy home that had lost its will to his father – rendering it the epitome of hell – and retrieved this hidden treasure. Eva had been a welcome support and, if she hadn't enticed him inside, he would undoubtedly have left and never unearthed these precious memories, though she would, understandably, underestimate her role. He became hard just thinking about her, but that brought about its own dilemma; immediate solitary relief or the wait for the soft touch of an, as yet, unknown female companion – why, the latter, of course!

A quick splash of water and he crossed to The Well. It was already busy, which boded well, but alcoholic sustenance was needed before deciding his prey.

"Hi, Joe, wasn't expecting you 'til tomorrow. Usual?"

"Yeah, thanks, Mike. Fancied a little company."

Mike spread his arms wide. "Well, you've come to the right place, my friend!"

Surveying the bar, Joe homed in on a small group of ladies in the far corner; he'd start there, but firstly, he'd need some nourishment. "I'll have a burger, Mike, if it's OK…"

"Yeah, course, give me a minute. Any particular female you'd like served with that?" He winked as he headed for the kitchen.

Minutes later, Joe had company. "Excuse me, do I know you?"

Studying the face beside him and deciding to pass, he replied, "Well, surely, you would know that." His sarcasm appeared, unfortunately, to be lost on his companion.

"Yeah: did you used to work at 'Bluebells'?" Joe nearly choked! 'Bluebells' was a club in the centre of town, best known for its alcohol-free stimulants and frequent police raids; a club he'd never entertained...though Eddie may well have done.

"No, I'm afraid not – not my style."

She laughed. "What, too good for the 'Bells'?"

"Yes. Absolutely." Impatience had triumphed.

"Alright, prick!" She sauntered off, shocked at her failure.

Laughing, he returned to his drink as dinner was served. "You want to watch her, mate; mouth like a sewer and the undercarriage ain't much better!"

"And how exactly would you know that?"

"I have my sources…"

"Sources or methods? If I'd known that before the other night, I may have reconsidered…"

Mike smiled. "No you wouldn't." With disregarded chauvinism, they proceeded to work their way through the bar, grading the women and a few of the men, as Joe attempted to finish his meal.

Mike refreshed his drink and as he removed Joe's plate, another female tried her luck. "Do you want to share the joke?" Her smile was naturally provocative and Joe was pleased he'd not had to wait too long.

"Always happy to share. What did you have in mind…?"

"Lillie. I hadn't thought that far, any suggestions?"

His smile disclosed more than his words, but to ensure he was clear, he leaned in close. "Oh, I have many suggestions, Lillie – would you like to hear them all, or shall I recommend the best ones?" He held her gaze, waiting for a response.

"Well, let's start with your recommendations and take it from there, shall we…?"

"Joe. Absolutely; here, or would you like a little privacy? I'm easy; I don't mind a crowd…"

Slightly shocked, she waited for the punchline, but it was conspicuously absent. "You're not suggesting right here?" His eyes didn't falter and his expression remained unchanged. Lillie laughed. "Well, I'm impressed by your confidence, Joe, but I think it's a little too public; let's try a little privacy."

Taking her hand, he signalled to Mike and watched his grin spread as he left with his prize. "I live across the road – is that private enough?"

"Yep, that'll do."

Closing the door quietly behind them, he fetched glasses and wine from the kitchen as Lillie reviewed the surroundings. "Are these family photos or girlfriends?" Not a jealous enquiry, more a reluctance to exploit his hospitality with the faces of prior conquests surrounding her.

"Family, and don't worry, they don't judge." Handing her a glass, he sat down and waited for her to join him. As she studied the room, he studied her figure, content with its form and, as she took her time, he could feel his dick becoming restive. "Have you seen enough?"

Spinning round, she smiled and, walking seductively towards him, slowly removed her dress, allowing it to drop to the floor. His eyes followed its progress before returning to its carrier and analysing what lay beneath. Abandoning her glass, she removed his and straddled him, feeling the hardness imprisoned in his jeans and, unbuttoning his shirt, she kissed him tentatively, placing his hand on her breast, squeezing gently whilst grinding hard on his cock. He responded aggressively, his tongue searching for hers, and pulled her down firmly. Her ill-concealed conceit flickered in her eyes, confident in the knowledge that she was responsible for what lurked below her pussy, and resolved to make him wait until she was ready; Joe, however, had other ideas and as he continued to squeeze her breast, he found her hand and ran it down his stomach, to his belt, but she resisted, choosing instead to stroke his chest and take her time and, unaccustomed to subservience, Joe's intolerance escalated and he pulled her closer, prising her hands from his chest. Uncomfortable with his response, she attempted, unsuccessfully, to pull away, but he found her hand, guided it to where it belonged and spoke quietly in her ear, "My suggestions, remember?" Intimidated by his menacing tone, she obeyed and gently removed his cock from his jeans whilst he watched her face and, satisfied she'd fulfilled her obligation, he pushed her back, forcing her to hold on, his jaw tense as he bypassed her underwear and drove his cock deep inside her. He propelled her hips towards him, affording a deeper penetration, pummelling her and appreciating the movement of her breasts, barely encased in their lacy enclosure, eager for either to break free, allowing a little extra stimulation for his tongue. Removing her hands from his legs, he placed one on her breast, gently encouraging her to massage and aid its escape, whilst he fed the other into her underwear, prompting her masturbation. Now relaxed, she was keen to see his reaction to her hands on her own body and as she watched him closely, as he did her, she was rewarded with the start of his climax. His thrusting became more violent, but she was unconcerned – her manipulation of his excitement would make him come.

"Harder, Joe. Make me come…"

Closing his eyes, he responded correctly, pushing her further back and himself deeper. "You want more, Abbie; you want it harder?" He opened his eyes and smiled as his words registered with her.

"What the fuck…?" But she'd got what she wanted.

He shuddered as he filled her with cum and sat still, feeling the throb of his cock and the glow of his face. "Thank you, Lillie."

"You bastard!"

As she raised her hand to strike him, he caught it, gripping her wrist tight. "You want to play rough?" He pushed her to the floor, lay on her and kissed her crudely, removing her breast with one hand, as the other pushed inside her. Her efforts to wriggle free were futile; he was too heavy and his hands restrained her, but she continued, determined to demonstrate her resolve. Removing his tongue from her mouth, he wrapped it around her nipple and sucked hard, as the other hand, wet from her cum-infused pussy, found its way into her mouth.

She pulled away. "Joe, don't, please."

He looked at her face and sneered. "But I'm not done, Lillie…and you wanted my recommendations." Shoving his hand inside her again, he devoured her mouth, revelling in the struggle he could feel below him, inflaming both his desire and derision and, as he moved his mouth to her ear, he began to lick before whispering softly, "Whilst I'm enjoying the feel of you writhing around beneath me…" He took her hand and folded it around his dick, sighing at her touch. "You won't get away until I let you and I haven't finished with you." He covered her hand, persuading more participation, and closed his eyes, visualising Abbie, hearing her sensual voice and her commanding words, wanking him until he came over her hand and she licked it clean. A little disappointed at Lillie's eventual submission, he focussed on his fantasy – the captivating scent that aroused him whenever Abbie was close; her touch, her wet pussy – and, as illusions and reality competed, the welcome growth of his cock rewarded his perseverance and he rolled off Lillie, pulled her head down to his crotch and rammed his cock to the back of her throat, controlling his own pleasure as she refused to participate, which, unwittingly increased his enjoyment, and within minutes he felt the surge of his climax vindicate his decision, groaning loudly and holding her still until the throbbing subsided. Feeling the tension in her body, he opened his eyes and released her, smiling victoriously as he buttoned his jeans. "I thought you'd be a little more adventurous, Lillie…"

She found her dress, and pulling it up quickly, she scowled at him. "So you remember my name? Who the fuck's Abbie?" Pointing at the photos she turned on him again. "Is that her?"

He laughed. "Why does that matter? You wanted to fuck me and you wanted to make me come; you did."

"But I didn't, she did! You fucked her, not me." With nothing to lose, she played his game. "Doesn't she want you, Joe? Not man enough for her?"

His face slowly contorted into a sneering grimace and his eyes narrowed. "I've been fucking her since I was twelve years old. Every woman, every man, every wank, every blow-job has been Abbie but, when she's not around, I need someone else to fill my time, and that, Lillie, is why you're here. You're a fill-in, a temporary replacement; you're just one step up from a wank, but a most pleasant one."

Incensed by her defeat and unnerved by his confession, she reached for the door, but Joe, amused by her impudence, grabbed her arm before she could leave, drawing her close and pulling her arms tight behind her back. "Please don't worry about my credentials. Abbie, like you, is very happy wherever I put my dick and even more so when I made her come, again… and again…and again…"

As Lillie fought to free her arms, she smiled smugly at him. "Well, you didn't make me come."

Returning her smile, he looked deep in to her eyes. "That's because you're not worth it."

Finally wrenching herself from his grip, she flung the door open wide and marched out.

Closing it quietly behind her, he finished his wine and hers, grabbed his keys and wandered back to The Well, updating Mike on his progress. "I'm going to lose all my female customers if you carry on like that!" Taking a more serious tone, he questioned

Joe, "Don't any of them mean anything to you? Don't worry, I'm not fishing, I just wonder what it'll take to make you settle down."

Charmed by his concern, Joe smiled. "She knew what she was getting in to, Mike – why should I be worried? If you proposition a stranger in a bar, you take a risk, but next time she might not be so lucky; she had no idea what I would do. If I had any desire to hurt her, she wouldn't have stood a chance, yet she's happy to go to my home without knowing a thing about me – that's fucking insane…but I'm not complaining." He sipped his drink. "Anyway, why do I need to settle down? Didn't you try that?"

"Yeah, good point. But you've had a more than your fair share, Joe. There must be someone you want to see again, spend more time with…" Joe's smile waned as he nursed his drink, but Mike's inquisition was incomplete. "Abbie?"

Slowly raising his eyes, Joe considered his response. "You know she's not here. She left and I told you: I have no idea if she's coming back."

"But if she does…?"

"Why are you so concerned, Mike?" With unambiguous impatience, he finished his drink and, thankfully, Mike knew when to stop.

"Well, I just wondered if she might like a threesome."

14

Joe woke early and went for a run. He couldn't remember the last time he had and could feel the difference but persevered and, after a considerable time, found himself outside Abbie's house. He paused, suddenly overwhelmed with evocations of the time he'd spent here and he struggled for breath. Sitting down, he closed his eyes and battled with the memories, blocking the images and stabilising his breathing, and as he was about to resume his run, his phone rang.

"Hey, Mark, how ya doing?"

"You OK, man. You sound out of breath…"

"Yeah, just been for a run. Christ, I'm out of shape!"

"Yeah, it shows!" If that was out of shape, Mark would have liked the recipe. "Well, all the guys are coming tonight but…"

"But…?"

"They want to bring their girlfriends!"

Joe laughed. "Girlfriends – who? I thought James was the only one tied down."

"Well, the last time we met at The Well, they all got lucky, so you and I are the only sad bastards now…well, Jamie, too, but he'd settle for either one of us, I think. Do you want to toss for him? Not literally…well, he'd probably be quite happy…"

Giggling childishly, Joe was happy to forego Jamie. "He's all yours, Mark. I'll take my chances tonight. What the hell's got into them?"

"We're all getting older Joe, can't play around forever…"

"No, why's that? Happy families don't suit everyone, my friend."

"Yeah: you keep telling yourself that, Joe! She's out there somewhere…waiting to get her claws in to you; ready to tame you, to stop your sexual exploits; no more sleeping around; sex, what, once a week, if you're lucky?"

"Yeah, fuck that!" Marriage held nothing for Joe. The thought of a relationship bored him – what the hell was the point? "Not for me, Mark, but knock yourself out!"

"Yeah, yeah, we'll see!" Despite his taunting, he believed his friend. "So can you call Mike and book a table for eleven for, what, eight, eight-thirty?"

"Sure, I'll see you at seven, then, so we can drink to the sad, lonely bastards we are!"

"Now there's a plan! See you later…maybe a little later, but definitely before the others. I might crash at yours tonight…so long as you don't have any company…"

"Well, I don't mind, Mark. You're welcome to join us, but the chances are, I'll get lucky in the bar so no need to bring anyone home." Whilst there was an element of truth to his words, he knew Mark would be amused.

"Thanks, Joe, you're a true friend, despite what everyone says! See you later, and try not to kill yourself running, old man!"

"Cheers, mate. Your concern is touching!"

The run home was a little easier, helped by the appreciative glances from female passers-by, and as tempting as it was to thank them all for their attention, Joe wasn't sure he'd have time, settling instead for an equally sweaty fellow jogger, happy to divert to the woods. Recalling his nights with Molly, he bent his companion over a fallen tree and fucked her from behind, unimpressed at the lack of movement from her taught and toned flesh, though not enough, however, to affect his performance…it just took a little longer. A quick kiss in thanks and he was on his way, grateful to finally be home and in the shower.

A hearty breakfast was followed by a quick call to work to ensure nothing important had been missed, but he was reminded that his car was due for servicing today. "So why did no one call me before?"

"We didn't want to disturb you, darling. If you missed it, it wasn't the end of the world, but as you called in…" His extremely loyal PA, Laura, had threatened death to anyone who dared to contact him.

"OK, thanks, Laura."

"When are you back, sweetheart?"

"Monday. I can't face another week without you – it's been hell." He was fully aware of her devotion to him and treated her to the same courtesy he bestowed on any other female.

She laughed. "Stop it, Joe – you know I'll have a flush! Have a good weekend and I'll see you Monday…and try to behave yourself."

"Always. Love you."

"I know."

He thought carefully about the service: the garage was close to the hospital and, whilst he'd be happy never crossing that threshold again, Eddie was still there…and he missed him… dreadfully. Staring at his phone, completely undecided, he knew he probably wouldn't get another chance, so he dialled.

Shaking, he ended the call and sat down; he'd never been to the hospital alone and now he was going voluntarily to a place that held nothing but fear for him; a place that currently housed his dead friend, as it had his dead mother…but this would be the last time.

Grabbing his keys, he left and drove slowly to the garage, seeking a reason to return home; an incident to prevent him from reaching his destination but nothing occurred, and after leaving the car in the parking bay and leaving his keys with the garage manager, he walked towards the hospital again, unhurried, preparing himself for the anxiety that would follow, but pausing outside, he could feel the sweat running down his back and his temples, fighting to convince himself this was a good idea. Ignoring his fear, he continued, with the promise it would all be over soon.

As he was led to the familiar observation room, he took a few deep breaths before entering. Eddie still looked different…in fact, more so now, and that was wrong. He needed to see Eddie, not an impersonation or a caricature; Eddie. But that was gone, no more; this was the closest he was going to get, so either stay and make-do or leave and never again get this close. The shock hit him, and hard. He'd known Eddie longer than he hadn't and, despite his hatred of his habit, he had been a true friend – his only friend – for many years. Mark, Andy, James – they were great mates, as were the others, but none of them would ever be Eddie and he was, again, alone, like he had been at seven, but this time, he would remain so; the pain of losing love wasn't worth the joy of having it. Sex would always be available and that was all he needed. He kissed his finger and gently touched his friend's cheek, recoiling at the cold, stony feel. He thanked Eddie for saving him and giving him a life, wiped away his tears and left without looking back.

Leaving the hospital, he gasped, uncertain of the last time he'd breathed, and he headed for the nearest bar. Two shots later, and a slightly hazy mind, he wandered to a burger bar to soak up some of the medicine before attempting to drive home. One meal to eat in and another to go, and luckily, the car was still on the ramps when he returned. After finishing his second course, he felt stable enough to navigate the car safely and, having arrived in one piece, he closed the front door and curled up on the sofa, sleeping soundly for the rest of the afternoon.

Waking just after six, he jumped in the shower again and wondered about the evening to come; the boys had always been just that and the addition of girlfriends would take some getting used to. He was intrigued, however, to meet Matt's new partner. He hadn't forgotten the man's lack of respect for Abbie and felt duty-bound to return the favour in his own inimitable style… and that made him hard. Relieving himself beneath the hot water, he smiled at the possibilities the night would bring.

Dressed and looking divine, he removed his boxed memories to his wardrobe; if Mark decided to stay, that was a conversation he wasn't ready for. He checked the spare bed was fresh and left for The Well.

No sign of Mark, but Mike greeted him warmly. "Well, this'll be interesting, Joe – girlfriends in the mix…"

"Yep, that's why I'm here now. Mark and I are the only one's standing our ground, apart from Jamie, but he's gay…"

"You could be in luck then…"

"Don't push it…"

"Well, if you're not interested…"

"Go for it, my friend, you have my blessing."

"Thanks, Joe, that means a lot! Now start drinking and make me some money!"

Mark arrived soon after and, as the bar was quiet, the three men joked and drank, enjoying the temporary lack of females, yet willing their imminent arrival, hopefully, in considerable quantities. Joe hinted at Mike's interest in Jamie, but Mark, unfamiliar with his history, remained oblivious.

Slowly, the boys arrived: smart, well-behaved and accompanied. Introductions were made and Joe, having no one to impress, was already enjoying the freedom of being uncommitted, and having met Matt's girlfriend, Lucy, was convinced he'd have some fun.

Drinks were bought and table offered, and as they took their seats, Joe managed to place himself with Lucy to one side and Miles to the other; Mark, thankfully, was opposite. As Mike left menus the conversation flowed and, to Joe's surprise, the boys were beginning to relax. He exchanged pleasantries with Lucy, waiting until later to fully launch his attack. He was sure, however, that he'd already made an impression.

Meals ordered and several drinks consumed, the atmosphere was light despite the many references to their absent friend. As they began to eat, Joe turned to Lucy and smiled irresistibly. "Is that good? It smells amazing; I'm wondering whether I've ordered incorrectly."

"It is – would you like to try it?"

With a face full of innocence, he placed one hand on the back of Lucy's chair. "Would you mind?"

"No, not at all." She filled her fork and as she offered it to him, he leaned in close, slowly removing the contents, whilst holding her gaze, and heard that familiar, involuntary female gasp, that made Lucy blush.

Still watching her intently, he smiled. "You're right, it's absolutely delicious. I'll have that next time. Thank you, Lucy." He returned to his own plate, aware of her discomposure and Matt's hostile stare.

He chatted to Mark and Miles for the rest of the meal and when coffee was served, several of the boys left to smoke outside; Matt, luckily, was one of them and as he left, his eyes remained fixed on Joe. But once he was out of sight, Joe returned to Lucy, inching closer, feeling his arm brushing hers. "Did I hear you say you were in recruitment, Lucy?"

"Yeah, I work for Sullivan's, in town."

"And what do they specialise in?"

"Construction professionals: surveyors, project managers, architects, planners…"

"Well, that's good to know. I'm an architect – maybe you could find me a new position…"

Lucy seemed genuinely surprised. "Really? I didn't see you as an architect; I think of them as being boring and middle-aged."

Leaning slightly closer, he spoke quietly. "And how do you

think of me?" Observing her hesitation, he smiled. "Let me give you my card; if anything comes up, you can always call me." She could feel the weight of his stare as she fumbled for her purse. Matt had warned her about him, but he was mistaken: Joe was gorgeous and charming and he smelled glorious! But his proximity unnerved her and she was aware that he knew it. As she placed her bag back on the floor, Matt returned and kissed her gently, marking his territory – a warning to Joe that would go completely unheeded.

As coffee finished, Miles suggested a pool rematch, giving him another chance to thrash Matt; Matt, unwilling to be beaten and incapable of suppressing his competitive nature, accepted, accompanied by James and girlfriend Charlie, Andy, and Miles' girlfriend Zoe, but Lucy, however, declined, preferring to remain at the table, irritating her partner and amusing Joe. Mark watched him and, as Lucy visited the conveniences, he leaned towards him. "Be careful, mate."

Smiling, he feigned ignorance. "You know me, Mark…"

"Yeah, that's the problem; Matt will kill you."

"I don't think so."

Leaving the table, he loitered outside the ladies until he was sure Lucy was alone and, closing the door behind him, leaned against it, waiting for her to respond. As she checked her make-up in the mirror, she spotted him and jumped, feeing a sudden glow of anticipation. Turning round, she headed for the drier, smiling at him. "Are you lost?"

Walking towards her, he shook his head: "Nope." He pushed against her and walked her back towards the washbasins, kissing her gently before picking her up and sitting her on the edge. Her breathing already deep, when he pulled her towards his crotch, she gasped, amazed at the hardness of his cock.

"What if someone comes in?"

"Then we'll have an audience."

With her still wet hands already unbuckling his belt, she

was impatient for him, and whilst he pulled up her dress and adjusted her underwear, she pulled his dick towards her pussy, pushing it inside, allowing him the freedom to thrust hard. Closing her eyes, she lost herself in her earlier fantasy, spurred by his propinquity and subtle flirtation and, mirroring his movements, she maximised the thrill of his cock inside her. "I dreamt about you…"

Finding her tongue and tasting her excitement, he concluded, understandably, she'd enjoyed her dream. "Really, like this? Is that why you're so wet? That's good to hear. So did I, Lucy; I dreamt about your mouth round my cock, sucking until I came…" Sighing, she looked in his eyes and imagined herself as he had, her face nuzzled in his groin, savouring the taste of his sumptuous dick, tempted to try it now, but equally keen to continue as they were. She was awoken from her trance by the door opening and she buried her face in his chest, concealing her infidelity.

Joe turned to look at the welcome visitor. "Sorry, we won't be too long. Feel free to enjoy the show…or join us…" The shocked gate-crasher quickly retreated and he laughed.

Torn between being appalled and being aroused, Lucy settled on the latter, swayed by Joe's punishing rhythm and the onset of her own climax and, sensing its imminence, he instinctively pushed harder, inciting the velocity of his own, enriched by its instigator…and her duplicity for her oblivious, yet deserving boyfriend.

Allowing the satisfying throb to finish its routine, he was conscious that his desire to punish Matt negated the need for Abbie's involvement: revenge was most definitely sweet.

His distraction introduced a little reservation into Lucy's mind – is this what Matt meant? "You OK?"

Oh yes! With the devil in his eyes, he smiled. "Absolutely." He buckled his belt and helped her down. "I better get back before somebody notices." Kissing her softly, he returned to the table under the intense glare of Mark.

"Where the fuck have you been? Matt came back to find Lucy and found the pair of you missing. Tell me you didn't…"

Slapping him on the back, powerless to prevent his guilty smile, Joe leaned towards him. "But I would be lying, Mark, and I don't lie." He wandered to the bar to order more wine and was met by a frosty Mike.

"I assume it was you…?"

Stifling his amusement, Joe tried his best to look innocent. "Mike…"

"Joe! You have the cubicles, you have the back room; why do you need to do it in public?"

"Silly question, Mike, you know I like an audience…" Given their recent activities in this very bar, Mike's attitude was a little unexpected.

"Yeah, well, you better hope your 'audience' doesn't report me."

"Sorry, man. Would you like me to go and pacify her…?" Despite the potential seriousness of the situation, he'd exploit any opportunity.

With no real hope of penitence, Mike shook his head. "No thanks, mate, you've done enough damage; I've already asked her to come back at closing time and she agreed, so I'd appreciate you being nowhere near!"

As Joe reappeared at the table, Matt was talking to Lucy and was clearly furious. Before he could sit down, Matt was by his side. "Outside!" With eyes full of contempt, Joe ignored him, finding his seat and refilling his glass, but Matt persevered and, grabbing Joe's shirt, he raised his voice. "I said, outside!"

He looked at Matt's hand and back at Matt, his voice calm and controlled. "Let go of my shirt, Matt…"

Mark shot round the table, attempting to diffuse the situation. "Come on guys, you'll get us thrown out; we don't want to end the night like this. Let's all go outside and calm down a bit, yeah? Matt, let him go." Grudgingly compliant, he led the way through the bar, followed by Mark and a rather arrogant Joe and, as the door closed behind them, Matt shoved his adversary against the wall and drew back his fist, but he was too slow. Mark's intervention wasn't quick enough to prevent Joe landing a blow to Matt's stomach, folding him in half, releasing himself from the brick-work.

"For fuck's sake, Joe!" Mark helped Matt down and rested him against the wall.

Enraged, Joe turned on him. "What, so you'd rather I let him hit me?" He hadn't anticipated such insolence from his friend. "Thanks, Mark. Remind me to look out for you next time."

"Oh, come on, Joe, do you blame him?"

"Well, if he'd paid a bit more attention to his bird, she wouldn't have gone looking elsewhere."

Matt grabbed at him again, but Mark pulled him back and, as he struggled to release himself from the restrictive grip, a smile slowly spread across his face. "It's alright, Mark, you can let me go." Reluctantly, Mark loosened his hold and watched, nervously, as Matt staggered to his feet. "You want to know what I like about Lucy, Joe?"

With complete disinterest, he looked scornfully at Matt. "What, that her pussy's so tight it makes your dick feel big?"

Matt laughed, ignoring the jibe. "She fucks like Abbie; she likes it hard, just like Abbie…and she's dirty…just like Abbie…" He watched as his words penetrated Joe's mind, relishing the effects of his confession, though somewhat underestimating the reaction they would provoke.

With a derisive smile, Joe dismissed him. "In your dreams, man! I've no doubt she's featured in many of them." He walked closer. "Fantasising about Abbie when you wank is not sex, Matt!" Mark anxiously stood close by in the hope he would be able to prevent a bloody massacre if Matt was, indeed, telling the truth.

"You've got a short memory, Joe – Eddie's eighteenth? You all went to the club, but I stayed to help her clear up –

remember? That didn't take too long so we found other ways to fill the time before Eddie got home…lots of ways. I've got to hand it to her, she taught me a lot that night, Joe, and she was up for anything; the dirtier, the better." He stood back, happy with his performance, full of conceit for finally screwing Joe over; at last, he got to fuck someone before Joe did. But as he stood congratulating himself, he didn't see the fist launched at his face. Fortunately, Mark grabbed Joe before he could throw another, bear-hugging him as he thrashed around like a mad-man.

"You lying cunt! She wouldn't go anywhere near you, you fucking piece of shit!"

Still reeling from pain, Matt managed a smile as he comforted his face. "Oh, she got very close, Joe, *very* close. Why don't you ask her when you see her next? In fact, give her a call now." He laughed in Joe's face before sauntering back inside.

Mark, still grappling with his friend, refused to let go until he was sure he wouldn't retaliate. "Just leave it, mate, let it go."

"Let it go? Were you fucking listening, Mark?"

"Of course I was! But why does it matter? It was five years ago and you don't own her, Joe, she can do whatever she wants." He knew he was treading a very thin line, but his words were true. "He's not worth it…and, to be fair, you've just screwed his girlfriend, so, you kinda got to let it go…"

"Girlfriend? Let's see how long that lasts." He grabbed the door and headed back to the table.

"Fuck!" Mark followed but was stopped by Mike.

"All OK, Mark? Don't bring it in here."

"Yeah, it's fine…it'll be fine. Can you bring us the bill?"

"Yep, be right there."

As Mark re-joined the group, the atmosphere was thick and he suggested they pay up and call it a night. Matt agreed and before Mike reached them, he was at the bar, with Lucy, paying his share. Once the remainder of the bill was settled, James and Charlie said their goodbyes, followed by Andy and Sophie.

Miles stayed a little longer with Zoe, and Jamie, quite taken with Mike's attention, hung around on the off-chance. They managed to keep the conversation light before Miles and Zoe made their excuses and left. Joe, less conversational than earlier, decided he'd had enough, and Mark, with the promise of a bed for the night, joined him, leaving Jamie at the bar with Mike…and Joe's disgruntled intruder.

Back at the apartment, Joe opened a bottle of wine and drank silently for a while. Mark, somewhat sympathetic to his annoyance, felt it probably best to mirror his friend's behaviour but was becoming bored. "You OK, man?"

Joe looked at him before responding. "Yeah, but you should have let me hit him again."

"That's not fair, Joe. You would have killed him; I could see it in your face. You should be thanking me for keeping you out of jail."

Joe smiled. "Well thanks, Mark. Looks like I owe you."

"Was she worth it?"

"Lucy? Oh, yeah!"

"You're unbelievable!"

"So they tell me!" His phone rang, but he didn't recognise the number. "Hello…?"

"Joe?"

As a smile spread across his face, he looked at Mark. "Hi, Lucy, are you OK?"

15

Mark sighed and shook his head as Joe continued his conversation.

Lucy, relieved he'd answered, enlightened him to her plight. "Yeah…no. I've just had a huge row with Matt and I've ended it, but he's not happy. He was quite nasty."

"You poor thing. Are you sure you're alright; do you want to come over? I can send a cab…"

Mark gesticulated his disapproval…to no avail.

"I don't know…that might make things worse…" She was sure Matt would find out.

"How could it be any worse, Lucy? Don't worry about him. I just want to make sure you're OK."

"OK…but are you sure it won't be a problem?"

"Of course – where are you?"

He took her address and called a cab, suitably pleased with the evening's outcome. Looking at Mark, he winked, still smiling at his handiwork. "Excuse me while I shower. Help yourself to more wine."

Clean, fresh and looking devastating, Joe returned, half-dressed.

"I'll take Lucy's cab back home, Joe. Don't want to cramp your style, mate!"

"No need, Mark. I said you could stay before this all started."

"Yeah, but that was before you got lucky!"

"Mark, my dear friend, luck has nothing to do with it, and

whether you're here or not, I shall get laid...unless it makes you feel uncomfortable...a little inadequate, maybe...?"

"What, you trying to piss everyone off tonight?"

Joe laughed. "Sorry, mate."

"So what are you playing at, why are you so concerned about someone else's girlfriend – someone *else's* girlfriend?"

"Well, you keep telling me I need a girlfriend myself; thought I might give it a go." He smiled cheekily.

"OK...but you're supposed to find your own, not take your mate's!"

"Christ, make your mind up."

As he heard Lucy's cab arrive, Joe greeted her at the door with a face full of concern and paid the driver. "Let me take your jacket."

Surprised at Mark's presence, she turned to Joe. "Oh, sorry, I didn't know you had company. Sorry, Mark, am I interrupting?"

"No, don't worry; I'll get out of your way."

"Stay, Mark, and have some more wine. I'm sure Lucy won't mind... Would you like some wine?"

"Uh...yeah...have you got some white?"

"Yes I do." Feeling slightly awkward, she sat down as Joe fetched another bottle. Returning, he sat down close and handed her a glass, touching her arm gently. "Are you OK? I'm sorry you had such a hard time."

Touched by his sincerity, she relaxed. "It's OK, he just said some horrible things and I know I was wrong, but he wasn't bothered about me tonight until he thought I'd...spent too much time with you. I obviously misjudged him."

"Did you tell him...?"

"No! God, no! But I think he may have guessed."

Mark laughed. "Oh, he would have worked it out – he's known Joe a long time!"

Lucy looked at him and then at Joe, wondering if Matt had been right. "What's that supposed to mean?"

"It's a joke; Mark's just joking." Joe gave him no choice.

"Sorry, Lucy, bad timing; it's not funny…sorry."

"No, it's not."

"It's OK, don't worry." Taking her wine, Joe placed it out of the way and pulled her on to his lap. "Forget about all that." He gently pushed his crotch into hers as she smiled but, looking a little embarrassed, she glanced sideways at Mark, as Joe continued his rhythm.

Mark finished his wine. "A little warning next time, Joe!"

He turned towards his friend. "You're alright, Mark. I'm sure Lucy doesn't mind you being here."

Despite his reservations, in no doubt as to what would transpire, he felt compelled to stay; maybe it was the wine, maybe it had been too long, but he could feel his dick growing, and he was starting to feel warm.

Looking back at Lucy, Joe awaited her protests, but when they didn't arise, he smiled in the knowledge that he was right and the prospect of a promising night. Increasing the tempo slightly, he kissed her softly, catching her tongue and licking slowly, watching expectantly, willing her to unbutton his fly. Eager to do so, her breathing was quick, but her hands were controlled and as she released his cock, she squeezed gently, rubbing it against her pussy, closing her eyes, already lost in her own ignominious world. Joe, allowing her to play, listened to his friend's movements, knowing Mark's hand was already occupied, and carefully adjusted Lucy's underwear so she could push his dick inside her; as he began to thrust deeper, she began to remove her dress, but he stopped her, still teasing her with his tongue, encouraging more vigour from her. "Leave it. I prefer to use my imagination – it's far more exciting…just like you, Lucy…" As she sighed in agreement, he smiled. "And I know you like Mark watching you, watching me fuck you… are you going to let him fuck you so I can watch?" He groaned dramatically. "That's something I'd like to see, Lucy…" He kissed her aggressively and she responded well, craving more, pulling at him, needing him closer and deeper. Removing her hands from his back, he placed them on her breasts, closing his hands round hers, squeezing gently and examining her face. "That's good." He grabbed her hips, pushing her down hard, elated at the turn of events, and she felt good: wet and tight. "Fuck me harder, Lucy, c'mon…harder…" He could hear Mark's rasping breaths and his hand moving faster, and was aroused further, knowing he was at the centre of this depravity, longing for more. "I want to watch you, Lucy. I want to watch Mark fuck you…" Hypnotised by his words, she was unable to object, willing to do whatever he proposed so long as it was sex – any sex, any way, anyone – and he was there, for he initiated the thrill, coercing her into undiscovered exhilaration. With Lucy's acquiescence seemingly effortless, was it possible he'd met his match? Matt had intimated her persuasion and Lucy's capitulation to his demands suggested she'd go to any lengths to satisfy him and, indeed, herself, and the endless possibilities excited him; he wanted more of her, stimulated now to establish her limits, and with his jaw set, he hammered her, pulling her closer, almost tearing her apart, but Mark's orgasm caught him unawares and he held his breath as he felt his own rampage through his body, bursting out inside Lucy. Trembling as his cock throbbed, he could feel her tongue searching for his and he engulfed her mouth, resuming his command.

Mark's temporary disappearance permitted a little intimacy and as Joe gently brushed the hair from Lucy's face, he searched for answers in her eyes…and she made no attempt to conceal them. Smiling, he realised she was as Molly had been: unrestrained, vehemently zealous; adventurous. Wasted on Matt, he would exploit her full potential, satisfy her yearnings and understand her perversions, manipulating her desires to afford him whatever he needed, no matter when, and abandoned by Abbie, she was currently essential. Upon Mark's return, Joe threw her down on the sofa and buried his face in her pussy, tasting his own cum, his tongue caressing the folds of her skin, taunting her clitoris as she sighed repeatedly, guiding him with her hands and, taking one of them, he gently pushed a finger inside her, released it and watched as she instinctively placed it in her mouth. Mark's appreciation was audible and with Lucy softly whispering his name, Joe gave her what she wanted, what he wanted, whilst she closed her legs around his neck, holding him tight to maximise her climax.

Granting her a few moments to recover, he slowly ran his tongue across her stomach before pulling up her dress and carefully removing it, licking her breasts, feeling the twitch of her body, sensitive to his touch. Removing his shirt, he dragged his body across hers, edging closer to her face, allowing his cock to tease her pussy once more, searching for its way in. She clasped her hand around it, looking indomitably at him, rubbing gently, seeking control and a quicker resurgence. Her initiative was compelling, but he had his own plans, and consenting to a few moments' privilege of her freedom, he kissed her neck and ran a finger along the inside of her bra, before whispering in her ear, "Now it's Mark's turn." He looked in her eyes as his tongue found its way deep in her mouth and, sitting her up, he gently pushed her towards Mark, moving to the edge of the sofa for the best vantage point. Mark, suddenly tentative, slowly pulled her down onto his cock, conscious of Joe's proximity, but Lucy, happy to comply, eased herself down and writhed around, grinding deep into Mark's crotch. Resisting the urge to mirror their actions with his hand, Joe studied her intently, examining her body, the way it looked and the way it moved and Mark's hands on it, caressing her curves, unfastening her bra and removing it cautiously, sucking a nipple and rubbing the other. Lucy, rocking back and forth, held his head still, throwing hers back, unabashed, immersed unequivocally in the inculcation of Joe's volition. Honing in on her arse, he longed to participate, competing as Mark fucked her pussy, both striving to make her scream more, make her come first, and he could feel himself there, his hands holding her firm as Mark battled for the same space, kissing her neck whilst his friend sucked her breasts. Feeling the throb of his dick, he knelt down behind her, brushing her skin, testing her response and, with no rejection, he proceeded warily, but intimidated by Joe's presence and his abilities, Mark caved. Joe, unconcerned by his ally's failure, removed Lucy and laid her back in the sofa, pushing her legs high above her head. "Where shall I go, Lucy? How do you want me to fuck you?" The concern in her eyes forced him to reconsider and he fought to control the desire to go his own way, ignoring her plea, but there was always next time. He drove hard in her pussy and, as he punished her fiercely for the wrong decision, driving deeper and faster, he leaned close to her ear, and through clenched teeth, spoke quietly, "You owe me." He swung back and pulled her across his lap, leaning her back far enough to watch the motion of his cock, disappearing and reappearing, rhythmically, crudely, and he smiled perversely as he looked at her. "Is this how Matt fucks you, Lucy?" He pulled her close, his hands on her arse, forcing her forward, quicker and quicker, still reeling from having to settle. "Is this how he does it? Is he good, Lucy, does he make you come?"

Her reply was unnecessary, but she sighed deeply and whispered, "No."

"No, not hard enough for you?"

Mark closed his eyes and welcomed another orgasm, listening to the performance he'd relinquished, torn between ecstasy and uneasiness. Unaccustomed to partaking in someone else's sex, there was something about Joe that drew him in, kept him fixated, but it made for an uncomfortable experience.

Joe, still consumed by the thrill he'd been denied and

totally unaware of Mark's presence, rescinded his generosity and pushed Lucy back on the sofa and her legs high again, ramming hard in her arse, resuming his pace, ignoring her piercing scream. "Is that what you wanted?" He came instantly and powerfully and the violence of his actions shook his whole body. Collapsed on Lucy, sweating profusely, he was oblivious to the discomfort she still felt.

Mark escaped to the bathroom, shocked at what he'd just witnessed, but uncertain whether he was appalled or aroused. Washing his hands, that familiar sensation in his crotch clarified his position and he sneaked to his room.

Recovering finally, Joe sat up and looked at Lucy as she rolled off the sofa and crept to the bathroom. Assessing his behaviour, he was unnerved; his self-control was the one thing he needed, the one thing he'd mastered from a young age, but tonight had controlled him and that made him uneasy. It was possible the evening's events had set him up: Matt's confession, Mark's presence, Lucy – God, Lucy! Convinced she'd be complicit in every way, he had to consider he may just have screwed that up. Contemplating his apology, he pulled up his jeans as she returned, and he watched the gentle movement of her bare breasts as she swayed towards him, not, as he anticipated, distraught or irate, but provocative and sultry, and as she sat astride him, she pushed her breasts towards his face, rocking back and forth. Apology forgotten, he took a nipple between his teeth as he gently squeezed the other breast.

"You're naughty, Joe, very naughty. You hurt me…"

Looking at her face, prepared for an admonishment, he was hit by an unexpected smile, and he kissed her, biting her lip as she pulled away. "Is that a problem?" He mirrored her movements, holding her firm as his cock hardened.

"No, but you now owe me…"

He laughed. "Owe you what, more? Is that what you want?"

She smiled again. "Yes."

He picked her up and carried her to the bathroom, turning on the shower and removing his jeans before dropping to his knees and slowly lowering her underwear, licking her as her did so. Watching him, she ran her hands across his neck and, with paroxysmal imploration, she accentuated her enjoyment by caressing her breasts, awaiting Joe's detection. Sensing her contribution, he stood up and walked her slowly back into the shower, pressing her against the tiles, his fingers replacing his tongue whilst the other hand pushed her breast towards her mouth, excited by the prospect of her self-stimulation, and rewarding him, her tongue appeared and curled around her nipple. With riveted eyes, he pushed his cock inside her whilst she sucked, continuing to fortify his exhilaration, breeding a new fascination in him and, with Joe ever closer to the mania he craved, she removed her mouth from her breast and kissed him seductively, tormenting him with the tongue that had just teased her own body but, too aroused to play games, he pulled away and forced her breast back to her mouth, impatient for her to resume her talented display. She waited, taunting him with her smile, watching as his control withered. "Do it, Lucy." But she prolonged his frustration, pursuing her torment until his aggression proliferated, and with his bellicosity secured and his jaw tightened, her tongue emerged and she first licked and then sucked, as dictated, scrutinising the face mesmerised by her mouth, ensuring exclusivity before squeezing her breasts together and licking them both, precipitating his defeat. He rested his head on hers as his orgasm deposited its culmination deep inside her and, still hungry for her exhibition, his whole body throbbed as he continued to watch her tongue, augmenting his reparation until, finding her mouth with his, he played with it, searching for his tormentor to fulfil his further need. Finally satisfied, he pulled away and looked in her eyes. "You bitch!"

She smiled at her own efficacy: she'd won. She'd manipulated him against his will and her success was intoxicating. She stroked his balls to prove her supremacy. "You can't always have it your way, Joe."

Pushing his body hard against hers and her hands against the tiles, his face changed, and the aggression she craved reappeared. "Yes I can – get used to it, Lucy. You got me this time; you won't do it again." He shut off the shower, grabbed a towel and threw one to her, watching her dry the body that had invigorated his own and, despite his protests, her abuse of his hunger was provocative...and she knew it.

Folding her towel neatly, she set it down before pressing against him and kissing him softly, but, aside from the rumblings of enervation, she'd had her fun and he was averse, at least for now, to allow her to prevail again.

"Shall I call you a cab?"

A little surprised, she stood back and stroked his chest. "If you want to..."

He grasped her hand and pulled her close, smiling as he spoke. "If you stay, I can't guarantee you'll get much sleep."

With innocent eyes, she returned his smile. "I can live with that."

"I'll get the wine." He pointed her in right direction as she collected their clothes and he collected glasses and bottles. Once she was out of view, he considered his position: in the years since he'd discovered Abbie and had made good use of Anna, he'd had a lot of fun, a lot of sex and way too many partners to count, but none had shared his bed, and now, Lucy was here, spending the night...and that unsettled him. Still, he could help himself to her body at any point and that eased his mind somewhat.

As he entered his bedroom, she was already on his bed, waiting patiently, too tempting to leave alone. Having filled their glasses and sipped his wine, he pulled her roughly onto her back, lay on top of her and kissed her fervently, his fatigue subtly dressed as contentment as he welcomed another opportunity to explore her boundaries, push them and introduce her to his appetite. Procuring easy access to its desired location, he assisted his cock in its path as his hands wandered over her skin, desperate to feel every curve, every crease, inside and out. Her body fascinated him: it was soft, it curved beautifully and it was full and warm. She embraced his investigation as he licked and squeezed, stroked and rubbed, whilst she lay still, silently anticipating his moves. Tracing a finger around her navel, he continued its journey down between her thigh and her pussy, watching its progress as it changed direction and rested at her clitoris, gently pressing down. As it withdrew, he was rewarded with the sight of his dick fulfilling its own obligations, monitoring its rhythm for a while before drawing his finger back up to her breasts, circling each one slowly, moving closer and closer to her nipple, where it lingered, barely touching, coercing her in arching her back to feel its touch again. With his gaze fixed on her face, his finger continued its voyage to her mouth, stroking her lip and finally pushing its way inside. Covering his hand with hers, she sucked his finger and sank her teeth in as far as she dared, drawing it back and forth, wrapping her tongue around it. Removing it completely, and his cock, Joe rolled onto his back and pulled her down to his crotch, closed his eyes and basked in the sensation of her mouth surrounding his erection, her tongue gently licking and her teeth, almost too painful to bear. He reached down to feel her breasts, resting heavily on his legs, and he eased them out from under her, pinching each nipple in time with her mouth, gradually increasing the pressure as her breathing gathered pace. She gently massaged his balls, tight and smooth, resisting the urge to crush them in her palm and, as he watched the movement of her head, and her hair spread across his stomach, he ran his fingers through it, tugging lightly, but holding his grip, and he clenched his teeth as he groaned softly. "I need to come in your mouth." He held her head firm and thrust deeper in her throat, harder, as her hand tightened around his balls and her tongue fought to get inside his cock. He could feel the movement of her breasts on his legs and, as he visualised them around his dick, he held her still, feeling the magnificent flood of his climax, still forcing himself in her face, executing its full potential. As he slowly disengaged, she crawled up his body, allowing her nipples to gently kiss his skin, while he shivered below them. She kissed him roughly, playing with his nipples, but her touch was too soft and unbearable, and he removed her hands, placing them, instead, on her own breasts and encased them with his, kneading harshly, smiling at her pleasure. "I like your style, Lucy, but by the time I'm done, you'll be so much worse. Say now if you want out…"

Although intrigued, she was thrilled by his words. "Do it, Joe."

He kissed her aggressively, holding her so tight she struggled to breathe. "Get some sleep while you can."

***

He stirred at five, disturbed by pleasant dreams and a raging hard-on, and he moved towards Lucy, pulling her close and slowly pushing his cock inside her, careful not to wake her. Caressing her breast with one hand whilst the other found her pussy, he closed his eyes, delighting in the feel of her body, still warm and soft yet seemingly unaware of his proximity and, thrusting gently, his excitement grew quickly – his breathing, heavier and deeper – as he reflected on her tranquil state, undisturbed by his desperate need. She sighed, appreciative of his presence, without her own knowledge, and he continued to enjoy his surreptitious indulgence, struggling with the customary urge to hammer his target, yet stimulated more by his self-imposed restraints. His secret gratification and his thoughts brought his climax closer until he could no longer prevent its arrival and, as he allowed it to consume him, awakening every nerve, every sinew in his body, it coursed through him like an avalanche, slowly settling as he finally realised the benefits of sharing his bed. Detaching himself from her, he turned over and fell asleep.

Waking just after eight-thirty, he jumped in the shower whilst Lucy continued to sleep, and discovering Mark had already left, he made his way to the kitchen, naked, and set about breakfast. Lucy, having woken shortly after, joined him fresh from the shower herself, dressed in his shirt. The thought of her bare body beneath it wasn't enough to convince his acceptance – isn't that what couples do? She, however, very much admired his attire and kissed him provocatively, her hand quick to find his dick.

"Did you sleep well?" He was happy to permit her teasing.

"Not bad…'til you woke me at five."

He laughed. "You knew the risks…" As he prised himself from her hand and filled the kettle, his phone rang. "Good morning, Rosie. I was just thinking about you." He smiled as he imagined her struggling conscience.

"Morning, Joe. How are you, my darling?"

"Very well. What a pleasant way to start the day."

"Start? Joe, it's gone nine – have I woken you?" Lie-ins were not his style and she hoped he was OK.

He looked at Lucy. "No, but I had a very busy night. Sit down and I'll tell you all about it – not sure it's safe for you to stand."

Rose laughed. "Thanks, Joe, but I don't need the details."

"No? Are you sure? I was thinking about you the whole time, Rosie…"

"Ok…"

Lucy, unsure who the intruder was, was incensed by what she'd heard. "Thanks, Joe!" She walked off towards the bedroom, but he grabbed her arm.

Hearing another voice, Rose was taken aback. "Is she still there?"

"Yes – are you jealous, Rosie?"

Ignoring his question, she was astonished by his admission. "Christ, what the hell happened to you? Since when did you start having girls stay over?"

"Well, I couldn't wait for you forever. Besides, I don't need permission; I'm a big boy now, Rosie, you know that…"

She smiled to herself. "Mmm…I think we should leave it there, sweetheart."

He smiled too. "I don't…"

"Look, call me when you're…free, OK?"

"OK, will do. I love you, Rosie…"

"No you don't."

Ending the call, she sat down. Joe had never shared his bed and she was concerned about Abbie's reaction, but there was no way she was going to be the one who broke the news.

Joe, however, had Lucy to pacify. "Who the fuck was that?"

"Relax, she's an old friend." This was the reason he avoided attachments.

"Really? I have a lot of 'old friends', Joe, but I don't speak to any of them like that, and I don't think about them when I'm fucking someone else!"

"For Christ's sake! I was joking, Lucy. If I wanted to fuck Rosie, I would have by now; I wouldn't just be fantasising about it." His patience was thinning quickly. "Look, I don't do relationships; in fact, you are the first person to spend the night, and I've had a lot of sex, so don't lecture me and don't expect me to change. If you want someone to tell you they love you, go and see your mother. If you want someone to hug you, or cry at some shitty movie, go and see your friends. Don't come here expecting to talk or snuggle up in bed; if you're here, you're here for sex, and if you want to watch a movie, great, but if I don't fuck you during it, I sure as hell will after it. Know this, Lucy:

this is my apartment, *my* apartment and I'll do exactly what I want; I'm going to fuck you whether you want me to or not, and I'll speak to whoever I like, however I like, whether or not it meets with your approval. I don't want dramas, I don't want sentiment, I just want an easy life and my dick in something or someone as much as possible – get used to it."

Aroused by his tirade, she moved in front of him and sat on the table, legs wide apart. "Come on then…"

He grabbed her and rammed deep inside her, staggered at her change of heart. "Fuck! You turn me on…and you owe me a shirt." Tearing it open, he grabbed her breasts crudely as he fucked her hard, watching her mouth, brushing it softly with his own. "This is it, Lucy; this is all I need." He studied her face for a moment before pushing her back onto the table and dragging his hand down her arched body. As he held her hips firm, he observed the movements of his cock, sliding easily back and forth, in an out of her as she wrapped her legs around him. Drawing his eyes up her body, he caught his breath at the sight of her breasts dancing to his beat, a sight that aroused him more each time he experienced it, and he found her hands to massage them for him until he pulled her close again, watching and feeling them rub against his chest. As he thrust quicker and his breathing increased, he eased his shirt off her shoulders and pulled it tight across her arms, restricting her and, closing her breasts together, crushing them with his arms, he lost his tongue in her cleavage. Closing his eyes, he pictured his cock there and he came instantly, caught between reality and fantasy, holding still until the throbbing eased, and as he released his grip on his shirt, he kissed her. "That's all you're going to get from me, Lucy and it's all I want from you."

She grasped his flaccid dick and pulled him towards her. "OK, but this is for me only, I'm not going to share it; if you start dipping it anywhere else, I'll find another to play with."

Smiling broadly, she'd unknowingly given him consent. "I

seem to remember you playing with another last night, and I didn't complain..."

"But that was your idea."

"But you didn't protest, so I have one in the bag."

"One what?"

He sighed deeply. "Let's just wait and see."

Breakfast devoured and ravenous appetites appeased, Lucy returned home, with promises to return for dinner and a further dissipative evening. She was happy to settle for The Well again, but next time, she wanted something else, and whilst unwilling to give in to the demands of a relationship, Joe was rather amused at her impudence...for now. She would learn that he would not take orders.

16

Forgetting Rose, Joe wandered across to the bar to book the table and catch up on Mike's evening. "Hey, man, how's it going?"

Mike smiled mischievously. "Very well, my dear friend, very well. Usual?"

"Yeah, a quick one. So...?"

Mike poured his drink and, as it was quiet, sat down next to him. "Well, it was rather interesting. Jamie hung around after you'd all left but, of course, thanks to you, I had somebody else to attend to...so, once the doors were locked, there we all were...and it seems Jamie isn't one-hundred-percent gay after all!"

"Really? Wow, didn't see that coming!" But the possibilities were already forming in Joe's mind. "Mmm...thanks for the tip there, Mike. So, is it going to be a regular arrangement...?"

He laughed. "You know what, I think it might! They both seemed quite keen to come back. So what happened between you and Matt? It's getting a little too frequent, Joe, and I don't need that sort of attention, mate. I assume it was his bird you were amusing in the ladies'..."

He smiled triumphantly. "Yep...but, in my defence, he wasn't giving her enough attention...so I did."

"Christ, Joe! Have you spoken to him today?"

"No, I don't think that's likely to happen – Lucy stayed at mine last night..."

Incredulous, Mike needed confirmation. "She *stayed* last

night? Fuck! What's happened to you, Joe?" He laughed loudly, still unsure whether he'd missed the joke.

Smiling, Joe was keen to defend his position. "Well, it solves those early morning hard-ons."

Mike slapped him on the back as he stood up. "Man's got a point!"

Finishing his drink, Joe remembered to book. "So I need a table tonight, but just for two, around eight?"

"You got it. Now bugger off and leave me to it; I'm going to have to break the news to a lot of my regulars, and it ain't gonna be pretty!"

Obeying, he left, and with plenty of time until Lucy returned, he strolled in to town to replace the shirt he'd destroyed that morning. Recalling those events, he smiled and felt his cock stirring – would he be able to wait for Lucy? Best to keep an open mind. After visiting several stores, he finally found his replacement and, searching for the correct size, a friendly voice arrived. "Can I help you, sir?"

The friendly voice had a rather pretty face, not lost on Joe, and his innocent smile and innocent eyes felt sure she could. "I do hope so. I'm not sure of my size, what would you suggest?"

Unable to resist his smile, she was already hooked. "Maybe…a large?"

"That sounds about right – where are your changing rooms?"

"I'll show you, sir." Appreciating the view, Joe followed, allowing the assistant to brush past him as she left the cubicle. "If it's not the right size, ring the bell and I'll bring another." She smiled sweetly and closed the door.

Deciding the size was wrong, however it fitted, he rang the bell and, as the voice returned, he unbuttoned the shirt before opening the door. "I'm sorry, we don't have a medium."

Removing it completely, his assistant's uneasiness amused him and he handed the shirt to her. "Could you order one for me…?"

"Kelly." Averting her eyes, she took the shirt and reached for the hanger.

"Kelly, thank you." He dressed as she returned the shirt and he met her at the desk.

"Would you like your order delivered to your house or the store?" She was hopeful.

"Here, I think. I may not be home when it's delivered. Shall I pay now?"

Happy with his decision, Kelly took his details and gave him his receipt. "It should be here next Saturday. Is there anything else I can help you with, Mr Francis?"

"How about lunch?"

She blushed. "I'm afraid I've already had my break."

"Then it'll have to wait 'til next Saturday. What time, one?"

"OK." She smiled as he left, already willing the week away.

Despite the luxury of Lucy on tap, Joe was already looking forward to something new and, letting his imagination play, he wandered home, jumped in the shower and visualised next Saturday's lunch with his hand responding appropriately.

When Lucy returned, he was ready for dinner and, although unaccustomed to dining as a couple, he was pleasantly surprised. Lucy had commandeered most of the conversation, but that suited him; he wasn't the reminiscing type and he was happy to keep his ghosts and demons under lock and key. Amused glances and occasional asides from Mike also entertained him, but largely bypassed Lucy, and as the bar emptied, leaving the three of them chatting, he was tempted to see if Mike would perform better than Mark. Lucy, however, feigned tiredness and dragged him back for an early night before he had a chance to offer his proposal.

Closing the front door, he watched her hands unbutton his shirt, before slowly removing her dress and tugging at his belt. She dropped to her knees, removed his cock and licked gently as he closed his eyes, picturing Kelly in the store changing room, wondering whether he should have propositioned her there, and as Lucy sucked, he swayed slightly and held her head for support, guiding it a little more vigorously than she had planned but, impatient, he thrust in her face needing to come quickly, fearing boredom would soon take over. Although a little taken aback, she welcomed the taste of his cum filling her mouth and the feel of his hands pulling her hair and, pleased with her efforts, unaware of the part his fantasies had played, she dragged her body up his, kissing his chest and neck, oblivious to his indifference.

She found his mouth and kissed him passionately, awaiting the exploration of his hands on her body, but when they refused, she pulled back, disappointed. "Are you OK?"

Following her lead, he sat down. "Yeah, just a little tired."

"Joe! I thought you were insatiable – don't let me down…" She wasn't prepared to settle for a mouth full of cum and, pulling him to the sofa, she straddled him, grinding hard into his crotch, knowing he'd be ready very soon.

Struck by his own disinterest, he reasoned now probably wasn't the right time to examine it, choosing instead to concentrate on her swaying breasts in the hope they would provide enough stimulation for him to perform and, in the process, pacify her; his options were somewhat limited and rather inhibited by her presence so he elected to utilise her availability. Running his hands from her hips, gently brushing her skin, he reached behind her and unclasped her bra, pulling it down slowly, analysing the exigency of her breasts as they sought their freedom and, enthused by their appearance, he focussed solely on entertaining himself at their expense, squeezing them as his tongue encompassed first one nipple, then the other, unconcerned for Lucy's pleasure, absorbed, only in rousing his own decadent gratification. Looking at her with undetected derision, he tested her confines with increasing force, compressing her flesh, waiting for her objections and, as the pain registered in her face, he could feel the excitement mounting in his groin, ready to attack the rest of her body with the same potency. Pushing her back onto the sofa, he removed her underwear and rammed his cock deep inside her, watching her face delight in his belligerence, and with her tongue pursuing his, he allowed her to continue whilst his hands assaulted her breasts long enough to demonstrate he'd fulfilled his commitment and, when he felt she was satisfied with her fuck, he willed his orgasm to start. Although it was real, his response to it was not, but he'd fooled her.

As her breathing eased, she smiled at him. "That's better, now you can go to bed."

Fastening his jeans, he was unable to avoid the inevitable: "Are you staying or…?" Preferring, tonight, to sleep alone, he knew it was unlikely.

"Yeah, is that OK?" Despite her successful persuasion, she was a little frustrated: he'd not been as demanding as she'd hoped, but figured he was, as he suggested, just tired.

"Yep."

***

With charming dreams of Kelly, he woke later than usual with a staggering hard-on and he pulled Lucy onto it, waking her as he did so, but she was happy to oblige, given the abrupt ending to her evening. Rocking sleepily back and forth, she smiled at him, but his face was stern. "Harder, Lucy." Grabbing her arse, he propelled her forward, demonstrating his instruction, and she obeyed, relieved he'd returned to his customary approach, enjoying the rigidity she could feel deep inside her. She performed her duties well, elated in her drowsy state, eager to please him, gripping his hands, still on her arse but, hypnotised by her swinging breasts, he pulled his hands from under hers and grabbed them, pulled her low, sucking her nipples and biting hard. She screamed, yet he held firm, sucking and biting harder as she struggled to alleviate her pain, but her attempts provided overwhelming provocation and, witnessing her discomfort, he closed his eyes for his orgasm to take hold, flooding his mind with erotic images and his body with euphoric sensations, triumphant and satiated with the assistance of her distress. She pulled away when he finally released her and got up from the bed.

"What the fuck, Joe?"

"What? Come on, Lucy, you like it rough." Smiling, he headed for the shower, untroubled by her concerns.

He made breakfast as she showered and when she joined him, they ate in silence: Lucy still irritated; Joe still oblivious. When she realised an apology was unlikely, she changed direction, albeit, sulkily. "What do you want to do today?"

"Well, I'm back to work tomorrow so I need to get straight: check emails, get an early night..."

"You don't want to do something, then?"

Puzzled, he looked at her. "'Do something'? Like what?" He thought he'd made himself clear.

"I don't know, go out somewhere, go for lunch, a walk..."

Laughing, he shook his head. "No, I don't. I told you, Lucy, I don't do relationships. I don't want to do couple things...other than have sex, but today, I have other things to do so sex is going to have to wait too. Did you not hear what I said yesterday?"

"Yes, Joe, I heard. You were very articulate, but I just thought..."

"Well, don't. It's not going to change, don't upset yourself hoping it will."

"OK, fine. I'll see you later." She finished her mouthful, grabbed her bag from the bedroom and left.

As he watched the door close, he was annoyed but relieved; the apartment was already feeling rather claustrophobic with her frequent presence over the past two days – how did that happen? Staying over occasionally was fine, but night after night and 'doing something' during the day – too much. Remembering his brief conversation with Rose the previous day, he called, ready to seduce her down the phone.

"Hey, Joe, how are you?"

"Good, Rosie; waiting for you. When are you coming round?"

She laughed: predictable as ever. No matter how much time she had, she wouldn't dare; she wasn't convinced she'd be able to resist him a second time. "I'm sorry, Joe, I've got Josie and Stephen coming for lunch, otherwise I'd be there in a shot, you know that. Why don't you join us?" She was aware of Josie's indiscretion, though not the detail, and would enjoy watching the tension between them.

"As lovely as that sounds, I want you to myself, Rosie. I don't want to share you with Josie and Stephen...well, not with Stephen...but you and Josie..." He smiled at thought: that would be worth exploring later.

"Well, I'm sorry, my love, not today...ooh, shit! Sorry, Joe, I've got to go; there's someone at the door. Can I call you tomorrow?"

"I'm back at work tomorrow, so it won't be easy, but I'll try to find some special time just for you."

Closing her eyes, she refused to allow her mind to wander. "Ok, sweetheart, call me when you can. Bye."

Staring at the wall, he visualised Rose with Josie and allowed himself a few minutes to indulge in a little self-gratification, drawing on first-hand knowledge and a large dose of fantasy and, for a moment, his thoughts returned to Abbie, long enough to set the orgasmic ball in motion, before returning to Josie and Rose to complete the sequence.

Distractions dealt with, he checked his diary for the week; all correspondence and minutes covered, he returned only those emails that were absolutely necessary and would probably win him favour and, being respectably close to lunchtime, he dressed and headed to The Well.

"Hey, Joe, this is becoming a bit of a habit." Although unlikely, Mike dared to hope it was more than just convenience but chose, wisely, to keep quiet. "Alone today? Bet she's not happy!" Unlike his client, he found Joe's plight rather amusing.

"Yeah, thanks, Mike. She's not particularly, but I won't be losing any sleep over it. What are you cooking today? Smells good."

"The usual, but I've got Jambalaya for the special – want some?"

"Yeah, thank you."

Lunch ordered and beverage delivered, Mike returned to Lucy; he couldn't neglect the opportunity. "So where is she today?"

"I don't know. She wanted to go for a walk or something and I told her I wasn't interested. She's already trying to create this relationship illusion, but it's not going to happen and if she thinks it is, she's going to be very disappointed. The only benefit in having her around is waking in the morning with the raging horn and she's lying beside me – saves a lot of time in the shower…not to mention the water!"

Mike laughed. "I was sure she'd get her claws into you and make you change; she's pretty hot, Joe."

"Yeah, I know, but I'm bored already. I need something new." He smiled mischievously. "I've got next weekend sorted so there's that to look forward to…"

"What?" Mike felt a little sympathy for Lucy. "Does she know what you're up to?"

"I don't know, but it doesn't include her."

"Joe!" Why was he surprised?

"Oh, c'mon, Mike, I was going to suggest we share her last night, just for a little excitement, before she dragged me back home."

Groaning softly, he was instantly frustrated. "Don't tell me what you *were* going to do, man, just tell me what you *are* going to do."

Joe leaned close, smiling devilishly and smelling divine. "Who would you have fucked first, Mike...?"

Feeling his jeans bulging, he shook his head. "Don't play with me, Joe..."

He sat back and laughed; it was good to know he could always fall back on his landlord. As his lunch arrived, his drink was refreshed before Mike moved away to find someone less provocative to talk to...at least until his jeans felt more comfortable. A couple of drinks later and Joe reluctantly returned home, preferring to tease Mike but knowing it would lead to a very late night.

***

Back to work Monday morning and it was refreshing to resume a routine, although having disciplined himself to limit his appetite at work to new-starters and overly-satisfied female clients, Joe struggled with the constraints he'd not experienced the previous week and a few extra 'comfort breaks' were necessary to ease the transition back. The week went quickly and, having tried a couple of times, unsuccessfully, to contact Mark, left messages to call back. Lucy, despite her attempt to cut him off, crawled back Friday night, hoping for a repeat of the previous weekend and, content with the freedom he'd had all week, Joe was happy to oblige, but with conditions: be gone by mid-morning and return late-afternoon; no relationship talk and no commitments whatsoever.

After a few drinks in the bar, he was ready to return home and for Lucy's breasts to engulf his dick. Watching her remove her clothes was a satisfying experience in itself, but the removal of her bra meant a luscious dissipation and he could barely contain himself and, pulling her breasts close, he guided them around his cock, willing her to take the bait, as she smiled seductively and accommodated his wish enthusiastically. Closing his eyes, he sat back and waited for the magic, glancing occasionally to remind himself of the delectable performance taking place, but preferring to feel it, feel the softness of her breasts rubbing his cock gently but effectively. As his breathing matched her movements, he smiled, aware that he would come very soon and very considerably, and rather than delay them he welcomed the sensations as they rippled through his body forcing him to vocalise his pleasure, and he watched as his cum covered her breasts, glistening in the muted light, before pulling her onto his lap, licking her chest clean as she stared, unsure whether to be disgusted or aroused, but before resolving her indecision, she was on her back with Joe planted firmly, and rather violently, in her pussy. Wriggling for more comfort, she was powerless to move, held firm by his interest only in his rules and, despite the agony, she came quickly, lost again in the eroticism of her pain.

With excuses of a busy week at work, Joe was in bed early and Lucy, without complaint, joined him and, in the early hours, when he woke with the ritualistic erection, she was waiting, pulling down the duvet and seizing it with her mouth. Joe, still drowsy, gasped and closed his eyes, leaving her to wake his body gently and gloriously, grateful, once again for the over-night company. Her soft touch and generous tongue were as comforting to his cock as the warm duvet was to his body and he luxuriated, half-dreaming, in the furore of his senses, playing no part in the exercise, waiting for the inevitable splendour that would soon follow. As she toiled for his gratification, his body rewarded her – and him – with his breath-taking climax, propelling him into a deliriously decadent state, setting what he hoped would be the mood for the day. Drifting back to sleep, he dreamed of Kelly, dressing and undressing him, for her pleasure, like a toy doll, teasing him until he forced her onto the desk and fucked her in view of the whole store. A quick shower to complete the story and he was in the kitchen making coffee.

By the time Lucy woke, he'd finished breakfast and left for a run, hoping she'd be gone by the time he returned and, receiving her sweet little text, he was relieved and took a longer route to pass the time. He knew she'd be back later, but before that, he had lunch with Kelly to look forward to. As he headed home, Rose called again.

"Joe, you were going to call me back. I need to speak to you…"

"Rosie, you know I'm just dying to speak to you, but right now I'm hot and sweaty, and you're welcome to join me, but it's not the best time to talk. I'm out for lunch later, but I promise I'll call the minute I get back and tell you every little detail…unless you want to come over and I can show you…"

"You do know lunch, for most people, involves eating food…?"

"But that's a waste of an hour."

"Well, you enjoy, and I'll speak to you later."

"I promise."

***

Showered and ready to go, Joe wandered into town early, found a nice restaurant and booked a table for lunch. A quick drink to sample the ambience and he wandered off to find Kelly and, heading straight to the order desk, he found an equally pleasant voice, smiling.

"Can I help you, sir?"

"Yes, is Kelly around?"

"I'll find her for you – is she expecting you?"

Beaming wickedly, he was pretty confident. "I do hope so; tell her lunch is ready."

"Oh, OK – lucky Kelly…" Somewhat jealous, the assistant set of in search of her colleague.

After considerable time, she appeared: a little nervous but looking sensational – appreciated, very much, by Joe. "Are you ready?"

"Yes, but I need to leave via the staff entrance; if you go out the front and turn left, it's down the alley, I'll meet you there."

"OK." He was feeling rather jubilant. He'd missed the exhilaration of a one-night-stand and, although he was sure she would be a challenge, he was certain he could persuade her.

Walking to the restaurant, he radiated charm, and she was quickly enamoured by his attention and compliments, and with drinks ordered, he was careful to select a light lunch to allow him time to get what he came for. Thankfully, she was desperate to impress him so opted for a salad and, despite her employer's no-alcohol policy, there was no management in store on a Saturday and she relented, with a little pressure from Joe. As he chatted effortlessly, she was completely captivated, guided a little by her large glass of wine, but mostly by the beauty of the face looking back at her, studying her, and the softness of the voice emanating from it, raising her temperature slightly, mesmerising her without warning, and when he paid the bill and offered to walk her back, she welcomed the extra time spent with him, and his suggestion to spend the rest of her break in the staff room, was well received: no one else would be there, so she would have him all to herself. Sneaking in like two naughty children, Joe locked the door behind them and pulled her close, kissing her softly yet passionately, pressing his groin into hers so she could feel the effect she had on him but, disconcerted at his speed, she stepped back, reluctant to continue. "Joe, I think we should stop…"

Placing a finger on her lips, he interrupted. "Shh, don't spoil it, Kelly." He kissed her again, pulling her back, determined to prove her wrong. "You've been turning me on all through lunch, I can't help it…"

"Yeah, but I'm not sure..."

He took her hand and rubbed the bulge in his jeans. "I am." Holding her tighter, he unbuckled his belt and unbuttoned his fly before she could protest further, and slowly raising her skirt, he pushed his cock towards her crotch, squeezing her arse, thrusting her forward. He could feel her tense, but that only aroused him more and, as she squirmed, he pulled her underwear to one side and forced himself inside her, smiling as he sighed deeply and carried her to the nearest vacant wall. Clinging on, she buried her face in his neck, uneasy with his perseverance. "You feel good, Kelly; you taste good." He found her mouth with his tongue, despite her opposition and looked deep in her eyes as he continued to thrust, gaining momentum and speed. "Don't pretend – did you think lunch would be free? Nothing's ever free..." This felt right; this is what he'd missed and Lucy would have to go. Consumed by the exhilaration he'd almost forgotten – the thrill of a new pussy, a new challenge – he was completely absorbed in the motion of his dick in this relative stranger, fuelled by her reluctance to participate and his determination to continue regardless, and his excitement grew, encouraging his orgasm, his prize, his *raison d'etre*.

Kelly gasped as she heard somebody at the door and her eyes were full of fear. "Joe, please..." But she was way too late, though her pleas weren't entirely wasted, triggering the end of her distress, but not as she would have hoped; Joe, however, achieved his aim and rammed her hard against the wall as he exploded inside her, breathing heavily, holding on as long as his climax dictated, unaffected by her concern, or, indeed, the unwelcome visitor.

Finally, he put her down, dressing himself as she quickly straightened her clothes and unlocked the door. The smiling assistant was less happy now. "Why the hell was the door locked? You're late, Kelly."

Joe stepped in with a devastating smile. "I'm sorry, that was my fault. I used to work in a store and it was a security thing – old habits…"

The smile returned as she looked at him. "I'm sorry, are you Kelly's…?"

Moving towards her, he reached for her hand. "We're friends; I'm Joe."

"Nice to meet you, Joe, I'm Lana. I'm afraid Kelly needs to get back to work so someone else can go to lunch."

"That's OK." He kissed her cheek. "Thank you for a most enjoyable time, Kelly."

Forcing a smile, she left, but she could hear him working on Lana and cringed, annoyed at her own stupidity and naivety; she could warn her colleague, but would she listen? And once she was out of the way, he turned his full attention to her co-worker. "Have you had lunch, Lana?"

"I have, unfortunately, but some other time…?" Already enticed by his enigmatic air, she was hopeful.

"Absolutely. But I must collect my order; shall I meet you at the desk?"

"I'll take you down; you really shouldn't be in here. Kelly should have known that."

"Oh, I'm sorry, but it wasn't her fault. I was very insistent." The innocence in his eyes had Lana easily fooled.

"OK, but don't do it again." She touched his arm gently, guiding him through the store.

"Whatever you say."

As he collected his shirt, Lana slipped her number into the bag and, leaving her with a smile, he found Kelly to say goodbye.

Satisfied with his accomplishments, he left and as he crossed the road and headed back home he saw her, standing in the middle of the pavement, watching him. Routed to the spot, he felt slightly unsteady…and then she smiled and he was instantly hard, needing to feel her, to be inside her, to feel her hands on his chest and his cock, her mouth, her tongue, her pussy. He walked towards her and covered her mouth with his, happy to take her right now, unaware of the passers-by, tutting and mumbling.

She was back and this time, there'd be no escape.

Acknowledgements

I would like to thank my long-suffering husband, David, and my beautiful family for their patience and encouragement when it was needed most, and my extended family for continuing that support, but particularly my mum, Judy, for being the one to help out…always, my dad, John, for his unrelenting commitment to the cause and my brother, Paul, for counselling my tattered nerves!

My close friend, Amanda, for complete and steadfast support, especially when uncertainty surfaced and her dad, Paul and my friend, Tracey, for their unquestioning assistance.

And, lastly, my oldest and closest friends, Marsha and Rob, for their enthusiasm and for proving that 'Anything Is Possible'.

You have all given me so much of your time and love, without restriction or judgement, and I could never truly express my gratitude to any of you…but I love you all xx